Onea,
N.M. Herbalist 1916

THE MEDICINE BEAR

by

Jesse Wolf Hardin

Recommendations For Jesse Wolf Hardin &

THE MEDICINE BEAR

376 pages – 75 illustrations

"The Medicine Bear is a powerful novel of love, healing, devotion, coming of age, and sense of place... but more than any single element, it is a tapestry of the vital medicine that connects the people to the land, and all of us to each other. The skillful hands of the Curandera heal even while the soldiers endure a bloody struggle. Through it all, the medicine of this tale is found in the power of personal transformation and bone-deep passion. Readers of novels as diverse as Frazier's Cold Mountain and Urrea's The Hummingbird's Daughter will be pulled into the mythic yet eerily relevant story of The Medicine Bear. The vibrant weaving of the many cultural elements that make of the American Southwest on the border are beautifully represented, transporting us to the lapis skies, red clay, and lush canyons of New Mexico but the tale is applicable and relatable to the reader wherever they might be.

Never has a story of magic and healing, clarity and wildness been so needed as now. Hardin's masterful approach to magical realism and history grants us a seldom seen view into the events that have shaped the borderlands and its people. So pull up a seat, and listen to a master storyteller's tale of an mestiza healer and her true love."

–Kiva Rose
(New Mexico Medicine Woman, Author,
CoFounder of TWHC & Plant Healer Magazine)

"Jesse's voice inspires our passion to take us further, seeing the world whole — even holy."

-Terry Tempest Williams
(Author of Coyote's Canyon and Refuge)

"The teachings of The Medicine Bear shine bright, like sunlight through a canopy of thickly branched trees. Here is found the deep wild wisdom of curanderas and curanderos of yesterday and today, disguised as story. One can almost smell the copal smoke and rain-dampened desert as we follow how Omen's "don" unfolds, encouraged first by the spirits of plant and tree, stone and animal; the true teachers of those called by the guardians of the medicine ways. Later, honed by the old yerbera, Doña Rosa. Like we Mestizas, it walks between worlds: the world of matter, the world of spirit and the world of culture and language. Of brujas and curanderas. Of European healing and Indigenous medicine. It is also a love story... a tender unfolding of the Aztec spiritual principle of balance and harmony, of Ome Cihuatl and Ome Tekutli, Two Woman and Two Man, complementary opposites who embody soulful unity."

–Grace Alvarez Sesma, Curandera

"The Medicine Bear is an unabashedly magical, sensual, and yes, romantic tale of love and loss, of longing and renewal. It is a paean to wildness within and the southwestern wilderness that Eland and Omen are married to, along with each other, and whose exquisite beauty we are drawn into through the soulful eyes and language of Eland.

Plants intertwine with the lives of the main characters in The Medicine Bear. Eland knows his plants well, and as he watches his beloved Omen, an herbalist, at work and play, we are shown that plants are healers and beings in their own right. This matches my own sense of plants as beings of deep spirit and great generosity. There is so much plant lore and wisdom shared in the book, along with hints at how to gather and work with herbs, that the Medicine Bear will be a pleasure for herbalists to read, and a great education for those who long to become more intimate with healing plants.

The plants, the mountains, and the medicine bear sing to us, calling us each to full aliveness. While the old west is fading and the grizzlies are dying, love inspires, even beyond death itself."

–Robin Rose Bennett
(Wise Woman Healing Ways, Author of Green Treasures)

"Wolf Hardin has a true understanding of embodied spirituality — the sacred spirit in nature and in human beings as natural, erotic, animal life forms on a living planet... sensual, practical, and transformative."
  -Starhawk (Author of <u>Truth Or Dare</u>)

"Hardin has a fascinating style... almost lyrical. His perspective on the Old West is both romantic and dramatic. I spent some of my formative years long ago on the banks of the Cimarron River listening to Navaho storytellers relate tales of their ancestors and the history of that part of New Mexico. Jesse's writing is worthy of those fascinating chronicles."
  -Ned Schwing (Author and editor, Krause Pub.)

"Jesse Wolf has a depth and breadth of insight, and a true writer's touch for bringing it to life. I hope other people will read this novel and understand the world that he sustains... and hears, in the Medicine Bear's rumble. A book of herbal teaching, healing, loss, love, and love of the land... a remarkable treasure of words... a jewel of a story!"
  –Virginia Adi (RN, Herbalist, Singer/Songwriter)

"This is a love story about a young anglo-born Eland Howell and Omen, a part Apache, part Spanish girl with a gift for plant medicine and curanderismo, the art of healing as practiced by the hispano Indians of the area. Its portrayal of the changing West at the beginning of the 20th Century is accurate, including Pancho Villa's invasion of the U.S. and attack on Columbus, New Mexico. What also rings authentic are the healing plants and ceremonies performed by the indigenous healers. Using the common names in Spanish, and a few in Yaqui or Apache, the reader learns of the surprising number of plants used for serious illness. Omen learns her healing craft from a the wise Curandera Doña Rosa who imbues in her not only the knowledge of plant healing but also the spiritual necessity of allowing the Bear spirit within her to guide her. If you have ever loved, healed or been healed, bemoaned a changing society, and felt the animal spirit within you, this tale is for you."
  –Charles Garcia
  (Curandero, Director, Calif. School of Traditional Hispanic Herbalism)

THE MEDICINE BEAR

Novel Text, Original Artwork, Photography, and Photo-manipulation of Vintage Images by Jesse Wolf Hardin
Write for permission to quote text or to freely reprint any of these images: mail@animacenter.org
The author also welcomes your comment and feedback, sent to the same email address.

Order Additional Copies Online at: www.TheMedicineBear.com

SWEET MEDICINE PRESS

The Medicine Bear is brought to you by Sweet Medicine Press, the publishing branch of the Anima School and Traditions In Western Herbalism... publishers of in-house books focused on herbalism and healing, natural history and sense of place, rural attitude and Old West history, awareness skills and cultural evolution, Loba's wondrous cookbooks as well as the magical realism of Kiva Rose and Jesse Wolf Hardin's earth-hearted novels.
To View Currently Available Titles, go to:
www.AnimaCenter.org/books

For a Selection of Free Articles by Kiva Rose & Jesse Wolf Hardin:
www.AnimaCenter.org/articles

Jesse Wolf's Illustrated Book for Kids, I'm A Medicine Woman Too!:
www.MedicineWomanToo.com

Subscribe to the free Anima Blog with the latest in diverse Writings by Jesse Wolf: www.animacenter.org/blog

To subscribe to Jesse & Kiva's acclaimed Plant Healer Magazine:
www.PlantHealerMagazine.com

For Anima Herbal and Lifeways Home Study Courses:
www.AnimaCenter.org/courses

Traditions In Western Herbalism – Conference & Community:
www.TraditionsInWesternHerbalism.org

Omen, 1900

ACKNOWLEDGEMENTS

Acknowledgements seem woefully insufficient to me, when it comes to thanking those people who inspire, support and assist with a project like this, and it is impossible to name everyone in the reading community who give reason for and purpose to this book.

This historical tale was written at least in part to inspire and affirm *you*, in particular – our expanding tribe of healing-minded, nature inspired, plant loving, passion hearted outliers doing the good work on the authentic edge of an often unhealthy, disingenuous and superficial contemporary reality. Thank you for being the real and aware ones, for caring and serving, savoring and celebrating, and for finding this tale of benefit in your purposeful lives.

I extend my deep gratitude to the cadre of volunteer editors/proofreaders who rallied to go over these pages in the hurried final weeks before we published: Lauren Stauber and Asa Henderson, and their team of Kiva Rose Hardin, Resolute Michaels, Inga Hulleberg, Danika Anderson, Traci Picard, and Katie Winston. Far more than merely catching annoying typos, their creative input resulted in chapters being reordered, incongruences repaired, and lines rewritten – resulting in a better book.

Most profound appreciation must go to my dear family: To our precious daughter Rhiannon, for whom Earth is a teacher and magic alive... what a great pleasure it is to be her Papa. To our devoted Loba, helping to sustain me with grounding woodstove-cooked meals as well as unflagging love, providing an inspiring example of attachment to place, natural contentment, and the savoring and celebrating of elemental life through over a year of dawn 'til dusk writing. And to loving partner Kiva Rose, providing valuable incisive feedback and managing the vital outreach, while serving as a real-life model for many of lead-character Omen's traits, experiences, and feelings... learning and growing from her wound, becoming better tempered through great efforts, committed to healing, nourishing and stretching herself as she helps with the healing and growth of others.

Finally, I would be sadly amiss if I did not bow to this land, the canyon wilderness that houses us, the larger enchanted Southwest, New Mexico and the inspired Gila (pronounced *hee-la*) in particular. An unbroken adventurer and eclectic anachronism like myself could never have made a home somewhere different, and nowhere else could have been home to this novel.

–Jesse Wolf Hardin
June 2012

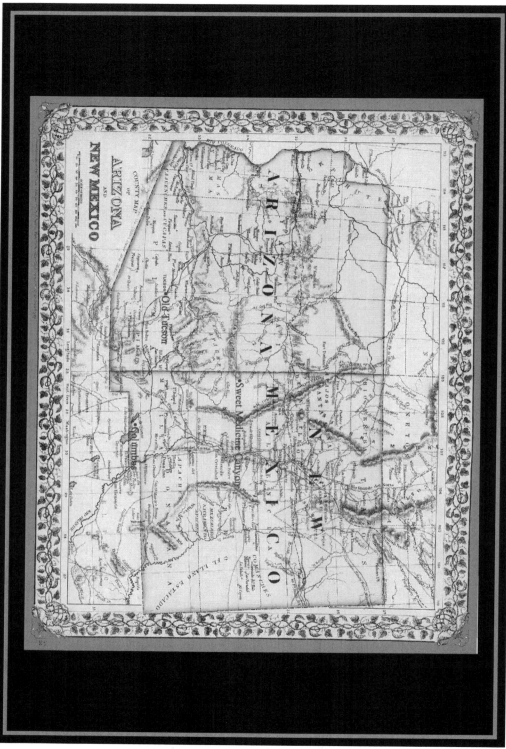

CONTENTS

PART II

PART III

PART IV

PART V

PART VI

PART VII

PROLOGUE

Sweet Medicine Botanical Sanctuary, S.W. New Mexico
August, 1966

At the first sound of his approach, the ravens stopped their croak and squawk, the squirrels their boisterous chatter.

And then seeing it was only Eland, they all started up again.

The old man found satisfaction in the assured resumption of their familiar songs: the melodies of the Canyon Wrens, and the crystalline notes of the Hermit Thrush. The sonatas of the Summer Tanager and Orange-Crowned Warbler, and the Gila Woodpecker rock and roll, all aural overlays atop a flowing river adagio. Tassel-eared nut chasers arguing over an acorn cache. The commentary of black-feathered gossips, bobbing up and down on the springy upper branches of silvered river Alders. These were the notes and tunes attending his continuing quest, once leading him through the bloody turf and tome of war, and lately no further than to a certain hallowed grove.

It was a special occasion that Eland had dressed for, thought one repeated every single day of his life... worthy of a clean white poet's shirt and jacquard vest, the Edwardian jacket with its wide brown lapels and beige bound edges. His custom made knee high boots of mule leather and favorite blue silk scarf. An old fashioned shoulder bag made from the skin of an elk, and the finest of his several treasured sugarloaf sombreros.

He progressed ever so slowly, though more because he savored every step and sight than due to any physical encumbrance his the decades might have wrought. He steadied himself with a carved Oak walking stick taller than his five-foot, eight-inch frame. There was no shuffling or dragging of the feet, only one deliberate step after the next, on what was clearly the most well used path in the canyon. It lay bound by rows of stacked rocks placed carefully, lichen side up, laden with heady Hop vines, and filled with soft river sand glowing golden in the last rays of the day.

On either side could be seen species of plants indicative of Eland's conscientious caretaking, as well as of his healing, including several varieties of calming *Salvia*, liver supportive Milk Thistle heavy with seed, clusters of multi-crowned Yarrow, spindly Artemisia that he'd long ago been convinced to call Moonwort. The trail was set just wide enough to accommodate an amorous couple walking hand in hand, and where it crossed the flat stretch of meadow, it seemed to twist and turn for no apparent reason. None, that is, but the creative exertions of two people determined never to have to walk the straight and narrow.

At the meadow's far edge, the path dropped off into a flood plain, then immediately entered into a shaded tunnel cut through an otherwise impassable band of white-barked Cottonwoods and red-stemmed Willows. On the first trunks to either side of the path were affixed decorations, befitting the gate posts of a secret garden, temple or shrine – or the entrance to a place of mystery, a revered grotto, a playground for goat-horned fauns and wise-eyed fairies more intense than they are cute or sweet. A pair of intimidating Aztec masks festooned with wild turkey feathers, male and female guardians fiercely carved from gentle palm. Driftwood Alder roots that wind around one another in an unbroken embrace. The bleached jawbones of a young deer. Bunches of dried Monarda blooms, tied with black velvet ribbon long faded from the sun.

The masks seemed to warn of consequences for the unaware or disrespectful, to insist on heightened consideration or even veneration for that which was housed within. The feathers bespoke movement and flight, the woven roots of devotion and place. The crumbling flowers and wind-polished bone were reminders of ever-transitioning beauty. Of the poetics of gesture and the possibility of meaning. Of pledges and bonds outlasting life. Of the necessity as well as the reward of aesthetic, courageous, celebratory living.

No priest or acolyte, Eland did not bow before walking in, yet his every move seemed to evince reverence and respect for this hallowed ground he daily visited and perpetually tended. And never did he seem more so than when he doffed his hat for a pausing rabbit, reached out to press the flesh of a Cottonwood or shake a Willow's hand. Whatever dues could make one truly welcome there – intention, focus, service, love – he had clearly paid, and continued to pay, in his stewardship of the land. In the gifting of wild seeds, tenderly dropped into holes made with the end of his walking stick. In those extra handfuls sprinkled onto the ground, intended for the hungry birds following branch to branch above him. In the tears that watered a lifetime's crop of hopes. In his whispered endearments and kind laughter. In that echoing promise: *forever*.

At the end of the tunnel gushed the silken river, its soothing, tumbling voice getting louder until he stood at its bank, rolled his pants up and stepped in. It could not have been considered safe for a man his age to be crossing even a shallow body of moving water such as that. But then, neither should it have been expected that the man in question would ever put safety ahead of either pleasure or purpose. Positioning his staff to his downriver side, he leaned into it as he crossed the ten-foot span, his hand gripping just beneath the chin of the broad headed animal that crowned it. The far, north-facing shore leaned back against an immense vertical cliff, its steep banks supported by a Celtic knot of interlacing Alder roots. Where they extended down into the water, they trailed long, blood red tendrils, an alphabet of dancing crimson swirls under opalescent layers of color, of breaking and repairing designs, reflected leaves and refracting light. At the place where Eland left the river, the same mass of roots that usually made a living wall created a series of gradual steps instead. At the fourth and uppermost sylvan stair, just above the reach of the highest floods, the trees opened out into a nearly perfect circle some thirty feet across. Woven through the spaces between the Alders were Wild Grape vines, from the branches of which were hung hooded brass candle lanterns, a brittle brown leather Sam Brown belt of World War I vintage, and bundles of medicinal herbs left not unlike the offerings of those natives who had lived and prayed there eight hundred years before he ever saw the canyon, tasted the water, or held in arms and heart there the bittersweet reality of love.

Eland lit candles that brightened the space's deep and constant shade – each a votive of his devotion – before sitting down in front of the well-dressed earth mound at the center. All around him was evidence of his affection, creating an altar of sorts, comprised of items no one but he could hope to know the significance of. To his immediate left, projected a clutch of creamy white Yarrow flowers from a cobalt blue medicine bottle, an assortment of nearly heart-shaped rocks, and gnarly Oshá root enthroned on a small fairytale plate. To his right, were carefully arrayed items associated with a creature that had been extinct in the Southwest for over three decades. A foot tall Hopi Bear-Mother sculpture featured a host of tiny children on her lap, a fired-clay "Storyteller" as they were called, regaling her charges with her ursine tales of deeds and quests. And a few inches away, lorded the giant yellowed skull of a Grizzly, minus its lower jaw, yet still sporting impressive front fangs that glistened in the glow of the nearest lit candle.

At the base of the mound and directly in front of Eland, there was a decorative brass and glass display case, protecting its contents while providing clues as to its purpose and meaning. Petite iridescent Hummingbird feathers nested inside the bosom of a fossilized shell, along with a Bear claw pendant strung on a necklace of seeds. Earrings shaped like a cluster of amber leaves, rested on sherds of native pottery painted white with brown spirals. And a gold plated pocket watch with an inscription on the back, incongruously resting atop some worthless paper money emblazoned in purple ink with the portrait of a onetime flamboyant Mexican revolutionary and bandit, Pancho Villa.

Eland slipped off his messenger's bag and sat the rest of the way down, leaning back against a familiar Alder. A minute later, he was lifting up the flap on his bag and reaching into it, first pulling out a glistening brass mortar and pestle such as a Middle Ages apothecary might use to grind various herbs and minerals for help in healing the sick. Setting it to one side, he put his hand back in the bag and came out with a mildewed envelope, the George Washington profiles on its stamps branded with a fifty year-old postmark. Eland leaned over, carefully positioned it in the glass case, and then reached towards his bag for yet a third item, a simple Apache Bear Fetish that had been carved out of green banded Ricolite, a serpentine found nowhere but in the Burro Mountains south of there. This and the mortar he moved to the mound, before stopping to rest and look around.

In the final moments of daylight, he could be seen lifting his head and softly smiling, as if having spotted a dear friend. Closing his eyes, as one might who had just caught a whiff of the most wonderful and reassuring scent. Tapping his feet, as if imagining himself running heartily to someone's side. Laughing, as if the whole canyon – the whole world! – laughed with him. And then, crying low and deep, on into the blacking night. Whispering a name that caused his whitening *bigote* – that proud mustache of his - to quiver, the name of someone magnificently acknowledged and incontrovertibly loved. A name hard to make out over the birds and river, one that sometimes sounded like *I'm comin'*, and other times like *home*.

"Omen. My Omen..."

While he'd been coming here for years, he'd seldom stayed so late, without a blanket wrap up in. And cool the evening must have felt, for he, shivering, then turned and lay belly down on his earthen bench, pressing his body into it until it calmed his shakes. It seemed to him that the soil there radiated heat to warm both body and soul, counteracting both bone chilling loneliness and cold night winds. Cheek to grassy dirt, Eland threw his arms around the mound and squeezed with all his might. He hugged, as if he were being hugged back. Kissed the raised ground as though it were responding lips. Stroked the Mint and Lemon Balm that grew there like he might a loving animal's coat... or a plant-loving wife's leaf-laden hair.

The moon rose half full of promise, and wholly empty of regret. When its light reached the grove, those bits that made it down through the thick canopy seemed to fall like ice crystals, like the sound of tiny bells, and then to spill like magic paint upon the ground. Down, onto the items on the altar. Down, onto the tear-streaked face of the man, and the black hat by his side. Down, onto the Bear skull, now seeming to grin and shine. And like fairy dust, it seemed to fill him, lift him, give him the wings by which all reach their Neverland, their personal "forever after". The moonlight played on the taut strings upon which all life was strung. And it was this music that caused him to rise, grasp the shoulder and waist of his walking staff as it were a cherished partner, and dance.

His was an old-timey waltz meant to be played with well worn instruments by damp-eyed musicians, a slow heart-stirring tune worthy of a groom on the happy day of his wedding. Or of the honored human guest at some midnight picnic for spirits. Or a battlefield survivor, after all others had been slain.

One-two-three, one-two-three, around and around the mound he went, until exhausted by pleasure and pain like an ecstatic sacred Sun Dancer bearing the weight of Buffalo skulls hung from a skewered chest. Sated and spent at last, the old man collapsed and spread-eagled on his back, his sombrero rolling and then resting in the grass. his head propped up by the base of the mound like an earthen pillow, watching for the myriad stars to cross the small openings between the enclosing Alder umbrella.

The first light of day revealed a normally keen-eyed veteran of conflicts both inner and outer, now with eyes closed, seemingly at peace with the world. He was clearly unaware of the family of raccoons that noisily sorted through the altar items, and then pulled the apple out of his coat pocket, as well as the big-eared doe that stepped into the clearing and snorted and stomped its hooves before bounding off. He made no movement at all, even when the Stellar Jays began squabbling overhead, as Stellar Jays were known to do. Nor when the nearby Ravens flew off, harried by a pair of angry little Tanagers. Nor when three young squirrels fished around in a hollow stump for nuts they'd stored, each carrying one in their mouth up into the safety of the trees before stopping to feed.

Rather than simply getting on with the business of enjoying their breakfast, however, these squirrels instead seemed to be working hard to disrupt each other's meal. As soon as one would take an acorn from its mouth and start to remove its shell, one of the others would rush in to try to take it away. In this manner, each in turn did its part to ensure that none of them would be able to eat.

And it was in this way that one of the nuts fell, much to the indignation and dismay of the furry host watching its descent, glancing off of one branch after another, until bouncing ignominiously off of the old man's head.

In an instant his eyes were open, and he was sitting up straight and alert. He smiled at the shenanigans of the squirrels, and used the staff to help himself up, but not before mischievously patting the soft bottom end of that well mounded and well tended grave.

"I'll be back," he said with conviction, as he always did before starting down the root-made steps.

Much to do today, he thought. *Much to take care of. Much to make more beautiful. Much to sit down and write.*

Moonheart – White Mt. Reservation
1897

PART I

Chapter I

A WILD SEED:
Omen & Moonheart

White Mountain Apache Reservation, S.E. Arizona, 1897

The day the one called Omen was born, Moon had determined to spend the morning walking. This, even though the hours spent among river Cattails or ridge-top Aspen were hours when no dough was being mixed to rise, no melons watered, no cistern cleaned. Her ruddy-faced husband lay sleeping off a hangover on the sitting room couch, and there would be no one to strip the leaves of the *Quelites* off their stalks or to set the trays out in the blazing July sun. Any number of tasks were predicated on the season and the weather, and she knew she approached the end of the drying season. In another week the annual monsoons could start, the long series of afternoon thunderstorms that would make all the White Mountains quake. But Moon needed time outside as much as she needed air to breathe. Not time away from chores, or even away from that "worthless" snoring man, but time out in restorative creation. It was only the child swelling her belly, she was sure, that kept her from smoking and drinking. And only the woods that kept her lifelong sadness in check.

Every chance she could, she'd visit the snares she set for rabbit, gather and spread the seeds of those plants preferred by the deer, and poke around for mushrooms in the forest litter. She fed on them, but made sure they in turn were fed. She tried to keep an eye on every creature and plant, and how well they were doing, taking on the responsibility for guarding their wellbeing and seeing to their needs. These walks had become a bit of a test over the last couple months, carrying the weight of her first child in front of her in a way that made balance difficult, a protrusion that got her tangled more often in the stands of brush and Willow.

The pregnancy never seemed anything less than right to her, even if it meant raising a baby alone. The stretching uterus felt as good and natural as taking a man inside her, regardless of the causes or consequences of either. Over the years, she exercised little more resistance to her instincts than a wild animal might to the cycles of rut and procreation, mostly in a series of monogamous relationships with generally abusive men. The best that would usually be said of her in these situations was that she was nearly as hard on her oppressors as they were on her.

Moon put on her olive wool poncho and headed out. What better way to prepare her nineteen-year-old body and spirit for what lay ahead, she thought, than a hike to the head of the valley, over the creek in front of her cabin, past the log outbuildings, through the fields of purple-crested Beeweed to the grove of Grandmother Ponderosas. Normally her head felt heavy as rock, a terrible burden to her neck, with a mind clouded by floodwaters of illusion and regret. But the further she walked, the lighter it inevitably felt... and clearer, until only a lens to see through, a conduit through which to reach out and connect. Barely out of sight of her abode, the incessant self-analysis had already slowed to a halt, with even the words in her thoughts beginning to break apart into snippets of wind and bird songs. Halfway through the

Beeweed, she was as a bee herself, giddy with pollen, tipping unsteadily but willingly on the very edge of the blossom of life. Entering the pines, there was neither comment nor qualification left, only hushed reverence for something she felt akin to, something huge and palpably thrumming. The woman who so depended on her boundaries and defenses, felt her walls quaver in its presence, and then dissolve around her.

It was in this opened and vulnerable state that she first heard the baying of dogs ahead, followed by unintelligible conversation. A few yards further, the trail spilled out into a glen circumscribed by a ghost-white choir of Quaking Aspens. She stood before what she took to be a pair of middle-aged Mormon settlers with clean-shaven faces, with lever-action rifles of some make or other leaning up against the nearest tree. One held back a pair of hounds struggling against the taut leather leashes, while a second knelt down in front of a huge blonde Bear with its skin half peeled back. She watched as he deftly cut strips of meat off the back, slapping them into a pile on a canvas tarp next to him.

Eerily, the dogs paid Moon no more mind than if she were a resident bush, and the settlers looked up only ever so briefly with looks of neither surprise nor interest, scarily devoid of feeling. Turning back towards home, she realized that it was this apparent absence of malice or love, passion or compassion, empathy or anger that scared her most about her human kind, and she sensed in their shadows an aura of detachment more perversely evil, even, than heated acts of hatred or conscious ill intent. She was a hunter herself, a taker of life and consumer of flesh. And while Grizzlies were always rare as hen's teeth, they were hell on livestock and could expect to get back a little of what they put out. But there was nonetheless something about this particular Bruin's death that gnawed at her guts. Something in it that followed her home.

Moon was barely out of the pine grove when the tears started to flow, and only halfway through the Beeweed before her water broke. The same oceanic fluids that floated all life gushed down her legs as she walked, soaked her Spanish dress, filled her sandals and drained out onto the welcoming ground. Before she got back to the creek the dress was already off, wadded together with her poncho.

She stepped naked into the crystalline current and sat down, first watching the patterns it made as it swirled around her distended belly, then the water striders that skimmed about on its surface. The water felt only slightly cooler than her own body, thanks to its day in the sun. She'd just started to relax when the painful contractions started, and Omen's life began.

Chapter 2

ELAND:

A Son Of New Mexico

Santa Fe, New Mexico Territory - 1892

Regardless of one's blood, being born in New Mexico was like being birthed to three mothers, one Anglo, one Hispanic, one Native.

Three hundred miles northeast of Omen's Gila was Santa Fe, a city of several thousand at the junction where the onetime Rocky Mountain fur trade met the California-bound wagon trains on the trail of the same name. It was the crossroads between Texas and eastwards, and the true West. Between ancient ways and modern times. By the time Eland made his appearance to the sound of his own mama's labored screams, it was a city made of equal parts of three distinct cultures, interactive but unmixed. Eland did not grow up a Santa Fean so much as a *Coyote*, embodying elements of character from all three.

Like most *Norteños* at that time, Eland's parents believed in what they called the melting pot, wherein citizens gladly gave up their various ethnic traditions and biases in exchange for membership in an enlightened monoculture. In this mythical vessel there would be no so-called hard-nosed Germans, practical English, sensuous French, savage Indians, or untrustworthy Mexicans... only Americans, defined not by their skin color or place of ancestry but by shared visions, priorities, work ethics and politics. By common fashions and purchasing trends. By believing in the same government, identifying with those on one side of the current national border, and defining themselves in contrast to those on the other side of the imaginary line.

Santa Fe turned out good for their souls, just as they'd thought, but it played hell with their minds. Ornate Catholic churches that welcomed the newcomers of Irish and Nordic descent, but confused them with its emphasis on a Black Madonna and Holy Mother, tempted some submerged part of their beings with the pagan *Copal* swinging in its golden incense burners. Half the community spoke a romantic language they could only partially make out, and celebrated something called *La Dia de la Muerte,* or Day Of The Dead. A portion still prayed to a Great Spirit, in Tewa, Hopi and Navajo. Another portion were English speaking anachronisms and iconoclasts, who nonetheless had their own language of renaissance and rebellion, eclectics ejected from the maw of any number of East or West Coast cities, feeling at home no where else than the city and state that most welcomed differences. New Mexico was a daily indication that the melting pot remained a lie. And Santa Fe was proof that diversity sometimes translated into a vibrant vitality, if one was only willing to believe one's eyes.

Eland grew up playing on the small Santa Fe River, a few hours from Sun Mountain, and within a day's ride of Santa Fe Baldy peak and the Pecos forest with its gushing crystalline river and ancient ruins. He grew up near still inhabited adobe pueblos, indigenous communities resplendent with tradition, noted for their costumed dances held in gratitude for the rain and the corn. The Spanish speakers all around him set an example of holding close to the earth in spite of the pressure to assimilate through the tumultuous winds of change.

Yet for all the diversity of Santa Fe, Eland's mother and father based their sense of continuity and belonging on their adherence to the social norms of their fellow English-speaking residents, their actions determined by the disapproval or compliments of their customers and neighbors. Both considered themselves progressive, defined back then as a condition of not only tolerance and magnanimity, but of advancing knowledge. It was their contention that if people lived in primitive conditions, or adhered to fascinating but quaint rituals, it was only because they didn't know any better... that all that was needed to raise the populous of the world from the state of ignorance, starvation or war, was education. And it was up to America, as both the repository of the world's wisdom and the leader in innovation, to take it to them, torch in hand, carrying the light into the huddled darkness of their lives.

Far as he knew, Eland was the one beneficiary of this enlightened attitude, having been surrounded since he was born by literally thousands of books. Shelves full in the bedrooms and den, piles of poetry and plays awaiting filing on the floor in the hall. For all the fine art statues and paintings hanging on the walls, a guest's first impression would be of a house made of text, tale and tome. While his friends were bouncing balls back and forth or endlessly knocking each other's marbles out of a ring, Eland was most content climbing on ladders to reach an unexplored volume, opening the heavy covers and reverently turning the paper or parchment pages. Their smells of leather and dust attracted him and he loved the illustrations, mostly line engravings of incredible detail, the lines bunched together to create the effect of shadows, bending and contorting in unison to delineate a form. But from day one, the words held a fascination for him as well. The squiggles and circles stood in for the wet feathered reality of heron and crane, for the smell of South Sea Islands and the earthen pottery of the Mimbres. They somehow contained the necessary magic to evoke the movement of wings in flight, the strike of the trout, the brave hero's act, the simple motion of getting up or sitting down. They communicated the crashing of thunder and the power of love.

Eland Howell - Santa Fe, NM - 1896

Long before he could read, he would trace over the letters with his curious mind, try to guess the sounds and meanings, to decipher the code that he was sure would reveal untold riches. Eland knew that words could direct one like a treasure map, to unimaginable discovery and reward. They could lead not endlessly further into the depths of the book, into objectification and disembodied language... but right out through the back cover, impelling the reader outside to the very subject and object, noun and verb of experienced life.

That was one of many ways that he was different from his parents. They had read most of the same books that he grew up reading, could recount the details of many of them, and had an opinion on the subject as well as the style and execution. Yet they were not moved in quite the same way. What reverberated in their heads, rumbled in his chest and bowels instead, drew his eyes in the direction of new sights, sent his nose in search of exotic odors, inspired his legs to take walks and his heart to take chances. A collection of Turkish poetry was not simply a lavish visit to the Near East, but a call to immediately and more sparsely write a poem. A treatise on the tracking skills of Indians meant identifying the marks in his backyard made by assorted wild denizens as well as domestic dogs and cats, then following them on hands and knees to see where they went, extrapolating where there were going and why. Tales of flying dragons had a four-year-old Eland climbing out of his window and up on the roof, with cookies and other dragon snacks in order to hopefully call one in. And stories like Ulysses and the search for the golden fleece drove Eland nearly crazy, until he, too, left a family and their expectations in a dangerous quest for adventure, meaning and purpose... and for what he hoped would someday be his partner and love.

Drawn. Copyright. Photogravure 1906 by E. S. Curtis

Chapter 3

PLANTS:
Omen's Proof of Miracles

Life for a growing Omen was exceptional and wondrous, but also anything but easy. It seemed to her that she had been swimming her entire life, since the very first moment she was expelled into the creek, umbilical still attached, arms instinctually and purposefully parting the waters. It was as if each time she broke through the surface, there was yet another ceiling above her to struggle towards and rise above, in endless succession. And as if with each surfacing she could see more clearly, not just around her and above her but down into the depths of being and meaning.

While she could not claim to remember the day of her delivery, she seemed to recall many occasions of dying and being born. Sometimes these apparent memories spoke only of soul-deadening traumas from which she'd rolled away and survived. Other times they took on unfamiliar shapes and contexts, referencing worlds she could not herself have seen, yet somehow she knew them. She recalled, from this deep well of knowing, what it meant to be truly at home in her skin, comfortable with her appearance and propensities, needs, desires and dreams... and she had spent her life trying to experience that again.

Omen was both informed and inspired by place. She grew not on the land so much as out of it, like Cottonwoods and Bear Grass. Each Fall a part of her collapsed and withered alongside the wildflowers and grape vines she loved. Each Spring some new part of her erupted just as the Globemallow and Mexican Poppies did, spreading her toes like roots in the truth and sustenance of ground, while branching out to the rest of the living world, and stretching upwards towards the light. In Summer she was all over the mountains and totally out of control... not unlike the outlaw Peppermint that spread from bank to bank, once contained in a single plot that Moon fertilized with Omen's afterbirth. By eighteen months, she'd escape out of the sitting room every time Moon forgot to keep the screen door latched. The only thing that reined her in was the need to take more and more care of her baby sister, the more that her mother drank.

Omen was the eldest of what would be five children all told, the products of an equal number of men Moon had briefly sought happiness with. There was, of these, one love that Moon refused to talk about, an adventurer so devoted to her that she had to cheat on him twice before he'd finally leave her to her bitter self-made prophecy... and tragically, a love so exceptional that it became the yardstick by which all other loves were found wanting. He who had contributed so much to the happiest two years of her life, became yet another reason for her profound sadness.

Omen appreciated inheriting Moonheart's powers and insight, as well as her affinity with plant spirits and her ability to heal, her wild spunk and formidable will. Like her mother, she would sometimes think words that others could hear in their heads, and continue to feel someone significant in her life even from far away. She'd concluded that this was a mixed blessing, however. She shared in the intense joy of a pair of Mourning Doves preening each other's neck feathers between taking bites from the hanging Wild Grapes. And the giddiness of a young Cliff Swallow, leaping for the first time from its nest a hundred feet up... the excitement of trusting one's instincts and attempting the seemingly impossible. But she ached as well, when it came time to clear trees from the new garden area, and when she had to cut her alcoholic mama off, even though she could still feel her calling.

Even as baby, it seemed that Omen felt close to – and a student of – the green growing beings. The first time Moon ever sat her outside, she immediately crawled over to a cluster of blooming Yarrow. Intently gazed at it from a mere inch or two away. Wiggled her little nose, as though to better take in its fragrance. Petted it, as if it could sense her and enjoy the strokes. Gently, as if it were capable of feeling hurt. Promising devotion with her soft blue eyes, as though it were possible for it to feel rejection in its tender green heart.

From earliest memory, Omen had considered all plants her teachers, allies and friends. It did not matter that they couldn't rise from their bed and knock at Moon's door to ask for her to come out and play, that she would instead have to always go to them. Nor did it seem to bother her that they spoke in a language much more hushed and difficult to hear than that of people or animals. If so, she would simply be quieter, more still, stay longer. It was in these ways that she absorbed their wisdom, their flowering gnosis, slowly pulling it up and into herself through the roots that she, like they, grew.

Omen honored plants, because they bloomed in the compost-heap of death, and got energy from light. She loved trees that could live for a hundred years, but no more so than those plants that graciously returned to the soil they came from in a single splendid season, in a Summer of no regret.

She loved trees for their cooling presence, for their gnarled appendages extending out of washed-out riverbanks, and the way their roots sometimes held rocks suspended in the air like an offering. And she was just as fond of bushes, for hiding her in their calm hollow centers when she wanted to be alone. It made her happy to pinch the spongy edible Cattail, and lick the sweet blossoms of the *Uña del Gato*, the Catclaw. Omen loved the way briars spread their Raspberry profundity through the entrails of sugar-drunk birds. The way oranges made her tongue tingle, and how she felt after a bowl of fresh Watercress. The seedy grin of the Sunflower. The vulva-like folds of the Datura blossoms.

She respected Dandelions for being feral and tasty, and more so after she'd heard of their ability to proliferate even in the manicured yards of Flagstaff or Albuquerque. The few times she'd gone to the small Mormon town of Springerville, she'd been thrilled to see them poking their cheery blossoms up through the cracks in their downtown sidewalks. Omen loved all so-called weeds, because they'd been judged and labeled, and so had she. Because they were irrepressible, blooming no matter how many seasons they were pulled or poisoned.

Omen was grateful to the Cholla Cactus and Stinging Nettle, for showing her where and how to step... no doubt pleasing those other life forms she might otherwise have trod upon and crushed. And she was wild about wildflowers, because of the look they brought to a lover's or grandmother's eye, how each smelled a little different from the rest. Because nobody planted them or paid for them, and they would have been content to shine their colors with or without human audience. Wildflowers seemed aware that flattery was often accompanied by swift-moving shears, which was something she was more than glad to be taught.

If it was her intention to hear and learn, it had always been the plants' intention to express, warn, entice. Flowers instructed insects to spread their pollen with a display of inviting colors and enticing smells. Fruit trees enlisted the help of an expressive language of sugar and flavor, but it went much further than that. Herbalists and wildcrafters had traditionally been taught how to locate, identify or narrow down the likely medicinal uses of a plant by reading its signature. Omen could often recognize the antibiotic or diuretic properties of an unfamiliar herb through careful observation of its color, leaf configuration, surface texture, and the specific environment in which it grew. When pressed as to how she knew such things, she would simply say the plant told her. And indeed it had.

The plant world spoke not just of practicalities but of magic, as some called it, or spirituality, as it was known by others. It was in the branches of knowledge that the indigenous shamans of many cultures would climb, making a symbolic entry into the universal tree of life: a composite of every vegetal form in existence, from which all life and knowledge sprout.

Such magic could be accessed through any available forest, since the roots of one intertwined with the roots of every other, the roots of tall grasses exchanging hormonal and electrical signals with Sunflowers, Barrel Cactus, and Canyon Grape, and linked by interwoven subterranean fungi. Region to region, one continent to the next. Together they made up a circumglobal mat of interconnected forms, creating a continuous field of accessible vegetal consciousness. Seeing the world that way meant there could be harvesting but no wholesale cutting. No wood or food taken without first giving thanks, and then giving back in turn... by replanting more than was cut or eaten.

It was hard for an Apache-raised girl to understand how some could see the planet as but a lifeless rock upon whose surface a bounty was distributed for the good of man. Who saw animals not as spirits but as steaks, fur and wool, pet or threat. Who saw trees only as lumber to be turned into buildings or to shade the sun. Who judged plants as being decorative or itchy, weeds or crops.

To Omen, they were not just wondrous sunshine-eating entities, without whom humans and most of the life on Earth would die.

They were proof of miracles, and reason for hope. The inspiration for a good and balanced life, and examples of how to live it.

They were her ever growing, ever reaching truth.

They were the medicine she would need.

Doña Rosa — Curandera

Chapter 4

APPRENTICE TO A CURANDERA:
The Herbalist Doña Rosa

Omen was 11 before she saw anyplace larger than the little Mormon town of Springerville. Moonheart had promised to introduce her to someone special in the growing city of Tucson, a day and half ride south of the reservation by horse. And Omen didn't mind the trip, since her mother seemed more than happy to go slow enough for her to stop and investigate those strange plants she'd never seen before.

The lower in elevation they got, the more fantastical the shapes of that which grew there. Catclaw Acacia. Twisty Ironwood and Mesquite. Spiked stalks of Ocotilla twenty feet high, topped with tubular red buds. Furry looking Teddy Bear Cholla, with many more stickers than the Walking Stick Cholla where she came from. And most outrageous of all, the giant, many-armed Saguaros standing like gods against the sky.

Being Spring, there was a profusion of flowers every which way she looked, celebratory eruptions of color for which she yet had no names– Larkspur and Poppy, Lupine and Jackass Clover, Venus Blazing Star and Wolfberry, Desert Senna and Rose Mallow. Some, like the Cereus, opened at night, while the majority slept in the dark and burst forth again with each new day. In order to be able to identify them later, she broke off small branches, collected leaves, gathered flowers and pressed them in the paperback book she'd brought for that purpose. Its title, in elaborate script, was Spellbound, though it hardly mattered since she couldn't read it, and since its highest literary achievement was to flatten and preserve desert blossoms with tender tales of beauty and life housed between every page.

As washed-out and hushed as the desert's hues could be in broad daylight, they took on entirely new tones at dusk and dawn, metallic copper greens ricocheting off of beaming golds, pinks and purples, all vibrating together, somehow getting brighter as the sun sank into its sea of sand. Her morning there was alive with music, with a multitude of songbirds vying for who could deliver the loudest or most complex tune. And her afternoons were more quiet than sleep, save for the footfall of their mounts, and the rustling of reptiles when the Horses were stilled. The mountains had held her tight to their bosom, and their forests had clothed her, but here she felt naked and exposed. She sensed how, unlike the prairie dogs and ground squirrels, snakes and toads, she could not burrow out of sight. But to her relief, she felt no judgment in that which was witness to her. Neither mercy, nor criticism.

She could nonetheless feel in the very core of her being that this was not her land, or rather, that she did not belong to it. It appeared infinitely strange, and she was a stranger passing through. But as such, Omen was a stranger bearing gifts, bringing with her awe, interest and gratitude as sweet as any Myrrh or Frankincense. Where others might have seen only harshness and thorn, she beheld instead a bouquet of landscape, a royal gown on the body of the Earth mother, jeweled, furred and feathered. Not desolate at all, as she'd heard some describe it, but teeming with life forms out of a child's dreams. Whip-tail Lizards and Kangaroo Rats. For Omen, observation was veneration, and a personal linking up of the watcher and the watched. She was the Harris Hawk madly flapping after a Cottontail, and the rabbit as it zigged and zagged to escape the grasping claws. The Roadrunner, as well as the pretty young girl with the squinting bear eyes.

Looking away from the craggy Catalina mountains and to the south and west, the unbroken expanse reminded her of infinity, a sky too big to contain, stars too numerous to count.

"Something else, isn't it?" Moon asked, enjoying her darling daughter's delight.

"It's wonderful! Amazing! I can't hardly believe it!" she answered in quick succession. "I could spend weeks or months just trying to see it all."

Omen found the town of Tucson every bit as fascinating, though considerably more intimidating. There were cars rushing back and forth on every thoroughfare, and more adobe houses that she had ever seen in close proximity. The downtown plaza was filled with children playing. Old men on decorative cast iron benches reading. Lovers strolling, heads pressed together. Someone strumming a guitar, with a mason jar out for tips. They rode on and into an ever-narrowing maze of streets, its houses older and smaller, with fewer cars and more horses. A boy led a burro loaded down with two racks of bricks, and a two or three year old girl looking serious and important on top. Omen followed her mother down an *acequia*, reining to a stop in front of a vine-covered house.

"Why are we stopping here?" Omen asked, her voice pinched with concern.

"I want you to stay here for a couple days, while I go tend to some business. Then we'll do some shopping and get you something special before we head back."

"I thought we were going to be together," Omen said accusingly, her face set in a frown.

There had already been too many occasions of her being farmed out, left with unpleasant strangers or resentful distant relatives when, for whatever reason, her grandmother was unable to take her. But this time proved different. It was not just anyone she was being consigned to, but Doña Rosa, one of the most well respected "Curanderas" or healers, of the rapidly growing town nicknamed Old Pueblo. She answered the knock on her door in loose white pants and a white *huipil*, making the tiny woman's brown skin and thick black hair appear all the darker in contrast. Her eyes were obsidian, though warmer, and indicated a smile the mouth had yet to express. Tiny lines and creases told tales of tears and laughter, consternation and concern well beyond her years. But it was her hands that Omen focused on, emanating power and will of their own, gripping the door handle, touching Moonheart gently on the forehead like a blessing, then both of them reaching out for her.

"So what have you brought me here, *querida*?" The Doña looked suddenly fiercer than Omen thought imaginable, causing her to recoil in alarm.

"You can't keep her," Moon said. "Only borrow her for a while."

Moonheart's smirk would have given away the ruse, if Omen had not been fixed on this unsmiling woman with the long single braid hanging down her back. Then, just as suddenly, the countenance of the Curandera shifted again, and she broke out laughing, slapped her leg, and nearly fell to the ground in unrestrained glee.

"Don't worry, the Doña won't hurt you," Moon said, nudging her towards this woman with her dark, expressive face and signature gold tooth. Rosita, as her friends called her, was only in her thirties, but to Omen she looked particularly old, or more alarmingly, ageless. She wore a white cotton tunic decorated with the floral embroidery of flower obsessed Mexico, with a piece of familiar looking Oshá root hanging from a cord around her neck that swung back and forth as she leaned over the frightened little girl. She carried it not to treat infection, as Omen would find out, but to ward off poisonous snakes. While she lived in rattler paradise, she'd reportedly yet to ever see one close to house.

Moon took wide eyed Omen's hand and walked her inside. The main room was dark except for a few candles, and what little light was able to filter in through the greenery that draped over the windows. A shelf featured a couple of overstuffed chairs sat on either side of a fireplace, above which was an altar combining the most dramatic symbols of two vastly different religions. Ten-inch high carvings of Aztec gods sat next to a crucifix with the martyred Jesus shown bleeding liberally from his head, feet, hands and side. And on the wall, a color portrait of the Virgin of Guadalupe in a stained wood frame, with Roses and Maguey at her feet connecting her not only to the Old World of Europa but also to the ancient Aztec rituals of the New. At her feet was salt for making instant Holy Water, an always convenient egg from a black chicken for a quick *barrida* sweeping of a sick adult or child, along with a cigar rolled in corn husk and cup kept half full of tequila as an offering, since the Virgin was known to appreciate a good smoke and drink, and next that a full bottle... "for medicinal purposes only."

The tradition of the *tepati*, the *tictlim*, the Aztec healer, had not vanished with the Spaniards' conquest of Mexico, but merely transformed, adopting some of the conquerors' rituals and forms. Tla'loc, Tonantzin and Quetzlcoatl were joined, not replaced, by the likes of San Judas Tadeo and San Martin de Porres. Now one could expect to hear the sweet etheric bars of Ave Maria follow ancient rumbling incantations. To the medicines and practices of the Olmecs, Mixtecs, Toltecs, Moors, Jews, Spaniards and Tarahumara were added the four humors of the early Greeks and

Romans. The modern Curandera blended the use of European herbs with those of the New World, Balkan Chamomile as well as jungle *Toloatizin,* Datura. Omen tried to isolate and identify all the exotic and mundane smells in the house, from a selection of fresh cut herbs to recently cooked chicken, from the Cocoa beans in the pestle to the smudge burning in a red clay bowl.

"Copal," the Doña said, when she saw Omen quizzically moving towards it. "Sage for cleansing, but Copal for prayer."

Omen took a tour of the room without bothering to ask, taking in every detail and trying to guess or intuit its significance in the Doña's life. The old tintype of a good-looking young man in a huge sombrero holding a rifle at his side. A framed photo of a small young woman with the Doña's features, standing among unfamiliar, twisting trees, a feather in her hair. And another tintype, this time of a tall woman with a powerful gaze, performing some kind of ritual over what appeared to be an ill old man.

"My husband," the healer explained, "before he was killed by assassins in Chihuahua. That's me in the middle, when I was fourteen, committing to *mi desarrollo,* my ten-year apprenticeship in the art of *curanderismo.* On the right is the legendary healer Santa Teresa de Cabora. The Mayo and Yaqui who resisted against *Presidente* Diaz with bows and arrows attacked his troops yelling '*Viva la Santa de Cabora',* making her their living patron saint."

Omen liked her already, and barely paid any attention when her mother knowingly nodded to the Doña and left for her planned rendezvous. The young lover of plants felt good in the abode of a Medicine Woman, not that different from her grandmother in her intensity and commitment to cures. She continued to admire the colorful yarn paintings, featuring the otherworldly visions of

Peyote-eating Huichols. She noticed the double barrel shotgun leaning in the corner, and noted the contents of an entire cupboard of tinctures and bottles of herbs.

"Aztecan *Pericón*," the Doña said, pointing to the first row of bottles. "My gardened plants, *Romero*, Rosemary, as smudge to disinfect and for rheumatism, and to keep away the plague. *Ruda*, Rue, used by midwives, and rubbed on the temples and neck to get rid of headache. *Manzanilla*, Chamomile, one of the most important. Calms the nerves, settles upset stomachs, cools burning eyes and skin, eases menstrual cramps. Minty *Yerba Buena*, the best thing we ever got from the Spanish friars, a wonderful tea for an ill stomach. *Mi Estafiate*, Wormwood. You see, it smells like Sage."

"It grows where we live," Omen said.

"Used for stomach complaints, a ceremonial herb, and to get rid of worms!"

"And this one?"

"What you call Marigold, *Cempasúchil*, good for fever and *mucho mas*. It's also called *Flor de Muerto*," the Doña said. "The flower of the dead."

Omen counted four dozing cats, as still as if slain. And a fifth with wide unblinking eyes, that looked like it never slept. Beneath one she saw a table, scattered with various parts of unknown plants. That made her think about the new specimens now in her saddlebags, and start imagining the questions she might ask.

"I hear you have been called to the plants. To be a *Yerbera*."

Doña Rosa — Curandera

It was special for Omen to hear that, out of such a powerful woman's lips.

"Oh, yes, I so want to! I know just what I want to do."

"*Si,*" the Doña said. "And first you will have to accept how little you know. And start asking the earth, and the plants, what they want from you."

Sensing Omen's defensiveness, she added that one cannot learn anything unless one drops all pretense and illusion, and accepts what really is. She dipped her finger in a small glass vial, and daubed a bit of lusciously fragrant Desert Lavender oil on her young charge's forehead.

"The mistake is thinking we exist to help people live longer, when our role is to remove the poisons that keep them from learning how to be more alive. More awake. With their spirits intact. To be healed is to become whole. That's what this calling is all about, young one. Whether you work with me, or learn it on your own."

"But you make all these medicines to cure those that are sick."

"These medicines don't cure the sickness, they help the body to mend itself. And what I do isn't to destroy the disease, it's to treat the *susto,* or the *desasombra,* the body's physical and emotional responses to trauma, as with the ritual of *limpia,* cleansing the impurities and making possible a return to balance. The three days of special diet. The herbs the patient chooses for the *barrida,* the ritual sweeping. The baths in Chamomile flowers and Rose petals. When the *tonalli,* the spirit, is cleansed, the life force prevails."

Omen was enthralled, yet for a moment she remembered her mother had ridden off for an activity too easily guessed. It was a sodden cloud, passing between her and the treasures she was being offered by the Doña. And the Doña knew it.

"Moon, she is very strong. But she suffers unquenchable yearnings. From *espanto*, the loss of spirit."

She paused a moment, before adding, "and *envidia, mi hijita...* jealousy of you."

Eland's Cabinet of Wonder

Chapter 5

A WEED:

Eland's Natural History Museum & The Forbidden Room

For some, dusk was a time of magic and transition.
Others thought it too dark to make out the path,
too light to see the stars.
-Eland Howell

What Eland appreciated most about his parents, besides their love, was their inclination to at least humor, if not actively support, his varied and (some said) odd interests, studies, hobbies, requests and demands. This included allowing him to take over the attic and turn it into a bedroom at age seven, and then to decorate it in the manner of a natural history museum or curiosity shop. It soon featured displays that all agreed were highly descriptive, but which his mother found increasingly disturbing. So many of the artifacts Eland gravitated to evoked for her not life, but death... and hence, her own inevitable passing. The broken Oak and Alder branches hung on twine from the ceiling, dressed in their brittle gold and russet leaves, acorns and catkins. The wings and claws of an Owl, a victim of the electric power lines. The complete skeleton of a Wood Rat, and the shed skin of a Bull Snake. Tail feathers from a turkey shotgunned for someone's holiday feast, and the bleached shell of a turtle, its flesh long ago a meal for eager teeth or beak. An unfortunate lizard who had gotten caught indoors, mummified in the heat of the sun, while looking out the window glass to the freedom that lay beyond. Dried flowers in a pitcher that needed no water.

No less troubling for her were the startling shaman masks that Eland often spent his generous allowance on: painted wooden faces with Jaguar features or with small, hinged creatures wagging from their mouths like tongues. And the foot-tall, red-eyed Bear Kachina, a human form with the furry head of Bear, holding a rattle and a clutch of sacred plants, hand-carved out of Cottonwood root by a Pueblo woman hoping to make a little money from the tourists on the plaza. Eland's father had looked as if Eland had stolen the kachina when he couldn't come up with a reasonable explanation for why a woman he had never met before would insist on giving such a thing to him.

It was, in fact, Eland's growing collection that discouraged his mother from going up the stairs to clean his room. The difficulty of dusting the feathers on the ragged, mounted eagle that a favorite teacher had given him. How upset Eland got when she didn't arrange everything back exactly the way he'd had it. Having to move the innumerable stones, bones and shells that covered the tabletops and shelves. Her last time up, she'd taken an interest in the recently added sherds of ancient pottery, with their geometric patterns done in black on white. She stopped and leaned over a counter, in order to read the poem on destiny that he'd tacked on his wall, then jumped when she dislodged a Timber Rattlesnake rattle, shaking out a warning all the way to the floor. She reached out a hand to steady herself, then involuntarily recoiled, imagining the hide she touched to be something alive. Swallowing hard, she slowly regained her composure, picked up her rags and duster and headed back downstairs.

That worked fine for Eland, who preferred to clean his own room, and who, like most kids, loved having a special place of his own outside the watchful eyes and judgments of supervising adults. A clubhouse requiring a secret password to enter. An opening into the land of the Fairies, too small for any but a child to enter. And a bastion of mystery, Merlin's inner *sanctus sanctorum*, a place free of cynicism, doubt and disbelief, and therefore a place where everything in the universe was still possible.

The skeletal remains and stretched furs were not macabre to him; they were design elements in the ever-evolving art of life. As alone and unaffiliated as he often felt in school, in town, in crowds of acquaintances talking excitedly about what he considered to be unimportant things... he felt connected there, a member in good standing in a brotherhood of the bones. Joined to the unseen future, as to the fossil past, through the calcified links arrayed around him and his own bone frame. As he loved the outdoors, so he loved this attic hideaway, and in some ways it was wilderness and adventure brought inside. Low as the steeply slanted ceilings were, they seemed to open out to an uninhibited sky.

What Eland gathered were elements of ritual, artifacts of a more-than-human culture, curiosities that awakened questions, contemplation and conclusion, that piqued his ponderings and excited ever new forms of thought and action. For him, boredom had always been impossible, since near as he could tell the entire world was so inescapably interesting. Every nuance and detail, the smallest life forms as well as the fiercest beasts, the constitution of the soil as much as the constellations in the sky. And he therefore measured friends, authority figures and mentors at least in part according to how much they noticed, how quickly they became enthralled and engaged, and how empathetic, enlivened and responsive they seemed to be. It was curiosity that fueled his traipsing through book after book, reading in the same way the story of the weather in the clouds, and people's hearts in their eyes.

And it was curiosity that always got him into trouble. It provoked him to ditch school, first for the relative wildness of the town *acequias* and overgrown cemeteries, then the outlying hills he could reach by bicycle, and then eventually the wilderness of the

Pecos and the ceremonies of the Pueblos via a ride bummed on the back of a ranch wagon or farm truck. It seduced him into reading purple prose and the chapter in the medical text that referred to the intricacies of the female body, which resulted in him being struck from the honor role, and then missing his name being called for the scholastic trophy because he was at a barbecue on Old Alameda listening to a bearded bohemian describe art as a life true to one's form. Curiosity about the effects of alcohol got him sick and soaked. And curiosity about girls got his little heart broke.

"I love you, but you've got to toe the line," his father had said. The line was that invisible edge that men in the military stepped up to when forming ranks. This, and a few other expressions his father used, betrayed the fact that he'd been in the army, though he had always stubbornly refused to elaborate.

Eland only smiled and said, "Oh Pa!"

This made his father think that he wasn't being taken seriously. To the contrary, his boy could see through his staid and sometimes unyielding exterior to his soft and caring center. Eland didn't do what his father asked out of fear of retribution, and in fact doubted his father had the ability to enact harsh restrictions, let alone ever strike his only child. And Eland could have normally suppressed the smile, if not for the ludicrousness of the expression. Eland didn't do anything according to a straight line. His path was curved, if not convoluted, his methods as twisty as the paths leading up Aspen Peak. He was attentive, but he would never snap to attention. He would step up when he felt it was right, but he was as incapable as a Wolf of recognizing human-made borders, limits, boundaries or lines. He was, as his few friends like to point out, a "friggin' weed", vigorous, incorrigible, impossible to control, always probing for openings and avenues, going and growing wherever it wants to.

Eland Howell - 1902

"I love you, Papa. I'll try to make you proud. I promise."

What Papa wanted for his son was not to do everything the same way he had, but to do better. To take better care of himself, his needs and hopes, than he himself had. To develop his own scruples, and then live by them. And to adjust sufficiently to the status quo that he would not be crushed by it.

What he didn't expect was that a 12-year-old Eland would one day pick the lock on the top drawer of his roll-down writing desk, remove the set of keys found there, and let himself into a back room..

"A bunch of crap," his father had said, though he hardly ever cussed. That was all there was in there, he insisted. Nothing he wanted to shared with others, least of all his family.

"Don't you ever even think about going in there," his father added.

Of course, declaring a yard weed-free was one of the quickest ways to invite a prolific bloom of feisty Mustard and Dandelion. Telling a child that something was off limits would, almost without fail, make the young'n want it all the more. And when they wonder long enough, they can find a way through any door.

Eland found the key that fit, held his breath for a moment, and let himself in. The room featured a single window but it had been nailed firmly shut, with the inside of its panes painted solid black. Carefully closing the door behind himself, he lit the kerosene lamp he'd brought and looked to see what it might illuminate. Eland's heart was thumping loud with fear, loud enough for him to worry that someone outside the room might hear. He felt as if at any moment Ali Baba and his forty thieves could show up in the doorway that was the only way in or out, swords drawn, enraged at the youthful interloper who had discovered their loot-laden cave. Worse than instant death, however, would be disappointing his father yet again, adding to whatever pain he already silently carried with him, destroying the hope of finding satisfaction and contentment through the fine character and honorable deeds of his son.

Eland was awestruck. In the yellow of the lamp glow he could see walls covered with the mysteries and ephemera of his father's past. Several violins, packed in their padded cases, amongst the voluminous accoutrements of the dedicated sportsman. Bamboo fly rods with labels proclaiming origin in places like Spain and Belgium, and archaic reels still flecked with the mud of legendary fishing trips. Large wooden fishing plugs painted to look like Frogs or Fish, with dangling treble hooks, betraying trips to the north country where Pike and Walleye had what it took to strike lures that size. Had he not been avoiding detection, he might have nonetheless been struck silent by the transportive smells of gun oil and old scabbard leather, the apparition of mounted, snarling carnivores' heads and jumble of massive elk antlers. There was nothing else in the house to indicate its owner had ever been an outdoorsman. No antler coat racks, or retired hunting horns. Even the furniture was done up in cotton tapestry rather than leather. In this room, Eland had found the chapter torn out of the book, the missing pages behind what he'd once thought of as his Papa's vacant eyes.

Before him a bench sat loaded with pearl handled pocketknives, gun cleaning equipment, percussion caps in oval tins and fully loaded shells. There were wooden duck decoys, attractive enough to put out just for display if one were so inclined. Tiny toy pistols and a ribbon for best junior sharpshooter. Straight razors and strops, and antiquated padlocks. A souvenir thermometer set in a small wooden tomahawk. Everything had to be dusted to be read, including the calendars of 1890's bathing beauties that his mother surely wouldn't have approved of. An ad with a drawing of a knickered boy on it, promoting Stevens guns to excitable kids. Passports showing him traveling alone or with Grandfather to Europe, Asia, and Africa while still in his teens. An opera program personally autographed to him by a lovely lead performer, emblazoned with a lipstick kiss. Between these bits of memorabilia were various black and white photos, the prints yellowed and curling. His father as an awkward boy, in a coat with only the top button fastened. Papa with some of his army buddies from El Paso, on leave for a hunting trip somewhere in the Black Range. Here was not just history, but proof that his father had indeed felt passionate, at least to the point of traveling the world on safari and making dangerous kills. That he had once been as interested and engaged in his own ways as was Eland, before whatever it was that killed the spirit inside him.

Turning around, he first surveyed the old rifles on the wall. A German Mauser shortened and refurnished for a man who cared about the shape and grade of its wooden stock. A high grade Parker double barrel shotgun, famous for its workmanship and what the published experts referred to as pointability. And below these, an odd odd-looking rifle such as Eland might not have recognized had he not read nearly as much about firearms as he had about history and nature. The bolt-action Norwegian Krags had been briefly adopted by the U.S. Army, as a transitional design between the single-shot trapdoor Springfields and the Model 1903 repeater. Their claim to fame had been their use in the brief war with Spain.

On the wall, to either side of the gun rack, were pinned more photographs, these of his father marching in boot camp, laughing as they loaded on to the transport ships, horsing around at base camp, and being commended from some unspecified action after... along with a copy of a letter from the War Department acknowledging receipt of the commendation he'd angrily sent back. On a table below was a stack of magazines dated 1898 and 1899, extolling brave servicemen, reporting on the treachery of the Spanish, the quick destruction of their fleet in Manila, a young politician named Theodore Roosevelt charging up San Juan Hill, and the resultant ceding to the U.S. of Cuba, Puerto Rico, Guam and the Philippines. Eland got a kick out of the advertisements for supposedly new smokeless gunpowder, hand cranked washing machines and a novel by H. G. Wells provocatively titled "The War Of The Worlds". Then his eyes fell on a letter.

It was from Eland's mother. If the man who would become his Papa wanted to find her waiting when he got back from Cuba, he would have to resign his commission. But that wasn't all. He would be required to give up hunting, since she certainly wasn't going with him. The bloodied guns would have to be stored or sold, so as not to alarm the well-to-do neighbors and literary figures she hoped would visit. And there would be no more of what she called that thing he did in the bedroom. Since normal sex was considered a wife's duty, Eland was amazed to conclude his father had ever lusted for anything more exotic or taboo.

Eland couldn't get over his father having been what society called a hero, perhaps taking a number of enemy lives in order to ensure those of his compatriots. It made sense now that his father felt traumatized, suspicious of causes, pacifistic to the point of being innocuous, to the point of impracticality. But while war was clearly anything but glorious, it was real in a way that his father's life no longer seemed to be. It demanded presence and awareness, put demands on every man to excel. There was no way of escaping reality on the battlefield other than to die, and no understating the importance of every decision made there. The soldiers' survival depended on it, as sometimes did the survival of innocents they were sent to protect. A war could be wrong, young Eland thought, and still have benefits for those who fought. Just caring that much about something, and being willing to risk everything. And even if you could draw no valuable lessons, surely you'd want to remember, instead of forgetting what you'd seen and done.

A tear came to Eland's eye. His father had turned away from the fullest living of life, and now seemed to mostly live just to avoid dying. Worse yet, he'd done it at the request of another... Eland's mother. Now he no longer played the violin, flipped a line and fly into a rushing stream, or hunted in the mountain ranges of faraway lands. Everything had long since been reduced to platitude and conjecture, opinion without the investment, risk or consequence. His parents even had separate bedrooms, appropriate considering what Eland's mother had unemotionally described to him as their evolving parallel lives.

Eland did indeed hear steps, and there was indeed no escape. Slowly the door swung open, but there stood in its frame no Ali Baba. Just a hurt and defeated papa.

A few things bothered his father the most at that moment: the memory of how he had blindly followed orders into a one-sided, unnecessary, and expansionist war. And the fact that not only had his own son chosen to disobey him, but that young Eland now knew the source of his shame.

Chapter 6

OMEN'S BEAR MEDICINE

Bear came into Omen's life in a big way again on the last day of her sacred puberty rite, known as the *Na'ii'ees* or Sunrise Ceremony. But as Omen put it years later, that's just how Bears can be. And that's part of what made them such powerful medicine.

Omen knelt in the special Willow lodge, the lodge itself secreted within a Willow grove due to the 1907 government ban on Indian spiritual practices. She looked otherworldly with her face completely covered in a mixture of clay and ash, and resplendent in the brain-tanned buckskin dress that Moon had spent weeks sewing together, decorated with tiny glass Czech trade beads, Bear fur, and Cowrie shells. She knew that she was not only playing the part of White Painted Woman, she *was* her, now and forevermore, becoming one with the She who brings not just transition, but life.

For the three days and nights previous, she had been guided by her godmother and the Medicine Man through the ceremony's more arduous elements and trials. She ran with all her might towards the rising sun every dawn, and then in each of the four directions, representing the four different stages she would go through in her life. She sang and prayed through most of the night and danced for hours on end, often until collapsing, with only an occasional help back up by a predesignated friend. These were the tests that taught the importance of intention, will, and perseverance, and a girl was judged not just by her performance, but also the pleasant attitude she showed others, and the dignity she demonstrated while undergoing hardship. To help remake her into White Painted Woman, Omen's godmother had massaged her body like clay, forming her into the woman of strength and vision that she needed to be. And perhaps most importantly, the creation story, the story of a people's birth and transformation, was reenacted once again.

Omen had of course heard the tale many, many times before, beginning when Grandmother carried her as a baby strapped tightly to her, mesmerized by the vibrations felt through her chest. Then again when still a toddler, luxuriating on her padded lap. And when she was ten, helping Grandmother walk up the mountain to gather plants again. White Painted Woman, also known as Esdzanadehe or Changing Woman, survives a worldwide flood aboard an iridescent Abalone shell until the waters finally start to recede. She then climbs the highest mountain, whereupon she is impregnated by the Sun, giving birth to a boy called Killer of Enemies. Not long after, she makes thunder-clapping love to the Rain, resulting in another child known as Son of Water. Together they kill the Owl Man Giant who had been terrorizing the people, and it was White Painted Woman's shouts of relief and triumph that the chosen godmother would imitate at the Sunrise Ceremony. It was the spirits, Grandmother said, who guided Esdzanadehe to establish the puberty rite, and the means for the future generations of young Apaches to learn the ways of sacred womanhood.

There was no more crucial ceremony than this, marking the start of menstruation and the onset of adult responsibilities to both Spirit and tribe. Being taught about sexuality. Learning the secrets of a woman's power, and how to use it for the good of others and the planet. And the rite seemed all the more important to Omen, a mixed-blood still hoping to earn the respect of clan and tribe... as well as the acceptance of envious peers, showing signs of her first moon two to three years ahead of her time.

The ceremony lasted four days and nights, but it had actually started eight or nine months earlier, with Moon taking a wagon load of her stone carvings to sell in Santa Fe. The money needed to pay for the Medicine Man and the Gans Crown Dancers, and to feed the guests, would come from rock chiseled and filed down to the flowing forms of Apache mothers huddled with their babies, mothers with little boys under their arms or little girls clinging to their backs. Graceful, grace-filled, idealized mothers. Mothers as incorruptible guardians of their beloved offspring, mothers that would never turn their head when something awful was happening to their daughters, mothers never more than a few inches away.

And too, it was her charms the tourists and collectors paid for, smiles as dimes and winks as quarters, a tolerated pinch on the bottom adding dollars in sales. If she gave those well-dressed white men more than a casual view of the wonder that was her, Omen sure didn't want to know. While she felt a little bad for thinking so, at eleven years old she was already the kind of girl who would rather rob those gentleman buyers at gun point than to have Moon's beautiful work trivialized or dishonored by what she imagined to be their shallow tastes and stuffed wallets. Those few times when she allowed herself to picture them touching her mother – the smirky way that men touched a woman when they thought they were being sneaky and dirty and getting away with something – she could also imagine pulling a trigger. Never just once, but four or five times. It was always as if she could feel the revolver trying to buck its way out of her little hands, as if she could see the wide-eyed looks of surprise as the bullets ripped through coats and vests, bones and flesh.

But that day Omen would imagine no such things, nor think about anything besides the metamorphosis she was then undergoing, the touch of Spirit and not the ways of commerce and men. It was the final day, when she would sprinkle her family and guests with the pollen she'd collected from wildflowers, and offer her healing blessings to any who asked for them. And they would give her gifts in turn, and wish her a long and wonderful life. Moon and Grandmother sat in front of her, the godmother standing proud at her side. Omen had often felt ostracized, for her own intemperance as well as her mother's deviations from the Apache norm, but with the closing of the ceremony it felt possible again to belong. For as long as Moon could recall, her daughter had swung day to day, week-to-week, between lows full of crushing self-doubt and highs animated by a surreal and unqualified confidence. Only four days earlier, she had been so anxious she could barely catch her breath, depressed to the point of not caring if she lived or if she died. Now she stood as sure as any wild creature, riding the apex of her emotional cycle like the imperturbable eagle rode the western skies.

The Medicine Man raised his painted rattle and opened his mouth to sing his last song, when suddenly a great crashing sound was heard. It came from outside the grove and up the hill to the north, most likely from the house of the holy man himself. It was accompanied by a steady wave of ever more agitated barking by all the area dogs.

Another crash, and then the distant tinkling of broken glass. Everyone stopped what they were doing, and ran to see what was happening. From the edge of the Willows there was a fairly clear view of his little house, a *jacal* constructed of upright Juniper *latillas* daubed with adobe mud, and at that moment suffering an assault by what all later agreed was the largest Bear any of them had ever beheld. When first spotted it was busy tossing everything off the porch, a relatively unproductive effort that could have been construed as either vengeance or bruin sport. A dog that had allowed its bravado to override its common sense, was swatted six feet into the air.

Omen and family watched in amazement as the beast then ambled over to the adjacent house, and quickly gobbled down the six loaves of fresh bread cooling on the picnic table. For reasons she never knew, she found herself running directly towards the giant vandal, while her uncles ran to retrieve the rifles from their rolling wreck of a Model T.

Moon yelled for her to come back, and then ran after her when neither pleas nor commands had an effect. Only fifteen yards from the Bear, Omen stopped, her mother halting only not more than another ten yards in back. Both stared with heaving breaths, as it rose up onto two legs as if in slow motion and turned to face them. Omen knew that living Bears never curled their lips like the mounted specimen in the agency office did, but it struck her that what she now saw in this Bear's huge oval face was nothing like a snarl. It was, if anything, surprise... followed by what she would ever after describe as a look of recognition. Two Bears, one woman-sized and one mammoth, both beautiful, resolute, and full of themselves, sharing an imperative to be ever more alive and realized. The beast dropped back onto all fours, dust roiling off its hide, the silver tips of its grizzled fur erect and ablaze in the sun. Somewhere behind them, Omen's uncles were struggling to get a clear shot without endangering the sister and niece strangely standing in their line of fire, while the most dangerous animal on the continent licked its chops and then casually ambled off.

Once they were sure that it was gone, everyone rushed to examine Omen, and to touch her head for good luck. Then, while they poked around the busted chairs and scattered bread pans, Moon and her daughter walked a ways in the direction it had gone. Bending down to measure one especially well defined track,

Omen found it nearly four of her hands in length. How appropriate, they agreed, for her transition to be marked by such a symbolic visit. It was, after all, the time for a girl to overcome her weaknesses and the dark forces of her nature, to come to terms with her sacredness and spiritual power.

The Bear had come, they realized, not just to anoint and bless, but to alert, inspire and disturb. Even the hint of a Grizzly was a gift of awareness, the mere sight of their tracks enough to get men out of their busy, distracted heads and thrust back into their responsive bodies and physical senses. The deer owed their alertness and speed to the Grizzly, and to this same being the men could credit their hard-earned humility. The people too, Moon said, needed there to be something that much bigger, stronger, and in some ways smarter than them to keep them on their toes, something as mysterious as it was ferocious, out stalking the dimly lit edges of their settlements and their minds. No one was exempt from the workings of nature. Not the Americans with their factories and guns, nor even the Medicine Man, surveying the wreckage of his ravaged home. There was always the reminder of real power, usually coming when it was least expected. A clever enemy, ambushing from a place of concealment or preying on one's trust. The aging process that would inevitably stalk them all. The invisible but deadly germs they'd been taught about in school. And the mighty Bear. Each of these, agents of change... like it or not.

Each time Esdzanadehe would get old, she would journey east until she met her maiden self again, meld with her, and in this way become young again. So it was with the people, generation to generation, one woman to the next, and so it seemed to be in all of life. With the virtual destruction of the *jacal*, another would be built in its place. The Medicine Man would return to his affairs with a renewed sense of purpose and a new perspective on the meaning of fortune, with even more gifts and lessons to share.

And thereafter, every time that Omen would find herself falling apart or under attack, she would get back up remade, re-formed. Now an embodiment of White Painted Woman, she would rise, dusted with ash from those pyres of transformation again, and again, and again.

Conflict with Bears, and the deification and emulation of the Bears had always gone hand in hand. Both hostility and reverence were rooted in the respect the bruins extracted from people through the earliest skirmishes over downed meat and coveted caves. The prehistoric Bears of North America did more than anything else to slow the steady tide of immigration over the Bering Strait from Asia. The ancestors of the Grizzlies following their two-legged prey on their sojourn into North America, competing with the indigenous Short Faced Bears for the available game. The successes of early hominid hunters were said to have been the single greatest factor in the extinction of several subspecies of buffalo, the mastodon, and the horse, but they met their match in the Grizz. The result of that contest was a healthy fear and lingering distrust... along with the creation of Bear clans, the development of Bear rituals, and the invoking of the Bear spirit. In old Europe, those who called in the power of the Bear had been known as berserkers, holy fighters dressed in the skins of Bears and slathered in their grease, charging the enemy while roaring like beasts. Among the Great Plains tribes of America they were called "Bear Dreamers" and "Bear Warriors" known for running headlong at their foes, at times with no more than a Bear-jaw knife. They believed the Bear spirit would protect them, which alone inspired great feats of courage.

Few of the grizzlies being killed in the early part of the 20th Century were any longer honored or prayed to, and were in fact usually dispatched in the most inglorious ways. Many trapped in giant double spring steel traps ringed with a wicked set of teeth, bawling in pain as they clawed the ground and flattened any bushes within reach, while others were shot at great dispassionate distances with high-powered rifles firing the latest smokeless powders and spire-point bullets. The majority were killed by government predator control agents, others by "sport" hunters who ran them with dogs to earn the rewards ranchers paid for their extermination from "their' range. Stillborn calves were laced with cyanide and left out for bears and other predators to eat. To the person trying to make a living raising cattle they were worse than Cougars and Mexican Grey Wolves, the devil itself. A single swipe of a Grizz paw could break the neck of a full-grown steer. With their sharp claws they could slit a cow's belly from one end to the other, as smoothly as if pulling down a zipper from which the still living animal's entrails would spill.

The big browns were still fairly common in New Mexico, and especially numerous in the Saliz Mountains when Moonheart moved Omen there in 1911. But so effective was the campaign to eradicate them, that only five years later experts were estimating a statewide Grizzly population of under fifty adults. While it was known that Bears would sometimes gather in groups to feed, such as during the Salmon runs in the Northwest, most of their lives were spent solo. It was believed that a single animal could require up to four hundred square miles of territory to thrive. But space was the one thing that the new paradigm, in the new century, was less and less able to provide.

In 1840 the human population west of the 100th meridian was sparse, but by 1900 over eleven million people lived there. Between 1900 and 1910, while the country's population jumped from 76 to 92 million, New Mexico's more than doubled in numbers. Most of that population was centered in large cities, not spread throughout the land. But the increasing demand for resources resulted in the clearing of eighty percent of native forests, widespread soil erosion and depletion, and wholesale destruction of wildlife habitat.

The big Bears may have taken it hardest, with increased human activity in their territory causing them to produce less young. This was problematic, given that they were the slowest reproducing of all large carnivores on the continent. How odd, and how terrible, Omen thought... that it would turn out to be the mighty Grizzly, not hairless man, who had the most to fear.

To Omen, a landscape without eagles felt discounted, cheapened, thinned. A desert was incomplete without cactus, even though she had to reconcile herself to the reality of its prickly spines. And the mountains would never again be the same, once the great disrupter – the great Bear – was gone from them.

Poultice

Chapter 7

POULTICE:
Grievous History & The Wound That Just Won't Heal

Moonheart never told Omen why she'd divorced her father, no matter how many times or in how many ways she was asked.

"He was a *sonovabitch*," was all she'd say. "I should've killed him when I had the chance."

She could have, too, in retribution for whatever terrible things he did. And she wouldn't have had to wait until he slept, so good was she with both a gun and a knife. A regular tiger, some said. But she didn't kill him, not even after he lost what they'd saved towards Winter in a crooked poker game, or after the swollen black eyes that Omen repeatedly tried to kiss into opening. Nor did she cut him deep, as she liked to say, when she was six months pregnant with Omen, and he kicked her in the stomach.

Moon reveled in a contest, and got excited about escalating conflicts anytime she'd had too many shots of whiskey. On the few occasions when shouting and disrespect devolved into out and out violence, it was said that she gave blows nearly as ferocious as those she received. A day later Omen's parents would be laughing and playing together again, protagonists unaffected by their bouts and back to sharing drinks. Never was there a threat to leave, or even the hint of a divorce. Omen then had to wonder whether, instead of something he'd done to Moon, the reason her father was kicked out might have been something he'd done to her instead.

People had often found Omen irresistible. Usually this affection came in the most healthy and faultless ways, the adoration of those relatives who fully accepted her, the neighbor who enjoyed teaching her to dance and to sing, and the affectionate hugs and clumsy kisses of other children. Occasionally it was not so innocent. It didn't help that she'd started to look like a woman at ten, biologically matured with wide hips and hard-to-conceal breasts by eleven. In the year leading up to her puberty ceremony, Omen had been the subject of, and had successfully resisted, several untoward advances. A mailman trying to handle more than his bags on a trip to Flagstaff. An unabashed proposition from the married owner of a nearby mercantile.

It was, at that time, a popular expression to call such men wolves. But Omen knew wolves to be intensely loyal, lifelong mates. They killed only for food, and unlike men and lions, seemed to take no pleasure in prolonging their victim's suffering. If these men were like any animal, she figured it must be the Black Footed Ferret... its embarrassingly brief and characteristically vicious sexual encounters with more than one female, and its susceptibility to behavior-altering distemper. It was dependent on and defined by its success with a specific prey species. But even that was unfair, because the Black Footed Ferret acted out of an evolutionary urge to procreate, not as a way to compensate for fears about manhood or feelings of insignificance. And other than during the breeding season, ferrets lived alone, content with themselves and their solitary lives.

Besides, from what she'd seen of her mother's lovers, men such as those were less like predators than parasites, drawn like fleas or ticks to the heat of a body and spark of a soul, making desperate sucking noises as they try to make her power their own. Omen had watched as one after the other clung to her mother for a short time, feeding from her blood until they reeled from its hallucinatory effects. Then, largely incapacitated, they would release their hold and fall away from her... their little legs pedaling madly in the air.

Already at age eleven, Omen had reason to believe she could handle any unwanted suitors. What she found more worrisome was what she might be carrying inside, in her genetics, and in her troubled mind. An energy pattern or pheromone that seemed to attract the worst kind of men to her, just as it had to her mother. She wondered what it was about her that made her feel so intrinsically and inherently guilty, seeming to seek punishment for some unnamed but unforgivable crime.

On the one hand, she loved herself the way she loved nature. She loved the nature within her, her true nature; the world of earth and spirit, blood and bone, animal and plant. She loved the way it felt when her strong little arms swung an axe nearly as long as she was tall. The sensation of straining leg muscles when she climbed the nearby peaks. The thrill of bodily senses when leaping into frigid water or baking in the heat of the canvas and hide covered sweat lodge. The curious nose and desiring tongue. She even liked the way she looked... if only in clothes whose cut visually subtracted rather than added on pounds. And only at a certain angle. With the soft under-part of her chin hidden by the tilt of a lowered head.

On the other hand, she never felt quite good enough. Even when she exceeded the expectations of everyone around her, by her own standards and demands she often felt like a failure. If she succeeded at a task, she reasoned it was because the chore or test was too simple. If people complimented her, it simply meant that compliments came too easily to them. Not even her powerful beauty could be trusted, drawing the starved like the pollen of the season's very last blooms... for so far, it had brought even more anguish than benefits and favors. A sense of dissatisfaction, hollowed not hallowed, had shadowed every flirtatious glance.

And disregard had followed most of the kind remarks that ever flattered her hoping heart.

Omen worried about things that no child her age should have to worry about. She couldn't help but wonder if her heart – like her mother's – might already be a wound that no known poultice could heal.

Salvia greggii

Chapter 8:

SALVIA:
Being Taught To Accept The Death Of Things

Omen's second stay with Doña Rosa, proved even more educational than the first. The deeply feeling youngster learned to come to terms with her mother's ever longer absences, the slow dying of the bond she so badly wanted to believe they had, and with the very idea of death itself... all seemingly played out in the mortal drama of a single favored plant.

"Is there nothing at all I can do for it?" she'd asked her mentor, fully in tears over the curling edges of the once brilliant leaves, the colorful petals falling softly onto the ground.

"Of course you can," was Doña Rosa's response, with a loving and understanding look on her face. "Touch her. Sing to her through her transition. Write a song about her when you think she is gone. And then find that she lives on inside of you."

"Oh, but I don't want her just inside of me, I want her to continue living in the flesh, right here! I want her to still be here when I come back."

Omen mourned the loss of almost any life, burying the little animals she found on her walks, or setting them on a wildlands altar for a scavenger to come eat. She always did so with a prayer, and felt a similar kind of anguish to that of the bereft who had lost a close friend, a precious aunt, a favorite cousin. She did not need to know the creature in order for her to feel it personally. It did not matter that she may have never seen it when it hopped or crawled, ran or flew, before it was still and cold. She mourned the still grimacing coyote flattened on the highway, not just the mild-mannered rabbits and squirrels that it had torn apart and ate. She was saddened by the Fall shedding of Cottonwood leaves, and the annual disappearance of her favorite medicine plants. She dreaded the thought of the pink and purple morning glories dying back, especially those that grew in an arch around Doña's front doorway. But this *Salvia* was special. In the short span of her second visit, it had already become her intimate and ally. She had made tinctures of the flowering tops, with their tiny red vaginal pouts, and she imagined she only had to sit with her face close to one in order to feel its calming medicinal effects. On the first really cold morning, she had carefully potted it and brought it in. It being a perennial, she could not think of any reason other than perhaps a disease for its premature demise.

"But Doña, you can heal almost anything! You could make rocks bloom!"

"No, I certainly cannot," she laughed, "although I am able to see that they are beautiful without flowers."

"But I've seen you heal people. And tend wilting Roses until they came back to life."

Omen come to believe that there was nothing that this adopted aunt was capable of. The Doña had to resist the desire to comfort her through her tears. Like a plant, a person, even a little girl, sometimes had to be stressed in order to grow strong and true to its direction.

"I will do what I can for it," Doña assured her, "but as with all things, it is inevitable that the *Salvia* will die. If not now, then sooner or later."

She tossed her dark braids behind her back with a shake of her head.

"Healing is a magical process," she explained slowly, giving each word its worth and weight. "We need no more proof than a bloody cut quickly healing until there is no mark, to know that our bodies are miraculous indeed. The things we use – our focused energy, skills, spells, prayers, practices, and knowledge of nutrition and herbs – can all assist with this miracle. But the intention of the Medicine Woman is neither to help people escape all pain, or help some being to forever avoid its mortal demise. Our work is to help other people to become as consciously balanced and whole as the ever-changing universe we are a part of. And with the plants, we can treat their ailments, but we also have to honor their sacred deaths."

It was, the Curandera could see, not only an attachment to this one wonderful plant, but also a huge need to control her environment, and thus her life. With Omen's mother, and therefore her home, never stable, it was stability she called out for. And she would stamp her foot like a spoiled goddess if things would not stay in their places, stay put, remain dependably the same. She desired a reality where it didn't feel like the ground was giving way beneath her, like the winds were about to carry her off... where that which mattered to her was not always in danger of falling, rolling, tumbling away. The wasting away of this plant was tragic not just for itself, but because it was not what she had expected or planned.

"But why, Doña?"

The healer could have answered her with more description of the necessity of compost and the promise of seed. Or listed the various diseases she knew could inflict this particular species. Or she might have spoken to her about the likelihood of root-shock that often happens when individuals are transplanted. Instead, she looked out the window as if waiting for some true love's return.

"The Salvia may simply be unhappy, or pledged to a process we don't understand. She may even have a lover out there who will succumb to the first frost of Winter. And it may be that she would rather remain out of doors and face his fate with him, than to be saved and sheltered inside."

Chapter 9

UPROOTED:
Dislocation & Prophecy

"Why, Mama?" Omen asked, her voice changing in pitch to match her rising panic.

"Why do we have to go?"

"Just pack," Moon said, her words sounding like the lid of a steamer trunk being slammed shut.

"But why? It's our home!"

"It *was* our home," Moonheart replied.

This was something Omen simply could not comprehend. As far as she was concerned, home could never be something one said in the past tense. It was a part of your very being, not a place to visit. You depended on knowing every edible plant and dangerous animal, and somehow they depended on you knowing them and caring. It was where you sprouted like a tree: the fertile ground that gave you life. And to pull up roots was to die.

"That's impossible!" Omen yelled, surprised by her own anger. "I can't bear it! I can't do it! I won't!"

"We're not welcome here any more."

"What do you mean?"

"You can't stay," Moon said, quietly but adamantly. "They'll end up shunning you like they do me."

Omen rushed past her mother, out the door and down the dusty trail, asking the same question of everyone she met. "Why? Why do we have to go?"

The kids she most liked to play with looked down in embarrassment or shame, then turned and ran away. Her aunts and uncles said nothing as they roasted their bags of chiles outside, looking back at their niece with sorrowful eyes. Out of everyone, only her godmother – who had so often held her close and stroked her brow, trying to ease her grief following each successive family trauma – told her the truth: that Moonheart was the cause of a terrible breakup. And worse yet, that she'd been caught with the chief's son. She spoke with equal amounts of understanding, disapproval and regret. Meanwhile, they both could hear a great wailing in the distance, the audible anguish of the wife who had the misfortune to walk in on them.

There were some who would have answered differently: that Moon had to leave because she was a witch. That was what they often called women they perceived to be a temptation to their husbands, and thus a threat to the stability and wellbeing of their families.

"Witch" was not a word to be used lightly, and witches were often very real to those who spoke of them. Theirs was an age when many of people of the Southwest – Indian, Spanish and Anglo – lived in terror of evil sorcerers. In periods of misfortune they'd often blame the same person that they'd been looking to for their healing. In their minds there existed a malevolent caster of spells, poised to strike deaf or make impotent anyone who threatened or displeased her. That fear sometimes spilled over onto any and all forms of healers innocently plying their trade, doing their best to serve the people of their villages without pay, for whatever the patient's family might want to give or trade. *"La Bruja,"* the people might warn, should a stranger inquire about finding a Medicine Woman among any of the smattering of small villages nested within the vastness of the rugged *Sierra Saliz*. Being labeled a witch had long been a cost associated with visions and medicine making, or inordinate success as a midwife. Omen knew, however, that when those same folk were in need, they'd use the word "Healer," "Medicine Woman" or "Curandera" instead: the welcomed wise woman who dispensed teas of bitters to settle foul stomachs, secret ointments to ease the pain of arthritis, or potions meant to bring increased hope for love... if not love itself.

Omen's Canyon

PART II

Chapter 10

TRANSPLANTS:
Omen's New Canyon Home

The ride took the better part of a day in Omen's uncle's truck, a clearly pregnant Moon riding up front, while a tearful Omen sat in the back on the very top of their pile of worldly belongings. They only stopped once for gas, in the high desert Mormon community of Springerville, Arizona, before spiraling down through the Spruce and Pine forests of Luna, New Mexico, down into a broad valley and several miles past the tiny village of Frisco. The truck's brakes squeaked as it finally lurched to a stop, about fifty yards short of where the Frisco River departed the expanse of valley and entered a quickly narrowing canyon. Omen's eyes blazed, still red from crying, with her hair wildly tossed and knotted from the windy drive. She sat there for a minute on her mobile perch, the strange throne from which she surveyed a truly enchanted kingdom.

"This is where we unload," Uncle said after getting out. "I'm afraid you'll have to borrow a horse locally, in order to get everything over the other side."

Moon could see that the river wasn't that deep, but the bottom was decidedly loose and the truck tires were both bald and skinny as goat's legs.

"Hop down, girl," Moonheart said. "We're here."

Omen was awestruck, excited beyond the ability to speak. She had fallen in love at first sight, not excluding what she could see of the run-down adobe house that used a section of rock face fifty feet high for its northern wall. It appeared partly covered in a skirt of Woodbine – what folks from other parts of the nation sometimes called Virginia Creeper. But what called her first was the river, purring in a language that Omen seemed born to understand. She felt, in fact, as if the river had called her to be its translator, summoned her to speak its will, worry and glee. To make the deafened listen.

She carried nothing the first time across, walking barefoot as she always did, crossing a stretch of stickers by jumping from one clear spot to the next, brushing off any clinging irritants with the shuffling motion of the following step. The water cooled her feet at once, its gentle waves lapping up onto her legs the way an attention-hungry cat might rub itself on a person's calves, raising its back to be touched.

"How much?" Moon asked her brother as he climbed back into his rig to go.

"What do you mean?"

"How much do we have to pay you for the rent?"

"Nothin'," he said, "except the cost of the county taxes. I haven't had no luck selling it, anyways, being as it's on the impractical side of the river and all. Some months it will be low enough to spit over, other times not even a horse can get across."

Moon looked at her brother with profound relief for having provided them with this escape and refuge. She looked beautiful with her swelling belly and her face uplifted, almost heroic, resilient if more than a little weary. For the eleven years following Omen's birth, Moon had used the regulating herbs Grandmother had taught them to prepare, and religiously followed the moon calendar to assure she wouldn't have a child out of wedlock. Now she carried within her the the reason they'd had to leave the reservation, a Chief's offspring.

Omen was already off exploring as her uncle's buggy rolled off and out of view. From the moment they'd pulled up, Omen had set about to familiarize herself with the land. Only a hundred and some miles east of the reservation, many of the topographical features were the same, but others were tantalizingly strange and even in some ways more interesting than the landscape she'd left behind.

First, there was the *Rio Frisco*, larger than the creek she'd grown up on, and shimmering like nothing she'd ever seen before. The tall pine forest she knew best was present on the cooler south side of the water, while on the sun-kissed north side the hills were laden with twisting Juniper, nut crusted Piñon, and Oak. In some places cliffs the color of blood and flame, of Lilacs and Sunflowers, rose straight up three to five hundred feet, forming a chapel that inspired both humility and wonder. At their base, native Canyon Grape vines draped across some of the canyon trees, with the pink and orange blossoms of Wild Buckwheat waving in the wind below them. And she would soon love the lush patches of magical Datura, seducing the long-tongued moths of the mystical Southwestern night. She felt drawn into associations of water plants like Cattails, Rushes, Duckweed and Watercress... in league with the Crawdads, Tree Frogs, and Gila Trout taking refuge in the deeper pools from the Summer's heat, with the Mallards raising their young in the river's shadow-draped nooks and gentle eddies, and the Great Blue Herons standing tall over their middens of speckled Crawdad shells. The Mule Deer, watching her without running. Sharp-toothed Javalina, grunting and rooting. Pounding swarms of Stellar Jays and dive-bombing Kestrels. Orange-winged clownish Northern Flickers and hardheaded Gila Woodpeckers. Kingfishers, Mourning Doves, and a Bald Eagle circling unhurriedly overhead. And everywhere Omen looked were the tracks of canyon-bred Raccoons and Ringtails, Bobcat and Muskrat, Coatimundi, Mountain Lion and Bear.... evidencing the many other unseen beings who also made their abodes there. She didn't look around so much as engage and enjoin, submitting and surrendering to irreversible linkage with the whole of this gifted home.

Nearby mountains rose up from primeval inland sea beds to around twelve thousand feet in height, laced with streams and spotted with a handful of especially enticing hot springs. Snaking through these peaks and hills were the beds of the region's life-giving waters, not only Omen's already beloved *Rio Frisco*, but also the Tularosa and Gila. Soon she would explore creeks with names like Palomas, Gilita, Iron, and Indian. Turkey, Bear, and Centerfire. Alamosa and Negrito. Oak and Willow. Mangas, Mineral, Deep, and Devil's Creeks. All waterways were magnets for plant and animal species, but nowhere was that more true than in the arid Southwest where other sources of moisture were sparse and seasonal at best. Water spilling out of artesian springs or draining from the snow-saturated soils of the high country. Trickles coupled with seeps to become rivers that might be calf deep in late June or December, and thirty feet deep and seventy-five yards across during a big Spring runoff. No lover is unmarked by love, and everywhere the flowing water touched there was a meander carved deep like memory. Where raging love or insistent waters cut deepest, the result would be a canyon, bone deep, the bedrock of human or earthen soul exposed and titillated by passion's churning currents.

The same precious flow coveted by those of root, feather, and paw, drew early humankind close as well. At the same time as the Tiber of Rome and the Euphrates of Asia supported the growth of civilizations, rivers like the San Francisco watered the palettes, the crops, the imagination, and spirit of their Earth-honoring residents. Omen could climb up from the river to almost any flat spot above the flood plain, and find herself atop the erosion-filled pit houses of those who loved and revered that canyon long before her arrival. The Sweet Medicine people had migrated in mass down to the Rio Grande approximately a thousand years earlier in response to raids by other tribes, a particularly long drought or the well-received vision of some messianic Shaman... at around the same time as the first boatloads of Norse Vikings were making landfall in Greenland.

Various digs had shown how the Old Ones' homes had been D-shaped underground rooms, and revealed how they had made lives of crafting basketry and pottery, hunting, and cultivating maize. Based on the ceremonial items left behind, it would seem they'd practiced a spiritual tradition that emphasized connection, reciprocity and interdependence. What little the archaeologists had figured out indicated a culture that habitually honored life through ritual and stewardship, song and dance, story and craft, intention and act. Painted pottery sherds scattered about on the ground were, for Omen, surviving testimony to that lineage of celebration, responsibility and prayer. Many of the trails she tread on during her explorations had been burnished smooth by the touch of countless sandal soles: the early villagers had probably made twice-daily trips from their dwellings to tend their irrigation ditches and carry back their pitch-lined Juniper baskets filled with sweet river water.

Canyon Mullein

Omen fell in love not just with the totality of the composition, but with every individual component. With each Lichen-covered rock, every hillock and log. With the Willows, Alders and *Alamos* that reminded her of the White Mountain creek where she'd grown up, and especially with a particular big-boned grandmother Cottonwood that would have taken more than a dozen adults to encircle hand in hand. She loved the communitarian conviviality of the innumerable varieties of grasses. The chorus lines of Morning Glories and Four-o'clocks, Indian Blanket and Starflower, Asters and Daisies, Prickly Poppy and Desert Paintbrush, Yarrow and Evening Primrose blossoms, Sunflowers and Beeplants coupling with multicolored butterflies. And she fell for the seductions of the fuzzy-leaved Mullein that camped in the flats. It wouldn't matter, when she later learned it was an introduced species spread by Cossack-looking Slav pioneers, for she was a transplant too. Putting roots down in new soil, learning from and adapting to the character of a place.

If, as she believed, that wild land came with its own natural set of values, priorities and hopes, then she was sure they were hers to learn. She followed the river to what was not only a roofless temple, but also an experiential school. Her questioning, and the answers that came, were her biology and science. The corollaries that came to mind were her sociology and psychology. Omen's hikes were journeys into history, not simply because she found herself cast into a mental and emotional state outside the normal constraints of linear time, but because a descent from above traced an actual regression through geologic eras for which she had no names, down to the very time and place of life's beginnings.

Omen ran, walked, and crawled about like a gentle beast digging up its secrets with her claws, grazing on its knowledge, hunting its truths, sampling again and again its unfolding miracle of life. It was not some child's unblemished innocence that won her a ticket to her personal, manifest paradise... it was her propensity to engage the world not just eye to eye but nose to nose, her openness to looking at the world in new ways, her willingness to deeply feel. She had arrived still "little" enough to connect through the immediacy of a child's universe, yet big enough to take some responsibility for the wellbeing of that which she felt so immediately and thoroughly connected to.

Home would be best fathomed up close, through intimate interaction with microcosms nestled between the thighs of hills, astraddle rocks, passing under a flood-exposed Ponderosa root, and inside the hollow of a lightning-struck tree. Home would not be just a place for her to be, but the crucial juncture between skin and soil, eye and sparkle, nose and flower. It would elicit patience and attention, entice sensual exploration, insist she slow down to best behold the blooming present. And from Day One it would be this canyon home that held her, when no boyfriend seemed kind or aware enough. She would be both a faithful lover and student to the canyon and its surrounding mountains, an acolyte of its magic, and one day, its wizened adept. The sentinel Rock Squirrels that announced the arrival of a Redtailed Hawk, Rattler, or human, impressed on her the importance of vigilance. The Ringtail Cats instructed her to play. Every plant taught her about its nature, its poisons, food or medicine... and in their own ways, about her essential self.

Omen was born with the instincts and inclinations of a *yerbera* for making and dispensing medicines, and this innate propensity was increasingly grounded in deep knowledge of each and every plant. Her first year in the canyon was taken up almost entirely by walks, in spirals that wound out a little further from their new adobe cabin each time, noting every species of plant and drawing their most important features in a pad of plain paper she took along. She'd come home panting like a Bear, too tired to easily chop the night's wood. And every weekend, she sought out the old Hispanic women who knew the most about the amazing plants that Grandmother hadn't already introduced her to.

There was something magical about Omen for sure. But every bit of it was good, as good as guiltless babies and wild berries. There was something of the spirit, or spirits, in how she held herself, and how she moved. In the way she could intuit the beneficial uses of a plant she'd never heard of and only just met. In how she floated unseen through crowds, and could draw someone's eye to her with a thought. In the inflections when she spoke, always implying something more than words alone could say.

The witchiest thing about Omen was her ability to predict. She foresaw great loss for herself when she was only six, and always seemed to be walking along the edge of that impending dark and bottomless abyss. In retrospect she was sure it was leaving the reservation and the White Mountains that her anxieties had foretold. She had willingly held her mother's hand, but it would forever feel like she'd been dragged. As if the roots she'd grown had been wrenched from the earth to hang limply from the bottom of her skirt, leaving a snaking trail in the dirt.

And while still in her teens, she saw a strange and powerful love coming her way. She had no idea what he would look like, but such details didn't really matter. She would show patience if he was younger than her, love his wrinkles if he were old. What she held onto through every lonely, solitary, or misunderstood moment, was the feeling that he existed somewhere, that amongst the thrumming throngs of humankind, in some city or on some desert isle, there was a man that Spirit specifically intended for her. The one who would know her for who she really was, inside and out. The man she could comfortably let roam inside her head and her soul, and who had since birth held her, in turn, inside of him. In need of affirmation, or confusing sex with love, she would let other men penetrate her body over the years to come... yet no one else could enter her being. What Omen had prophesied was both a miraculous binding together, and a great opening. A mutual grafting of flesh, and a falling away of the chains she increasingly wrapped around her heart.

She also prophesied that while being away from that special canyon could kill her, committing, promising, and staying could help her live.

As terrible as it had been for her to leave the place of her birth, Omen never once regretted the shift. She might well have snubbed this new bit of land, disregarded its obvious qualities, ignored its spirit and allure out of loyalty to what she'd always known. It was only human nature to trust what was familiar - to cling to an identity, even if it were an inaccurate or incomplete one, rather than face disruption - especially when one's identity was associated with and attached to a place. Omen had often heard the stories of Warm Springs Apaches, forcibly removed from the mountains of Eastern Arizona and resettled on nearly treeless reservations in Oklahoma. Many deliberately starved themselves when they got there. But the river canyon she had come to felt like an extension of the same body of mountains that had birthed her, perhaps even its heart.

Things were different for her than they were for her unfortunate relatives. In her forced migration from the White Mountains, she'd found not a reason to die, but the promise of a full and satisfying life.

Chapter 11

OUT OF THIS CAULDRON:
The Makings Of A Romantic Individualist

Eland's public schooling concluded early when his mother could see his boredom was getting him into trouble as he'd completely lost patience with the rate at which he was being taught. She knew he absorbed information the way the parched desert sucked up any rainfall that hit the ground, leaving nothing to evaporate. After considerable discussion, his parents agreed to sell what was an increasingly valuable piece of downtown real estate, and enroll him in the prestigious Boy's Preparatory School.

"There's a chance he'll like it, and it will get him back on track," his father had said. "He was certainly wasting his time in class last year."

"He'll go, like it or not," his mother concluded, pressing her lips tightly together.

The education some kids got at the turn of the century might have seemed to an observer less about mathematics and English than the fine points of folding paper airplanes, forging notes from home, and getting along with the various contentious classmates. Paying for a high-dollar private school was therefore meant to be a reward and not a punishment for the insatiable Eland, even if he experienced it as a bit of both. The teachers imported from back East and even Europe were of the highest quality, ready to indulge any excited line of inquiry, but the sheer number of regulations alone proved daunting. Eland responded by pestering the instructors with questions, while experimenting with ever more creative ways of breaking school rules.

The hardest part turned out to be not the social or academic stress, but the implied pressure he'd felt from his parents since he was very young. They never actually voiced in words that he had to find some profitable and noteworthy venue for his abilities and succeed in it… or that he must dress, think and act in a manner that would bring him esteem, and his parents credit. Nor did they directly imply that if he accomplished any less, or comported himself with any less dignity, they would be ashamed of him for the rest of his life. But that was the way it felt. There was something in his mother's stern glances whenever he slipped below his usual high standards. Her recurrent references to the neighbor's boy, how he made his mother proud, how he'd been honored by his church. Eland felt like her showpiece when he did well. When he didn't, he felt like hell.

He could admit to himself a certain pleasure in ruffling his mother's feathers, and he sometimes feigned a bad grade or pretended to flub a certain task for no other reason than to see her neck stiffen, her eyes widen in dismay, and her right eyebrow go up. To witness the twitching forehead that indicated a speeding pulse, as she worked to civilly suppress either indignation or anger. Not so his father, who reacted to Eland's indiscretions and mistakes with silence that was hard not to hear, and heart-rending depression that Eland could scarcely bear. As much as he'd fought it, he'd largely taken on the cross of his father's unnamed and unresolved needs, of undefined responsibilities and fading hopes, carrying it until his back literally ached from the weight, forever figuratively picking its wooden splinters from his bruised shoulder.

It seemed to Eland that his father was expected to both make his fortune, and make a son who would in turn do the same. It certainly hadn't helped that he was the last in a line of Howells who had made sizable sums at various enterprises, including coming up with an improved process for the production of ball bearings. Little could the family have known when they sold the rights how quickly the bearing market would grow, thanks to a burgeoning automobile industry, or that the wheels of a world war would one day roll on them. And little could they have guessed that the last male heir of their line would grow up out West, with little interest in profits, preferring a horse or wagon to being transported by an innovative machine.

Eland took refuge in his studies and the camping trips he enjoyed on the weekends, and in the few young women in town who didn't think him either too shy or too intimidating. He found it in camaraderie as well, having fairly quickly assimilated into a group of intellectually stimulated, if socially challenged, students. He and these brethren misfits gathered daily to work on assignments, share historical tales and the latest news and scientific discoveries, and to discuss radical sociology, classical poetry, contemporary politics, new and old theories of art... and any physiological fact, class rumor or boyish humor related to the forbidden subject of sex. They would meet every afternoon after the last bell rang, either in the school's wood-paneled studio next to the window or fireplace, at one of their homes, or outdoors under some shady tree whenever it was Eland's suggestion that held sway.

By his second year the discussions had evolved to encompass Blake and Baudelaire, the Gnostic Gospels and the Tibetan Book Of The Dead, Egyptian beliefs regarding reincarnation, Native American spirituality and the Peyote Church. And his personal and often solo explorations had widened, featuring studies with an elder of the Taos Pueblo, acceptance among an informal salon of budding poets and writers, and time with the artists who were arriving from all over to paint what they saw as the last natural peoples in the territory's magical light.

Since the close of the 1870's New Mexico had been promoted as a Mecca of sorts, first as a surefire tonic for the restoration of mind and body. Pamphlets touted the miraculous curative properties of its clean air, persistent sun and artesian hot springs. Later appeals to visitors and possible investors hinged on its decidedly mystical appeal, the pueblos appearing much as they had for hundreds of years before except for the addition of cars, the Indian women often still swaddled in hand-woven blankets. The appeal of the continuing indigenous ceremonies, the intense landscapes that somehow defied capture by either the poet's pen or painter's brush. While all things western were being written about and marketed in the East, so too were the most romantic and restless, dissatisfied and hopeful, creative and atypical drawn from both coasts and the European continent to the same land of enchantment that had housed, formed, and inspired Eland.

It was into this cauldron that Eland was delivered, then continuously dunked and stirred throughout his formative years. The diversity and character of that land, its spirit and lessons, the embrace as well as the abrasion, the struggle mixed with delight gave him almost everything he needed. And it was to that school of reality that he transferred at age seventeen, when he dropped out of the institutions of learning for the last time and signed up for the poignant lessons of life. Over the next eight years he explored most of the state, the eastern half of Arizona, and the mountains of southern Colorado. Eland worked as a big game guide until he was disgusted by the disrespect shown to the animals by some of his clients. Then he worked for a lithographer as his apprentice. He felt drawn to the Mexican revolution and briefly considered becoming a mercenary, but realized he could only kill another human in defense of what he most cherished, not for money, and certainly not to enforce someone else's beliefs or protect their interests. He tried assistant teaching for two years, antique appraisal for six months, amateur boxing for a week, factory work for a day, and bronco busting for something under five minutes... none of which he counted as failures. Not even the bronco riding. He was sampling the possibilities, broadening through variety and vagary, and learning from difficulties and mistakes what course to take and what corrections to make.

The special nature of New Mexico had gifted Eland with a sense that he was not only called, but surely if oddly equipped... that he was meant to be of some great help or provide some crucial service, even if he had no clue what sort of ailment or absence a potion like him might heal.

Ligusticum porteri (Osha)

Chapter 12

OSHÁ:
The Medicine Bear Pharmacy

The first couple of years in the new cabin went well enough. A week after arrival, they'd traded for an old but serviceable horse, and begun working hard to get the old house repaired and in order. Three hundred pounds of corn and wheat lasted most of those first four seasons, supplemented by the concerted gathering of acorns and Piñon nuts, and a steady harvest of Wild Dock, Mountain Nettle, and Watercress. Add to that an occasional deer brought down by Moon's cherished Marlin lever action rifle, with its unusual half-octagon barrel and Buckhorn sights. And a bounty of tasty if not always tender rabbit, thanks to the snares that Omen set.

The birth of Moon's second daughter was relatively quick and easy compared to how difficult of a time she had with Omen. She gave her a long Apache name that everyone in their new community had trouble pronouncing, and that was somehow shortened to "Hannah". Omen looked up to Moonheart in many ways, and ways in which she admired few others, respected her for her unbridled passion, sheer guts, and uncrushed connection to Spirit... as well as the spunk she demonstrated packing Hannah around in a sling everywhere she went, while she worked at the loom, cleaned the kitchen, or cut and bucked logs to build the chicken coop. While Omen had little patience for things she found personally unpleasant and aggravatingly necessary, Moon would unhesitatingly jump on any project that needed doing –

and whether it was considered to "man's work" or not – everything from digging an outhouse hole to repairing a wagon axle. Omen was equally impressed with how her mother endured suffering without complaint, and quietly withstood pain that would have had Omen cussing and hollering. Less endearing were those characteristics that Omen was terrified she might be taking on and developing herself, either through example or inheritance, such as her tendency to simultaneously, intensely attract and repel both genders. And her insistence on being always right, and being miserable whenever she wasn't.

In these ways and others, Omen sought not to emulate her mother, but to free herself, and then build the necessary walls to defend herself... from the return of any of those traits that conspired to consume them both. To the degree that Moon got too talkative in mixed company, her volume rising with the increasing tempo, her daughter was intent on picking her words, lowering her voice, picking her pace. Unlike the months her mother spent with abusive men in her life, Omen would never allow herself to be grabbed or struck without immediately ending the affair. Watching Moon turn away from anything resembling nourishing, healthy relationships, while repeatedly carrying the children of the disinterested and unworthy, Omen determined to do otherwise. She would do whatever it took to avoid pregnancy, hold tight to her independence until she met the mate that would give her what she felt she needed and deserved. And Moon's habit of self-sabotaging her most cherished dreams and plans would prove the inspiration for Omen's relentless search for magic, the pledging of her entire life to a place and purpose.

New Mexico offered plenty to try a person, from periods of drought to Scorpions and so called Kissing Beetles, who sucked a sizable volume of one's blood before what would prove to be an unbearable full-body itch set in. And the simply difficult tasks of life. The distance they carried water from the river in order to live fully out of the flood plain. The rainwater collected from the roof for when storms left the river too muddy to drink. A river too high to cross when they needed to get the wagon to town, or too low when they needed to irrigate. Land that bore minimal corn, and most years produced scant hay for any horses. Raccoons, elk, deer, ravens, Black Bears, and Beetle Bugs all competing for the garden they worked so hard to plant. Their first big test didn't come however until March, their seventeenth month in their new home at the mouth of canyon.

Little Hannah, as they called her, came down with what was starting to look like a dangerous flu. She'd stopped running up and down the river, and rummaging through the kitchen cabinets like she always did. Omen was used to having to chase after her constantly, used to making the face of the tiny girl perk up and look happy even when nothing else in the world seemed to please her. It wasn't as if Moon had saddled Omen with the role of number one mama. It had happened quite naturally, the baby Hannah reaching for her big sister for everything but the breast. Hannah scaring Moonheart by following Omen on her long walks to explore and harvest plants. A beautiful child, carried back home asleep. A one year old girl, hiding behind Omen's long skirt the first time a gentleman from town showed up to court their stubbornly attractive mother.

On the third day Hannah screamed out from nightmares no child should ever have to face, afraid of things she'd never witnessed as if they were real... or still coming. On the fourth she developed a terrible coughing, while appearing listless and uninvested between bouts, her flawless spirit already thinning like morning clouds at the insistence of the sun. Moon turned away their only visitor, uninterested in their attentions if they could be of no help, and they'd already found out that the nearest town of Frisco had no doctor even if they could somehow come up with the money to pay one. Each night they traded off sitting up and watching the being they both loved, and both mothered, dabbing her head with a rag dipped in lemon scented water. They had already tried all of the teas that they thought the old Spanish women were likely to suggest, as well as others that they'd learned about and brought with them from the reservation. None had the usual beneficial effect. Before waiting for her condition to get any worse, Moonheart called Omen over to her side on the fifth morning, and placed her palm over the area of her elder daughter's heart. Her breath smelled of the whiskey that had again become her solace and companion, but both her eyes and her words were clear.

"You can take your horse, Cholla, on up the mountain," Moon instructed, "and see if there are any Spring plants that talk to you. If you're praying, if your heart is open enough and you can quiet that head of yours, you might find something that could help. A lot of strong plant medicine happens with the first thaw in the high country. I'll pack your things, and get together some food."

Moon never really told Omen to do anything, she'd just ask, or wait for her daughter to notice what needed to be done and feel the pride of that. Sometimes Omen actually wished that her mama would have imposed more structure, but it had always been do as you like up to the point that I have to yell at you. Nor was she giving orders now, only making a suggestion that seemed far too right to contest. What else was there to do, but attempt the impossible?

Omen saddled up, and then strapped on the leather saddlebags stuffed with more food than she wanted to eat. Next, Moon attached a rifle scabbard so that most of it extended under the protection of the saddle skirt, then slid into it her prized Marlin.

"Here's my last half a box of .38-55's," Moon said, handing them to Omen as she leaned over for a long hug. "This is just in case you have any trouble. I don't suppose you have time to be getting us any meat."

"I love you Mama," said Omen, as she broke away, put her left foot in the stirrup and got up on the old gelded horse.

"I know you do sweetie. And I love you so much. Hannah loves you too."

Yes, Omen thought. And she needs me, like you need me too. But what she actually said was, "I love her too."

A hundred yards past the first river crossing there was a road that took you alternately either to the sleepy village of Frisco, or in a sharp incline up to the nearby peaks. Each mile she rode, the country shifted noticeably, one strata of plant species melding seamlessly into the next, transitioning from hight desert biome to Pinon/Juniper, elfin woodland overlapping with Ponderosa Pine thanks to the effect of the river running through. Next came the giant Fir and Spruce forest. And further up still, the trees began to look stunted and weather worn until at the top, treeless crags tore at a racing sky. But she would go no farther than the patches of white barked Aspen just beginning to leaf, and the high lush meadows between.

When it felt right to do so, Omen veered off to the East, following a ridgeline from which she could see clear back to the hilltops that marked her canyon, as well as the top of the almost ten thousand foot high Bear Wallow Mountain. She rode parallel and close to the edge, perhaps too close given the slickness of the rocks due to the overwash of fresh snowmelt. Approaching a particularly lush meadow from above, Omen suddenly felt it was time to stop and look around. Felt it in her gut, and someplace substantially deeper. She attached a rope from Cholla's halter to a medium sized Aspen, and offered the increasingly nervous gelding a handful of grain. Turning towards the meadow, it seemed to glow greener even than the other sprouted openings that graced the nearby bottoms, dips, and swells.

Slipping off her boots, she stepped slowly and deliberately down the slope, trying to hush her thoughts and enter sacred plant time. An eternal, and eternally changing present. Cycles of fermentative dark and sustaining light, seeding, dying, being born. Now was the time of new birth, when the grasses were full but unseeded, and only a few flowers yet blooming. She felt what she stepped on, sensed what grew and blew in the breezes before her. Sometimes stooping to touch or better see. Always smelling for the plant type, trying to discern with nose as well as eyes some message that will tell her what plant, and what part of the plant, to try.

From experience she knew that certain shapes, odors, colors or family groupings could mean poison. She knew what characteristics to look for in species she'd yet to identify, that might indicate a potential application for surface infections, menopause, or arthritis. And maybe, of some that could help with fevers and cough. But if they couldn't come up with its name, they would have to try it on themselves first, and that would all take time. All she could do was to look, hope, and listen... to what more and more sounded like a tone she could home in on, a signature vibration, a song.

Omen walked through the grass intoxicated, blissful and blessed. Like an Our Lady Of The Plants, she seemed not just a Medicine Woman but a holy apparition gracing and being graced by the green growing world around her. Someone watching could have forgiven themselves for the excess of imagination she inspired, the vision of a dress made up of a host of living, intertwining plants rather than mere cloth. Roots pulled up with each step forward, reattaching every time she stopped. And hair, no longer feather or even fur, but at least for the moment a twist and tangle of hopeful budding branches. The montane complexion and alpine gait. The nectar smile. Not a queen reigning over, but a relative and representative.

But even in that moment of seamless connection, of sentient bliss, Omen sensed something more than the movements, entreaties and gifts of plants. Something distinctly, unequivocally creature, with a strong and familiar odor. It was during her Na'ii'ees, her Sunrise Ceremony, that she had smelled it last. It was Shash, the Bear, and she could see it now as it stepped out of the tree line some forty yards in front of and below her. It was a Grizzly, she was sure, easily triple the size of the Black Bears she'd been seeing over the last year. Omen then watched as it began zig-zagging back and forth in her direction, its head swiveling side to side, its eyes on the ground. At first she thought it might be hunting some dodging rodent, but the beast was moving entirely too slowly for that. She thought about the rifle back on the horse, but then it would break her heart to have to use it.

Omen squatted down as the Bear, now less than thirty yards from her, started making satisfied huffing sounds, then began rolling around on the ground. Like a cat in a plot of fragrant Catnip, it wiggled and shook, leaped about and crawled forward on its belly with what could only be described as an ecstatic look on its furry face. From time to time it would thrust its huge muzzle into the ground, pull out some kind of plant by its roots, chew it up, and then spray it on its paws, spreading it around and massaging itself with the white frothy material. Omen enjoyed watching as the bruin as it sat down on its rump, wiping its face like a toddler, rubbing the chewed roots all over its ears and belly. She laughed to herself as it dug yet another root up from the ground and playfully tossed it in the air, adroitly catching it with its mouth. For an hour or more it fed and frolicked, until sauntering back through the valley. Omen admired the sway of it haunches, and how beauty wasn't always petite.

She waited what seemed like a polite if not entirely safe interval, then got up and walked over to the site. Much of the grass was trampled, although it would soon straighten itself back up again. Here and there were divots where it had used its claws and jaws to dig, spitting out the dirt, savoring its prize each time. Omen could see that the source of its meal and delight had been a plant obviously in the Carrot family. Surely this was what she had ridden all day for. The plant that had been singing was the one the Shash had showed her.

It was not, however, wholly unfamiliar. She had learned about it first from her Apache grandmother, and more recently from Doña Rosa. Oshá, not surprisingly called Bear Root or Bear Medicine. The common Mexican name for it was *Chuchupate*, as the curandera had taught her. It was considered the very best thing for many respiratory ailments, fevers and flu, although of such power that it had to be used wisely and in measured amounts. By July they would be dressed in beautiful clusters of little white flowers not unlike Yarrow. The bruins ate Oshá exclusively for the first two or three days after coming out of their Winter rest. And the old women of the village claimed that the male Bears would dig up the roots and offer them to their favorite female as part of a magical courting rite, a thought that tickled Omen no small amount.

Riding back across the river well after dark, Moon heard the hooves and came out to help her unsaddle, carrying a kerosene railroad lantern. Omen saw that Moonheart looked especially worried, while the mother noticed immediately that her daughter's face was filled with hope. The food in the saddlebags appeared uneaten, and a cloth back hung over them filled with close to ten pounds of some kind of root.

"Oshá, Mama," Omen said, holding out the roots in her hand. "We forgot about Oshá! How's sister?"

"Hannah's fever hasn't gotten any worse," Moon answered. "But it's been taking a toll on her."

As soon as the saddle and bridle were off, Omen closed the corral gate and rushed in to see her sister. She knelt down with her hand placed lightly on Hannah's laboring chest, taking comfort in her stubborn clinging to life while Moon cleaned and began to chop up a particularly bear claw shaped root.

She would have another year to help raise her before her mother hooked up with a hard drinking fellow across the valley, took her Hannah, and left.

Just about the time Moon's third child started showing.

And shortly after Omen started getting more attention than her mother from the men who came and went.

Omen – Sweet Medicine Canyon, NM, 1911

Chapter 13

INFESTATION & BLIGHT:
The Dissolution Of A Family, 1912

Omen had feared this day would come, ever since her persistently comely mother began spending more nights of the week with her latest man than she did with her children... and ever since it became clear that Moonheart was pregnant for the third time, unable to button the fly on her straining Levis. Things were still good when they were together, the two of them as much partners in a posse as mother and daughter, and baby Hannah getting to play with them both. But together was becoming rarer and rarer.

Moon was heavy with the child of Ty Hardcastle, a supposed cowboy who seldom got on a horse except to show off, and who seemed as intent on wasting what was left of the family nest egg as his daddy had been to build it up for his offspring and likeness. Once his parents passed away, he made a habit of letting his fences sag, seldom bothering to move his herd from one pasture to the next, then blamed his financial losses on government, foreign influence on a fickle market, and predation by blood-thirsty wolves. Omen considered him an infestation, a scale and blight inflicting the garden of their lives.

Omen wasn't sure if her Ma had really been sucked in by Hardcastle's exaggerated adoration and gratuitous manner. Or if he was merely a convenient drinking buddy, with the benefit of a large spread and fancy house. It was certainly more than her simply being mercenary, or an opportunist. Perhaps, Omen thought, she was with him for the same reasons she seemed to have been with most of the others: to risk exposure, public ridicule ,or personal debasement or abuse in order to explore her own extreme frontiers of sensation... or debasement. Or to suffer what she somehow believed she deserved.

One thing was for sure, Omen would have none of him. It nearly drove her to violence when he'd pick up the squirming toddler Hannah, and make whiskey inspired baby sounds in her aptly disapproving face. And worst of all were his repeated clumsy come-ons in front of her mother. He would slink over to Omen every chance he got, like the foam from an overflowing pot of beans quickly creeping across an enameled stove top.

"Get the hell away from me," she'd growl at him, before he could find any opportunity or excuse to initiate physical contact.

Or, "Stay away," she'd say, always spinning around to face him.

She deliberately wore loose fitting garments whenever he or any other man came around, sometimes binding her growing breasts to her body the same way she did when she planned on doing any running. There was, however, no concealing the fruits of her adolescence, or the power of her appeal. And the vigorous way in which she refused him had the unintended effect of making him want her all the more.

The absolute last time that Ty visited, Omen had avoided the house all day long, only coming in to help with supper. Afterwards, he restrained Moon from helping Omen with the dishes, then sat her down and began to regale her with tall tales about himself, periodically stomping the clay floor in his lizard skin boots. He was several years younger than her mother, and might have been handsome if not for how he held himself, motioned and spoke. Or the fact that his broad smile looked to Omen like a rip in the unshaved fabric of his face. The Chicken-headed Fucker, she had named him, in recognition of the way his head seemed to bob around, loosely moored to his neck.

"I'm heading out to the root cellar to look for another bottle and some cheese," Moonheart announced at last, scooting out the door so fast that Hardcastle found himself finishing his sentence with no one there to hear it or care.

He started to sit down, and then thought better of it and half stumbled over to where Omen stood at the sink washing plates. It was pitch dark outside, and the multiple window panes above the sink were like mirrors for her, reflecting his approach.

"Whatcha doing there honey, with those pretty little hands of yours in that nasty looking water?"

Omen snatched a kitchen knife from the drying board and secreted it beneath the suds, while never taking her eyes off him, there, menacing, in the window in front of her.

"You look a lot like your mama," he said, while grabbing her arms from behind.

I'm nothing like her, she thought in a rage, gripping still tighter the knife's comforting wooden handle.

"Let me be, Ty," Omen hissed through clenched teeth... a second after she'd begun to lift her blade from the water, and only a split second before the two foot chunk of oak wood smashed into the back of his head.

Moon was good that way, able to hit a running rabbit with a balanced throwing stick, or a philandering boyfriend from across the room, even when she was heavy in the drink. Hardcastle's head quit bobbing, and he crashed to the floor. Omen couldn't tell how much her mother had acted to protect her, and how much of it was jealousy over the competition she unintentionally posed. Omen stepped over the unconscious form with a proud indifference, in a show of disdain more characteristic of her mother than she would have liked.

From that day onwards, Moon visited the Chicken-headed Fucker at his house instead of theirs, first for afternoons, then afternoons and evenings, and finally for regular all-nighters. Hannah got to where she didn't want to go to her mother when she returned home in the mornings, clinging to Omen when Moon reached out for love. She clung the day of Moon's departure as well, screaming at the top of her lungs as Omen loosened the diminutive fingers clutching at her dress, before handing her over to her anxious mother.

"Everything is packed and in Ty's car," Moon said, raising her voice only as much as was needed to be heard over Hannah's squall.

"I wish you wouldn't go, Mama," Omen answered, herself louder than she wanted to be on such a somber occasion.

"You could probably come with us," Moon added, panicking herself with the thought. "I could make Ty give you the bunkhouse, and you wouldn't even have to see him if you didn't want to."

Neither of them believed that was true. Nor did Moon really imagine that the daughter who was so connected and devoted to place would give up her sanctuary after having already had to surrender her childhood home. They fell into each other, pressing the still crying Hannah between them, then Moon walked off with Omen left framed in the doorway.

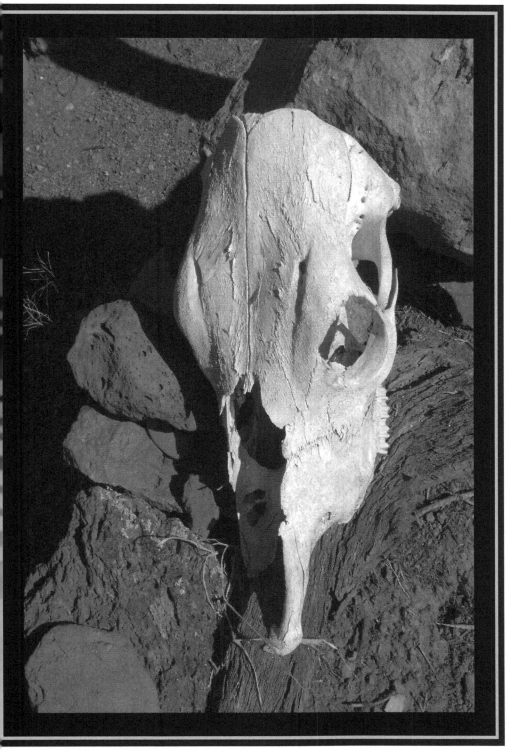

Chapter 14

MYTHOS & ALLURE:
The Real Spirit Of The West

Eland grew up with two often conflicting desires, one being to describe the struggle, truth, and beauty of life, to deepen, awaken and inspire through the magnifying lens of his dear and wild West... the second, paradoxically, being to grapple with, embrace and wholly experience a reality that no words could ever describe.

The ramifications of the latter were many, including his dropping out of school even after he was promised a scholarship to a university, refusing sensible jobs that failed to appeal to his senses, insisting on actually doing some of those things that most of his schoolmates were content to simply read about... and taking various creative, thrilling, and totally unnecessary risks: patching together an old wooden guide boat and crashing his way through the narrow Taos Box, where the Rio Grande rushed grey with snowmelt through an obstacle course of pointed granite incisors and molar-like boulders. Sitting outdoors in a wood-fired bathtub during the frightful slash and crash of a full-blown lightning storm, mostly to feel the rain on his face while he soaked.

The consequences of the former were in their own way no fewer, resulting in Eland never going anywhere without pen and paper, spending hours writing and thus missing out on time with the very sunsets and river courses he wrote about and extolled. The girls he dated thinking he was corny for giving them what were meant to be intoxicating poems instead of heady wine.

It would be more excusable, he thought, if what I was trying to do hadn't already been done so damn many times before.

People had been writing about and reading about all things Western since before any but the so-called "Red Man" even knew what this amazing region looked like. The literate citizens of an entire continent had been enthralled by stories of the American frontier from the moment the Spaniards' first sketchy reports of the New World were publicized in the metropolises of Europe, and they eagerly ate up every bit of news related to the immigrants' rapid exploration and settling of those wondrous lands beyond the Appalachians. Nostalgia for what was being lost had set in well over a decade before a final end to the Indian wars and the settlement of their lands. It was this overlap that made possible the anomaly of Sitting Bull touring with the Wild West Show between confrontations with the Bluecoats' army, and the showman Buffalo Bill taking time off from performing to assist in an attack on the Cheyenne after the incendiary victory over Gen. George Armstrong Custer. History had colluded with legend to create a West that was so much more than a mere idea, or even a place. It had fed on the juices of the imagination, to grow into a myth for the ages, an alternative paradigm, a glowing vision that burned like the fiery halos of ghost riders waving from the silken prairies of an unfenced western sky.

That was the allure for Eland as well, and growing up in the very center of it did nothing to diminish its mythical and mystical appeal. But his mission, as he saw it, was to reveal the intricacy and potential of human nature by painting a portrait of the soul of the West in words. To evoke a living and evolving thing, not to capture it, as was so often said of photographs and vignettes. That would be to unnaturally freeze and incarcerate what was meant to be free, revolving like Tumbleweed to reveal endless facets and sides. And if anything was meant to be free - not only of cruel imposition, but falsity and fabrication - it was the West.

Eland felt that far too many of its chroniclers had romanticized and sanitized it, reducing the protagonists to one dimensional characters, reducing events to simple right and wrong, black and white.

There could be no arguing with the appeal of a place where no one ever fell off their horse, barmaids provided comfort and counsel instead of sass and sex, and all stray dogs found homes. Where trouble was the fault of outsiders and miscreants rather than people who were known and trusted. Where justice and goodness inevitably prevailed, and those who loved enough never failed. Where a clear good-guy would sometimes shoot the gun out of an evildoer's hand without hardly bruising his fingers. Eland considered that kind of romantic approach delusional, short-changing an always complex and dynamic, often dangerous West. If, as the popular song claimed, there was someplace where nary a discouraging word was heard, that place was definitely not the frontier he knew.

Westerners had from the very beginning faced a number of challenges, hardships and tragedies that inevitably tested both their patience and good cheer: A scary percentage of children died between delivery and five years of age. Many who survived had medical and dental problems for the rest of their lives as a result of a shortage of doctors and the limited knowledge of their day. Epidemics took out entire communities. Good fresh water was often hard to come by, even for communities occasionally ravaged by storms and scoured by floods. Few towns escaped the scourge of fire and many had to be rebuilt from scratch every ten years or so. Crops often failed or were gobbled up by Locusts, while foods imported from the East were always expensive and too often stale. Alkaline seeps and poisonous weeds led to the deaths of many of those sheep and cattle not bar-b-cued by Indians, stolen and sold by rustlers, or shredded by the canine teeth of Prairie Wolves and Mountain Lions.

It was, as the saying went, rough out West. But the folks most likely to use that expression, did so with their tongue firmly in cheek. After all, if there were going to be difficulties in life, it was there that the rural Westerners want to suffer them. For many, a weathered porch provided an incredible view, the hum and howl of the wind, a rafter from which hung fresh meat, and the squealing of delighted children as buttermilk biscuits were brought out on a tray.

All in all, the West was never as tranquil, pastoral, or resolved as books and articles would lead one to think... nor was it generally as violent as writers liked to claim. At their peak of lawlessness, towns like Silver City, Albuquerque, or Socorro had no more murders than comparatively sized, gang-infested neighborhoods in the Eastern inner cities. Most guns discharged inside town limits were fired in the air, just for the fun of it. And the majority of shots actually fired in anger missed their intended targets. Aside from the Indian wars, poor gun handling was the number one cause of firearms related fatalities. Accidental discharges provided frontier undertakers with far more business than assassinations and shootouts combined, even if they made poor subject matter for newspaper articles or books.

Many claimed that the West was little more than a state of mind, something to be twisted and tweaked into convenient, practicable and marketable forms. The real West, however, was made of particular landscapes and a characteristic wildness, wonder and verve that made it different from other settings and other times. The lessons and tests, celebrations and tragedies were peculiar to the region and its way of being. Events, like characters, had personality. And Eland believed the West's "happenins and doins" to be a campfire story considerably more enthralling than the most entertaining fabrications ever to grace a printed page or silver screen, more momentous than even the best told lies.

A long & lonesome trail

Certainly, the West's promoters had not always been its truest proponents. The prevaricating Ned Buntline and dozens of other authors of Victorian feel-good drivel both enhanced the legend and gutted its truths. Buffalo Bill Cody, who did more than any other single person to both further and profit from the mythology of the West, nonetheless claimed his tour to Great Britain was an expedition to prove that the vast territory of the United States was finally and effectively settled by the English speaking race. The paradox was that the settling he touted had included not only the pacification of the indigenous peoples, but also the diluting and denaturing of the very crucible from which Cody himself was cast. There could have been no Buffalo Bill grown out of the concrete of thoroughly civilized environs. There could have been no Calamity Jane without a calamity or two. No heroes without villains to test their mettle, to keep them honest and give them purpose. No Ben Lilly without Bears. No Wild Bill Hickock without a West to be wild within.

The people Eland found most fascinating weren't the ones that toed the line, but those who at one time or another stepped a good ways over it. The women who flouted convention. The lawmen that skirted the law in order to bring to ground a killer, and the *banditos* who found such creative ways of breaking it. The word "order" in the expression "law and order" meant keeping every element of society in its place, on an even keel, working together with little friction, like the greased wheels and cogs of a great machine. That wasn't, however, necessarily what made for strong character... or even a good story. The story of real life anywhere, not just on Eland's dear frontier, was complex and filled with elements of both good and bad. Life's intensity and vitality was a product of diversity and challenge. It was tension and opposition that defined the lines of its art, and the power of one's life.

Not all historic Western characters had been the best role models, but that wasn't the point. Eland felt called upon to take what was most impressive and noble about the past, and embody it in his own day... and to go even further when it came to consciousness and compassion, forgiveness and understanding. He wanted to be an improvement, but that didn't mean he judged those who preceded him harshly. They were measured according to the context and customs of their time.

Eland felt the characters of the West he grew up with required neither sympathy nor adulation, but empathy. For the writer and reader to walk in their shoes for just a spell, to understand what their lives were like, what they went through, sustained, enjoyed and endured. Their trials and tribulations, minor accomplishments and major satisfactions. Their habits and traits, peculiarities and mannerisms. Their fears and hopes, needs and desires. The anger that fired their heart's furnace, the love that quenched and sated it. The countryside and weather that drew a knife down them like a sculptor, and lifted them up straight as Hopi Corn, tall as the Ponderosa Pines lining a rocky ridge. The stories that influenced their opinions, salved their anger or inflamed their prejudices. The dreams that they lived, and sometimes died for.

Chapter 15

AN UNEXPECTED OUTGROWTH:
Gift & Responsibility

A man in a long dark coat and ragged felt hat walked silently up to Omen's door, the wind masking any sound from his practiced steps. He appeared to have foreknowledge of the layout and terrain, and moved like an old hunter who had grown up getting within arrow's distance of big-eared elk and deer, as quiet as an assassin trained in the art of noiseless entry and death. He did not knock, but reached instead for the handle with a wrinkled hand, knuckles caked with blood.

Omen sat inside, writing symbols on each of several cobalt blue medicine bottles to mark their content, then adding the day's date in the kind of handwriting you'd expect from a happy-go-lucky eight year old girl... not a sexually developing teen set on exploring and understanding every aspect of her world. Her mind raced, the same way that her conversations often did. And her wide little feet, when the winds stirred in her the urge to run. For all the ways that her mind and body differed, the one imagining and the other doing, in at least one way they were alike. Both had just two speeds, besides motionless: hurried, and barely moving. Rushing, and relaxing. The mad scamper, and the intimate crawl. Slow as a well-loved Bear with a belly full of grass, fast as that same animal in the lightning moment when it rushed its panicked prey. She could have as many as four trains of thought going at once, in four different directions, with all revealing something about the source if not the destination. On this afternoon it was the bizarre-looking Coatamundi she'd seen up the dry wash, a rare and secretive animal that she thought looked like a cross between a Raccoon and an Anteater. Envisioning how she would draw it, while criticizing herself for what she considered her deficiencies as an artist. Trying to figure out if it would be best to prepare the Redroot for Ramon's liver medicine into a tincture or decoction, and who she could trade with to get the raw goat cheese that she wanted so bad she could almost smell it. Into this busy arena came the sound of her door being opened, and then all other thoughts stopped.

"Uncle!" she exclaimed, before running into his arms. She hugged him so hard he groaned. Then she took up his hand in hers to look at it.

"Just a scratch, from that damn car door," he said in his low and quiet voice. "My skin is thin as paper these days."

It was not age or weakness in his voice, but some sense of dignity, or perhaps not wanting to disturb the surrounding web, the sanctity, the perfection. Omen remembered herself as a child, climbing up on him to be nearer his mouth, and so better to hear him.

"I have some *Caléndula* ointment, Uncle," Omen said, turning to get a cloth and water.

The old man sat down in the rocker, near the fireplace, and looked around the room as he rocked. His eyes, that had for a score of decades taken so much in, now drank of the way the house looked and felt, the indications of how the house was cared for and loved. The flowers on the table and curtains on the windows, the shelves of neatly arrayed medicines she'd made, the tribal art and textiles hung up on the walls.

"You haven't asked about Mama," she said, returning to gently wash the scrape on his hand.

"Who is she staying with this time?"

"How did you know," Omen asked, looking away in embarrassment.

"You have no reason to be ashamed. My sister does what she does. It's not up to you."

"I've never been able to understand," Omen said, grabbing his hand and smearing on the forest-smelling salve.

"Of course you do," he said, still speaking just as slowly. "She has an extra belly, that maybe no food can fill. And you have that hunger too, although you have let it take you to a different place than your mother did."

He smiled at her, then at his mended hand. She was alone, he knew, only because there was something different in her than in Moonheart. Something that sabotaged any agreement that didn't serve her spirit, that ensured no man would or could stay unless it was one that could heal her. Not with medicine, but with powerful understanding, alliance, and love.

They talked no more about Moon's challenges, only her abilities and power. Come evening he asked Omen to tell him stories, reminding her how much he enjoyed hearing her voice. And she was forthcoming, with familiar tales learned from her grandmother that showed how she had not forgotten her early roots and gifts. Tales of Hannah, whom she only managed to see once or twice a month. Some that made him cry, and some that made him laugh. And tales of the canyon she had already grown inseparably close to... or rather, that she knew and belonged to before she first got to see, smell, and touch it. Come morning they ate cold biscuits in order to get outside quicker, then spent the day walking up and down the river, sharing with each other what they knew about the plants and animals that showed themselves, and sharing how they felt.

But as always, she knew the bright so well only thanks to her painful familiarity with the dark. She worried that she could not survive being moved again, and never from this enchanted place. That even if he gave the cabin to her mother, there was no way of being sure she wouldn't sell it in the future, mortgage it to pay for some great mistake or bankroll some wild whim. Omen worried about losing her home, as much as she did about the possibility of never finding her romantic match, her destined partner, her true love. And somehow the two were connected, as if she had always needed them together.

Omen squeezed the old man yet again, handed him a bag of special ointments and baked rolls, and then watched as he walked back and across the river just as quietly as he had come. She held her hand up as if to wave, though certain he would get into his car and drive off without waving back. The good-bye was his hug. Now it was time to go. She closed the door, then sat back down to her cup of hot Clover tea.

From clear across the room she could see a sheet of yellowing paper on the table with some sort of official looking header. Somehow she knew that it was her uncle's legal deed to the land and house.

She had no idea yet that it had been signed over - not to her mother, but to her. Nor was she yet aware of the responsibilities that came with it, or the further changes that it would lead to.

Eland, 1914

PART III

Chapter 16

THE MEETING:
Ramon's Fateful Party

June 11th, 1914, was a day Eland would not forget for as long as he lived. It had only been a short while since papers were filled with the assassination of the heir to the Austrian throne, Archduke Francis Ferdinand, and was only a month before the start of the horrendous World War that it would help to precipitate. He'd found significant disadvantages to working for his own father, but the bright side was his being able to get away for up to two weeks at a time. And being able to afford a black convertible, just in time for his first ever trip to the southwestern corner of the New Mexico territory.

Anything under a hundred miles and he would have taken one of their half dozen horses, or even a team and buggy. Unlike most of his schoolmates, he could hear little music in the roar of the pipes, and found no pleasure in the perpetual maintenance and repair of machines. But a 350 mile trip was a different matter entirely, as he didn't want to spend most of his vacation on the road going and coming.

The morning began with his putting on a light tan shirt to reflect the hot sun, an easy-to-remove sleeveless wool pullover vest for the early chill, and a knit cap instead of his usual round-topped cowboy hat, in order to keep his flowing hair from knotting in the wind. Next, the careful packing of food, clothes and the sections of his cane fly fishing pole into his trunk, and the slamming of the lid. He would always remember that slow climb up La Bahada Hill, with Santa Fe jiggling in and out of focus in his rear view mirror. South, past San Felipe and then Sandia Pueblos. Filling the tank in the increasing bustle of Albuquerque. Proceeding over yet another large hill, then the view opening up to reveal hundreds of miles of the treeless Rio Grande Valley in shades of umber and sienna, with a thin, crooked slash of green and blue where the grand river sliced ever southward. Passing Isleta Pueblo, with the Manzano Mountains and Mount Taylor to the east. Huge flocks of Waterfowl lifting and descending on the bosque, the precious wetlands where the big river seasonally spilled out into those Cottonwood and Willow groves not yet grazed down by Cattle. The landmarks Eland sighted in on were South Baldy and Ladron Peak. Between them lay the village of Socorro, where he made the turn west to the frontier railhead of Magdalena. Leaving the valley behind, winding up through the Gallinas, then across the high Plains of San Agustin which had once been an inland sea. Angling off at Datil as a Redtail Hawk careened overhead, then wheeling higher still over the heavily forested continental divide, and down the twisty gravel road that ran between the Tularosa and San Francisco Mountains.

How wonderful – how it filled him with wonder – to be entering a mountain-scape wilder than his familiar Pecos, millions of acres with far more elk than people. He felt his spirits elevated with each new rise and fall of the poorly paved road, and each mile seemed not so much like the approach of a destination as a return to somewhere he already knew and belonged to. He drove slowly most of the day, savoring the smells of Summer with the top rolled down. But the closer he got, the faster he went, his heart racing and a huge smile on his face. It made him think of barn-spoiled horses, how you can barely get them to go when you start away from the house, yet can't pull the reins in hard enough to keep them from running hard on the way back. Eland was nearly giddy, already intoxicated with the elixir of such a wild destination.

The road followed what he soon learned was the infant Tularosa River, from the springs that formed its headwaters near Aragon to where it was joined by Apache Creek, then left the Tularosa for a few miles before crossing a bridge over the Rio Frisco. In the village of Frisco the main route turned to the West, but Eland continued south on a smaller track, stopping at the Texaco across from Milligan's Saloon just long enough to fill his tank from the glass reservoir atop its lone pump.

The locals in their bib overalls seemed friendly enough, but he wasn't looking for camaraderie or community on this trip, or at least not from his own two-legged, reasoning kind. He was on his way to what he believed to be the forest least impacted by humanity, to the company of unthinking creatures setting an example with their adherence to their wordless natures and untamed emotions. He needed to be someplace where, when he spoke, what echoed back was river whoosh, bird song, and cricket chirps. He wanted the opposite of comfort, he wanted a place where even beauty was so intense that it was excruciating. Where there was no distraction from reality, Spirit, or his scalding emotions. He sought not just a wild and powerful place, but an awareness from which there would be no escape.

Eland had to pump the brakes as various wagons, cars, and trucks were parked on both sides of the lane, leaving very little room to pass between. In addition, a steady stream of children ran back and forth chasing a ball, while a bemused burro rested on its belly in the center of the right of way, and two dogs lay sleeping in the dirt. Eland backed up to the first available space, parked, and then got out to see what he could do about clearing the road.

As he approached, the dogs barely looked up, and the burro seemed to be be ignoring him completely. From a house to his left he could make out the melody of a *corridos*, a *ballada rurala* sung in plaintive Spanish to the accompaniment of a *bajo* and six string guitar. And from his right came the rush of children, yelling and laughing, grabbing both of his hands and propelling him towards what appeared to be a neighborhood party.

"Bienvenidos! Welcome!"

Several older folk were beckoning for him to come over, shouting their encouragement. Eland savored the atmosphere, the sincere welcome, the smell of broiling chicken and acrid chile. One little girl about four years old continued to hold his hand with both of hers, looking up at him with dark, adoring eyes.

"Have some food! Have a drink! There's plenty to go around!"

Before Eland could answer, someone leaped up and handed him a plate.

"Hi, I'm Ramon, he said, pronouncing it 'Raah-mon' in true Hispanic fashion."

"This is my *casa*, and my party, and whoever you are you're welcome here."

Ramon was a short man in his fifties or sixties, it was hard to tell. Two slightly battered hens kept as close to him as they could, moving when he did, being careful not to get stepped on, and clearly considering him their champion and protector from a rooster who glared nearby. He reached out and squeezed Eland's forearm, instead of shaking his hand.

"Good strong pulse," Ramon said, as if he knew how to tell something fundamental about a man that way.

For the next two hours Eland feasted and visited, all the while with the little girl at his side, on his lap, or riding on his shoulders. Characteristically quiet and observant at first, Eland was soon fascinating the group with his descriptive tales, stories gleaned through his obsession with the peculiarities of history and attention to the infinite curiosities of the world.

As he talked, he scanned not only the hearts and responses of his audience, but also the faces of the women for what he'd always called "Her." A typical young man on the prowl for sex or love would most likely look for such distinctions as married or unmarried, old enough or too young, thin or heavy, attractive or not. Eland increasingly focused on one question only: was it "Her"? Her, that he imagined waited for him someplace, though where he didn't know. Not just a fine choice for a date, or mate... but the one who would understand him. Work with him. Partner with him. Her, that would intensely, completely, loyally devote herself to that which they would be together. And while he didn't have a certain picture of what she would look like, he felt certain that he would recognize her once the time finally came.

There was no longer any chance of Eland making it to the trailhead before it was time to sleep, so he thought he might as well plan on making camp a few miles up the road. He still felt good, even though he'd been diverted and derailed... with a sense that the gold of life awaited him still, and that the party, the people there, that little girl and the mountains arcing around them were the path, the way, the rainbow.

Eland picked up his new friend, held her out, and looked her in the eyes a last time before handing her to her mother. Over the child's shoulder and just past her smile, he noticed a hill aglow from the receding sun, sheltering a flower-covered swale. Whenever something like that captured his attention – whether a river at the bottom of a difficult canyon to descend, or an inconvenient but enticing cave noticed while driving – Eland would almost always drop everything and immediately go to it. And now he crossed the fence, climbing between its four strands of taut barbed wire, proceeding up the hill to its golden summit.

Eland stood on the far side in the wind, just out of sight of the people below. He looked out to the North, at the Piñon and Oak and a handful of horses contentedly grazing, and then slowly turned to the East and its pine clad peaks. The South, and the shadow-draped gorges indicating a river, held him rapt for the longest time. Then he swiveled towards the sun beginning to dip in the West. Squinting to see through its glare, Eland's eyes were drawn towards something dark among the flexing rows of Bunch Grass. He'd be happy to see a deer, thrilled to spot a bear. The sun seemed to drop the last little ways quickly, bringing into focus what was now clearly a woman with long black hair, hair that glinted with the color of fire in the day's last rays. Backlit as she was, he could see the smoothness of her skin, arms that he already hungered to feel in his grasp, underneath his fingers, against his palms. Her broad cheekbones. Her wise, sparkling eyes. Her child-like smile, and her mouth the small bud of a flower waiting to open.

The woman stood motionless in the thigh-high grass, locks of hair blowing across her forehead and cheeks, with a large Willow basket under her arm. She'd come to honor Ramon on his birthday, but after the appropriate *embrazos* and wishes, ended up giving her afternoon to gathering several plants that she hadn't been able to find closer to home. Eland could see she wore a full length burgundy skirt, bound at the waist by a stout leather belt, and bearing a small knife in an engraved silver sheath. Some kind of ivory tooth hung from a cord around her neck, and a serpentine bracelet on one wrist. Her weighty breasts were concealed and supported by a black silk scarf featuring the evocative folds and petals of large red roses, helping frame the alluring roundness of her exposed belly. She continued watching him as he eased down the hill in her direction, as still as a tree just until he got to her, and then moving only a foot or two in his direction.

She'd seen him at the same instant that he'd first noticed her, silhouetted against the sky on a hill where she often came to collect plant medicines. But the way the light was, she could see him more clearly sooner. His confident but relaxed stance. The billowing sleeves of the tan shirt, the old fashioned breeches tied below his knees. Dark brown hair swirling down to a point just below his wide buccaneer collar. The auburn mustache she thought looked boyish without a beard, overlapping soft expressive lips. His penetrating gaze. She felt her heart begin to speed up, and her palms and thighs start to sweat. It wasn't his looks, as striking as she found them, so much as the feeling she got the moment their eyes met. Similar to the feeling she had gotten when she'd spotted the Bear that led her to the healing Oshá. And when her uncle drove the truck full of their belongings around the last curve before the mouth of the canyon that was meant to be the center of her world.

"Eland," he said.

"What?"

"My name. Eland."

"I'm Omen," she responded, in what seemed at once to be the voice of a tiny child, the plaintive crying of a forlorn wood sprite, and the seductive whisperings of a maiden... with a mixed-culture accent that he found utterly enchanting.

Usually she would not be so accepting of approach, nor so tolerant of boldness. Bold too often meant macho. Bold was the talk of war makers, and of the men who had hit her mother. "Be bold," some President always said, right before leading the whole country into doing some stupid thing. Boldness could be a mask that hid cruelty, or stupidity. The more cock-sure a man was, the quicker she usually was to turn him away. Not that she liked tentative either, as she distrusted those who didn't know or trust themselves. That was one explanation for why she had lived alone for the months since Moonheart left to go live with the Chicken-headed Ty, in spite of Omen attracting the interest of nearly all of the available or compromised men in the region.

Fifteen years old was when a lot of women got married, and the menfolk could be forgiven for their desires, if not their assumptions. Eland seemed somehow different. Even his confidence sat well with her. None of the normal warning signs triggered her usual defensive response. There was none of the tingling of her sixth sense that often warned her of danger, and so the walls had yet to go up. She continued to hold still, except for a small grin erupting from one corner of her mouth. Then even her grin froze, as, without asking her permission, Eland slowly and deliberately moved his hands towards her... and her basket full of plants fell to the grass.

Omen began breathing heavier and heavier, her lungs supplying the additional oxygen needed for running or fighting... or for giving in to her passions with this stranger who felt anything but strange to her. The hands stopped, palms out, a quarter inch or less from her breasts. So connected were she and Eland at that moment, that when he moved his hands in a circular motion she could feel them as if they were directly on her bare skin, and her nipples stiffened in response. Ever so gradually, he moved his hands out toward her shoulders, then down her arms as he squatted down before her, then back up again without ever once making physical contact. Then he moved his hands over to her stomach, the part hardest for many women to love, gently massaging without touching, honoring that blessed part of her body in a way that relieved her fears and stroked parts of her soul. A hand down each leg, so that by that time he reached her feet, his forehead was pressing on the ground in an attitude of reverence. By now Omen was visibly shaking, her breaths getting progressively shorter and quicker as both palms followed her legs back up and then came together into the shape of a heart directly over her pubic bone.

Eland too was panting, struggling to maintain that narrow margin of space between his palms and the burning pout beneath her skirt as she convulsed involuntarily, his hands dancing backwards whenever her hips thrust forward. Then with a cry and shudder her desires climaxed, and the tension in her body released.

Without pulling back, Eland's hands moved upward again, giving her shivers as they passed over her belly, through the channel between her breasts and to her upper chest, over her heart. It was only then that Omen found it unbearable, stepped back and stumbled away.

"I missed you," she said, before turning towards the party. I missed you, she said to a man she'd never met before.

Chapter 17

PROBING TENDRILS:
Questing For Omen

Eland squeezed back into the circle of men, just as Ramon finished sawing through the pig's neck, sending the head rolling in his general direction. As smart as dogs, he remembered reading somewhere, as he stared into its expressionless, dirt-flecked eyes. But then, people from the Celts of Britain to many Native American tribes had raised dogs for food as well, and no one could debate the fact that people needed to eat. No one subsisted on air, dirt, or rock.

We're all food as much as we are eaters, he thought, the dined upon as well as that which dines. Parasites feed on us while we're still breathing, and the worms and microbes get their fill of us once we're not. Blunder between a Grizzly mother and her offspring, and we find out we are nowhere near the top of the food chain. To the Bear we're a potential snack. And above all else, he figured, was the living soil. It got to eat everybody.

With Ramon busy butchering, Eland turned instead to a pair of nearby women to make his inquiry. They were having a great time bouncing and perforating a line of tin cans on the side of the hill, target practicing with their little octagon-barreled .22's. He watched as they slid the fore-end backwards and then forwards again after every shot, pumping round after round from the tubular magazines until each was emptied.

"Excuse me, if you would."

They turned to see who was addressing them, then looked the Anglo up and down.

"I was wondering," he continued, "if you could tell me where that *muchacha* has gone, the one with the basket full of plants."

The women both smiled knowingly, the one with the wedding ring walking off to set their cans back up, the other taking the liberty to answer.

"You mean the Bear Woman," she said. "Her name is Omen. She just left."

"That's right," he said. Omen.

His mind raced, going over in a flash much of the Bear mythology he knew, wondering just what her connection to the bruin might be.

"She's sort of a Curandera," the woman added, "been living downriver of here for a couple years or less. You sick? If you are, that's close enough! Or maybe you're just looking for potion that could put a little lead in your *lápiz*."

"Everything's in satisfactory working order, but thank you ,Ma'm", he replied. "I've got something of hers I want to give her."

He had no idea what that something might be, or even where the words came from. But as always, once he'd said something, he felt committed to making it true.

"Can you tell me how I might find my way to her place?"

"You were already heading the right way. Another two miles down, the road turns into a trail. If you go up the hill, you're going the wrong way. Take the lower fork to where it crosses the San Francisco, and you'll be able to see her house from there."

Eland's map showed a trail leading east, that came out to the road a little ways before where he expected Omen's house to be. He decided to take it at the very last second, braking and careening to make the turn. He followed it for a while up a small creek called the Negrito, then parked under some Cottonwood trees next to a series of holes deep enough to hold Trout. From the trunk he pulled out his bedroll and cotton-duck tarp, his fishing rod and creel, and then the small leather briefcase that held some of the projects he was working on, extra tablets for his journal, oil paints, brushes, and other supplies. It smelled of turpentine when he opened it, and he had to check to see if the ream of hand-pressed paper was alright. Assured that it was, he gathered up a small saw, a cloth bag of wood carving knives, files of various shapes and sizes, and U- and V-shaped gouges.

Temporarily forgetting the fishing pole, he wandered over to a fallen Black Walnut tree and selected a satisfactory section of branch. With the foot long hand saw, Eland cut the branch in two, and then cut from the base two fairly even slabs approximately one quarter of an inch in thickness. These he sawed into six by nine inch rectangles, rounding and beveling the corners, spending over an hour sanding them smooth, and using jeweler's hand-drill to make holes along one side of each. Setting one slab aside, he took out his Sheffield pocket knife and began scratching a picture of some sort on the other, slowly bringing to life his vision by removing any wood which did not contribute to its expression, recessing the background until only the dream stood forth.

It was noon the next day before he finished carving, with only a little sleep, and nothing else to eat. He followed by smoothing and polishing with ever-finer grades of sandpaper, and finally buffing it by rubbing it hard with a small piece of sheepskin. Eland especially enjoyed that part, massaging the wood, massaging his hopes. He then cut the paper the nuns had made into five by seven inch pieces, lined them up between the slabs, and punched a series of holes in the appropriate places with a leather awl. Through these he ran thick elk hide laces, binding all the components into a united mission.

Paper he'd thought he might divide between a dozen missives for friends – or for women he imagined he'd neither fully love nor stay with – was now bound into a single volume of possibility, awaiting the caress of her small, soft hands, and her marks upon it.

Only a few miles away, those little hands were picking up pieces of ancient Mogollon pottery, turning them so the painted designs faced first one way and then another, trying her best to make some sense out of all she'd seen and felt.

Chapter 18

A GRAFTING REJECTED:
Threatened By Love

From first sight, Eland was able to think of little else. Not the many things he'd read about or done, the facts of history or his projections of the future. Neither regrets, nor accomplishments. Not the mountain he'd thought he would climb, or when he was expected back in Santa Fe. Not the process of writing, or his desire to be read. It was Omen, only Omen, that filled his heart and head.

Eland carefully wrapped up his project and put it in his shoulder bag, securing the last of his hand tools into their case, and putting them and his rolled up bedding back into the trunk. Eland almost always felt elements of joy, even when he was having the hardest times, but smiling wasn't something that came natural to him. A wild laugh when called for, yes, but seldom the simple smile that meant one was simply amused or pleased. Now he couldn't stop smiling. He smiled at the dirt on the blankets, and the shine on the convertible's window glass. Grinned at the white butterflies taking a spin in the Saliz Mountains on their way south for the Winter. He beamed at the Rio Negrito, on its way to joining the Rio Frisco, and then, another few miles downstream, passing before the house he hoped to find: the home of young Omen.

The car started up first crank, thanks to having sat warming up all morning in the sun. That's what black vehicles were best for, soaking up the heat, although one could really bake in the Summer in a black hardtop. Eland returned the crank to its place, and then hopped over the door rather than open it to get in. In some ways he didn't even like cars, but now he smiled at the way it carried him towards his destiny, and the song of its tires spinning on gravel. He smiled largest of all, when he came into view of the river, the geologic pillars at the opening to a canyon that gave him shivers just to see... and recognized at the base of one, a hundred and some yards away, the house he'd heard described.

Feeling suddenly self-conscious, he drove slowly past, then continued on up a fork to the east a little ways before parking. Calming himself, he took the shoulder bag from the seat next to him and stepped out of the car, then closed the door quieter than he needed to. Walking back down to the fork, he slipped his boots off and carried them as he walked through water that rolled just above his knees. Once on the other side of the river, he started getting more nervous again, wondering if she might be in denial of what transpired between them, or worse yet, that she might not even be there, with no way for Eland to find out where she'd gone. Eland slipped off the side and into a row of Willows, rather than proceeding straight to the house, then circled around to its far side and on downriver to where a single round rock caught his attention. It proved a perfect seat near the wind swept water, surrounded by a great rustling of trees like a supernatural Medicine Man's rattle. From his bag he pulled first a curved burl pipe and fixings, then a match to light it. To an observer upstream, it would also have appeared that he reached his hand down behind the rock before getting back up... but there was no one to see.

When Omen first spotted him, she was walking down the dry wash by her house. She was coming back from a search for Oregon Grape, not really a Grape at all, but a small ground-plant with sour Grape-looking berries and roots useful for surface infections as well as liver ailments. The last thing she expected

151

was to see a person, and the last person she expected to see was Eland, even though she'd been thinking about him even as he walked up. Wishing she had gotten his address. Wishing she hadn't allowed him to do what he did to her, and at the same time wishing that he would do it again. She would have loved to possibly get to know him better, but preferably on her terms, at her pace, in a place she would choose. Not unplanned and unannounced. Not in her sanctuary, her home. And not yet.

Most alarming was that his car was nowhere to be seen, and he approached from below instead of from the direction of the road. This immediately put her on guard, the hackles on the back of her neck raising like the fur on some disturbed creature.

"What are you doing here?"

She half shouted, as he continued walking purposefully and silently towards her. And then, quietly but adamantly, she said for him to "Hold it right there."

"I have something to show you," he blurted out, as he stopped in front of her.

She wondered what he was talking about. Her mind raced at the possibilities, at scenarios both sweet and deadly, of true love and base rape. His request seemed so farfetched, so inherently dangerous, but something inside her responded to him like never before.

"Okay," she said, "but just for a little ways."

They started walking together, back the way he'd come.

"Where's your car, and how did you get downriver here?"

"It's parked on the road," he said. "I wanted to surprise you. Surprise you, or avoid you, I didn't know. But I haven't been able to concentrate on anything or anybody but you."

Omen thought to herself that this could be either a wonderful thing, or an unhealthy obsession. How could he be so fixated after only a brief encounter, and without touching or talking? And how deep could this man's attraction really be, if he was only basing it on her looks, or from some feeling he got from her. Something didn't seem quite right.

Eland reached out and grabbed her hand, which she almost snatched back away, but then relented and gave. She could feel him wanting her, feel the tug that could be a mental need, or a physical craving as forceful as the crushing bonding of jungle beasts or ancient dinosaurs. Eland lifted her hand up even as they walked, and kissed the top of it. He felt the molecules of their skin and muscle melding, like the grafting of one tree to another that fuses the essence and qualities of two into one single, flourishing being.

"I think we've gone far enough," she began to protest.

It was understandable for a fellow to have sex on his mind, if that's what he wanted, but Omen had no stomach for a ruse. If he had just said "let's go out in the trees and get naked," that would have been one thing. And she might have even said yes. Her body certainly desired him, responding not just to the sight of him, but his voice, his combination of sensitivity and strength. It heated her up, a wildflower bending toward Eland, the sun. Her body was sure, and maybe something deeper was sure as well, but her bruised and tumbling emotions remained worried, her mind conflicted. She didn't even have to look at him to feel his energy extending from his side to hers. Even before they held hands, there already seemed to be a physical connection bridging the space between them, a completed circuit carrying a mysterious and in some ways intimidating charge. But Omen had already been with too many eager boys who professed love when all they really wanted was to press their bodies into hers. Or young men who had really loved her to the degree they were capable of, but who, due to whatever inner weakness or deadly self-doubt, wound up expressing that love in cruel acts or dishonest bluster.

The more she thought about it, the more confused she became. And confusion was likely to lead to anger, especially in a woman whose sense of wellbeing depended on her ability to maintain control of herself and her environs.

"That's it!" Omen said sharply. Eland looked shocked, but still determined.

"Just a few more yards, we're almost there," he said, continuing to pull on her hand even as she gradually began to hold back.

She could see not just admiration and desire in him now, but also the first hint of desperation.

"Come along," he prodded. "Really, Omen, I have something you might want to see."

Sure you do, she thought, pulling back in earnest now, no longer just an increasing weight for him to pull along, but an uncooperative participant. And a participant in just what she didn't know. She had her belt knife as always, but that might not always make the difference.

Eland stopped, then grabbed her by her shoulders. She couldn't tell if he wanted to shake her in frustration, or if he meant to fling her to the ground.

"Back off, Eland," Omen growled, slipping her arms between his and breaking his hold on her. The graft rejected.

He stared at her with what she took for a mad and very possibly hostile look, his eyes narrowed and blinking more rapidly than she would expect of a man in charge of his complex feelings and eruptive creature impulses. Then just when she thought he would snap, he turned silently and left.

Omen felt weak as soon as he'd gone, and sat down on the flat rock that had been their supposed destination. She knew she often got light-headed after an encounter or threat, and fortunately never during an emergency or altercation. Something seemed to get into her blood that kept her clear-headed in the decisive moments where it mattered, and that drove her to strike out like a Bear when challenged. It was in the twenty or so minutes after that she would feel faint or ill, as the chemicals burned themselves out, and the aroused bruin within her lay back down.

Omen leaned back on her hands, her head tilted back to taste the rejuvenating sparkles of sunlight wriggling down through the canopy of leaves. What happened, she wondered, and had she done right? But of course she couldn't just go along. He shouldn't have pulled on her that way, even if he hadn't lured her there to hurt her.

The exact moment that word lured popped into her mind, Omen heard the sound of hurried walking coming from the trail on which Eland had left. Expecting the worst, she leapt to her feet and clutched the handle on her skinning knife, just as a large Javelina stepped into view. A nervous smile formed on Omen's face, as the near-sighted boar stomped and snorted, announcing his courage while testing and evaluating any smells in the air.

"Off! Go on now," Omen shouted, at the quickly departing animal. It had spun about in a complete circle twice, and was now retreating in what all concerned agreed was the right direction.

Omen sat back down again, putting her hand almost exactly on top of what looked like a book sticking out from under the rock. Pulling it out, she was surprised to see that it was a hand crafted volume with wood slat covers, featuring a bas-relief carving of Bear inset with a red stone heart. Opening it with trembling hands, she was amazed by the thick paper impressed with local flowers and leaves, and the beautiful script that formed the dedication. If she had bothered to learn to read, she would have found out that it had been dedicated to the purpose of her plant work, a journal for her drawings of her precious botanical and medicinal finds.

For all her psychic powers, her ability to sometimes predict what was far away and coming, Omen could also miss the truth of what was close. All her life she had wanted to think of herself as having foolproof intuition, but several bad boyfriends had proven it wasn't always so. As well as she could usually read people, through their inflections, gestures and body language, she could also be the victim of her knowledge, expectations and assumptions.

It didn't make her any less of a Medicine Woman, as Eland would in time convince her. The evidence that she was a wise woman was that she would find her truth and power without laying any false claim, planting her identity in an incredible true self and not in the medium of unstable illusion or teetering wish. Honesty and wisdom, however, did not come without character-building mistakes... and occasional regret. Omen closed her leaking eyes and ran her fingertips over the contours of the Bear carved on the cover, tracing again and again the raised heart at its center.

the wood covered book

Chapter 19

THE WOOD-BOUND BOOK:
Reconsideration & Hope

Omen walked up the trail and back inside her house, still holding the gift Eland had given her tightly to her chest. Sitting down on the sofa, she smoothed the wrinkles out of her brown velvet skirt and laid the book on her lap. She admired its carved wooden cover, and simultaneously comforted and tortured herself by imagining the hand that held the knife and all the motions it would have made to create the finished product. The careful slicing and scraping, the intimate rubbing required to bring out its color, grain and sheen. Then she opened it up and felt the texture of the thick paper, made so that there were still actual leaves and plant fibers visible within it.

The pages were blank, as if waiting for her to write the stories that would make it a book. Maybe he intended it to be a diary of her struggles and joys, without realizing she didn't know how to write. It made her want to learn her letters, as nothing before had been able to do. And it inspired her, in the meantime, to take it into the field to do drawings of those plants she gathered and sometimes helped propagate.

Speaking of plants, she said to herself, I'd better take care of that Oregon Grape.

Omen moved over to the dinner table, took a chair, and sat the special book next to roots she'd just gathered up the wash. Some might have advised her to get over her grief by distracting herself with busyness, but she had no intention of letting go of the painful way she missed Eland. It was more than a feeling, it was a way of holding on to him still. No, she got busy with her work because it needed to be done, not to avoid or forget. The simple fact was that the fresher the material, the stronger and more effective her medicines would be. For the sake of those she treated, and to properly honor the plant, that meant processing it as quickly after harvesting as possible.

Omen spread out the roots on a cutting board and chopped them up into thin slices with her knife, putting the point of the blade down on the board first and then rocking it backwards.

But, she wondered, how had he had the time to make a book like that? Since only the previous afternoon? What did he do for a living, to be so good with his hands?

Next she made a mound of the pieces, and cut into them again until all were as small as she cared to get them.

Why, she continued wondering, couldn't he have simply parked in view instead of spooking me so? Where does he live? How will I ever find him again?

Omen used a sheet of newspaper as a funnel, pouring the finely chopped pieces of Oregon Grape into several antique, cobalt-blue bottles, filling each up almost to the rim. Then she filled the bottles with brandy until the roots were completely covered.

"And how," she asked herself, "could he have possibly figured out that the Bear was my totem?"

Lastly, Omen inserted a tapered cork into the mouth of each bottle, pressing each one down firmly with her thumb.

"And," she wondered, "even if someone had told him about me and Bears... just what could have possessed him to go to such effort?"

Possessed was indeed an accurate description, for love now owned Eland, possessed him wholly. He would do anything it told him. It was not free will now, so much as will freely given. If he never saw her again, he could not be described as a free agent, but as an agent of love. This would prove to satisfy Eland like nothing else possibly could, but also to torment him as a challenge to his independence.

It was not uncommon for men to fear losing their power when they submitted to passion, let alone to caring and commitment. That which they craved most, they could pull away hardest from: the bonding of hearts in the scent and thrust of mated flesh.

Here too, it was the Bear that came to symbolize that which was most attractive, and most feared. Love was the elusive Medicine Animal they sought, often getting no closer than its week-old tracks. Sex was the hairy beast they followed, panting, into the darkest cave... that would, if allowed, consume and subsume, leaving nothing but semen and bone.

While Omen's White Mountain relatives held the Bear to be sacred, as the purveyor of cures, they also expressed their fear of both bruin and Woman. She knew well the story of the Bear Wife, also called the Overwhelming Vagina. Bijosh Yeda'a was said to have appeared to a certain warrior in the form of a young woman with an insatiable sexual urge that no man could satisfy. The husband-to-be was warned by his grandmother that she was really a Bear, and had razor sharp teeth in her crotch. He was told about the many men who'd previously succumbed to the dangerous allure of the vulva. Each that had given in to it had been lost forever, surrendering to the experience, then paying for it with his masculinity, and hence losing his life. The forewarned husband, sometimes said to have been a Yavapai, fashioned himself a stone penis. He then used it to knock out the vaginal teeth, symbolically removing the power that women had over him. Otherwise he might not have survived the truth of her hunger.

The whole subject made Omen livid, flushed with anger not shame. She thought that surely one of the worst aspects of any civilizing culture, including her own, was the separating of women from their natures, and from their natural appetites. For many, the Grizzly Woman came to embody the temptation, the lure, of the basic drives of the animal world. Uncontrolled and uncontrollable. Unhampered by any taming influence. As such, she represented a lure they could worry might spread, an infectious temptation passed from woman to woman. Long had females been considered to have the persuasive power to bewilder. Most threatening of all, then, may have been her power to change every other woman she met into a Grizzly Bear Woman like herself.

Omen drew sweet little pictures of Oregon Grape plants, cut them out, and pasted one on each bottle as an identification label. She then moved them to a small silver tray, and carried them into her pantry for long-term storage. That was one of the big advantages of alcohol tinctures. A hot water infusion made from some plant might last only a couple days in the Summer before going bad. So long as it was protected away from high temperatures and direct sunlight, the healing ingredients in a tincture remained viable for many years or more... though that was hardly an issue for Omen or the other healers in the area. There were always more people in need than there were medicines to share. And enough wrong to give someone committed to healing plenty to do.

Omen walked back out of the darkened pantry, and through the arched passageway between the kitchen and the combination dining room and den. Instead of a back wall, the ceiling was bolted directly to an exposed cliff face, a rocky surface that hosted still-living plants, with several slabs jutting out far and flat enough to decorate with a kerosene lamp, and some of the green Ricolite sculptures of Apache mothers that Moon had made. Close to the center, and illuminated by the lamp, was her *hornacina*, an arched alcove, a niche, a recessed ambry for the housing and displaying of some of Omen's most meaningful things. Objects from nature gathered on her walks, including bubbly quartz, dried Devil's Claw seed husks, and an arrangement of dried purple flowers. A bright orange Crawdad shell with claws still attached. Bear teeth, and a grinning Ringtail skull. Next to them were human artifacts, some ancient, some merely memorable, like a Mogollon stone axe and piece of woven basket, draped with the beaded headband she'd worn at her Sunrise Ceremony. A funny clay figurine of a woman that a four-year-old Hannah had made for her, and a photograph of her sister and mother in a frame made of knobby Juniper bark. It was there that Omen put the book with Bear on the cover, standing it up so it could easily be seen.

Men had brought her flowers before. Bottles of wine of course. Perfume once, that she passed on to Moonheart, offering gifts they believed would be valued, in hopes of being given something that they desired in return. But never had she been given anything that a boy or man had made their selves, and never something that mirrored who she really was.

Omen had never been so sad as now, having sent the man Eland off. And never so happy, now knowing he existed. Her dream was real, her premonition alive.

Omen
N.M. Herbalist 1916

Chapter 20

CAJETA:
Sweetening To The Idea

"Damn my pride," Omen muttered, to the canyon as much as to herself.

She hurried back into her house with her mind made up. She would ride to Ramon's and then on into Frisco, all in the hope that there would be some sign of either passage or destination. Perhaps the grass lay over and flattened so as to indicate direction. A set of tracks she could follow. A faint scent that might miraculously lead her, nose first, to the dream that she had chased off. After all, someone may have talked to him. He could have paid a gas or grocery bill with an out of town check, which would surely have an address printed somewhere on it. Anything was better than doing nothing.

Omen walked over to where her clothes hung, while pulling at various plant parts that had gotten stuck in her hair. She couldn't go for a walk without part of the woodlands coming back with her, little green beings holding on for all they were worth with their tiny tendril hands, hoping to never let her go. Enamored leafen friends, who gave up the sun in order to follow her home. And she separated them gently, acknowledging each twig, blade or bit of frond with a loving look. Identifying those she could, and calling out loud their names. Kissing them as though on the head of a needy child, before setting them back outside.

Omen slipped on a pair of baggy riding pants, then ran a brush through her locks, a little quicker and more roughly than she would have normally liked. She still wasn't comfortable with tending to and loving herself, and now she was in a hurry. She picked out and held up a top, turning towards her old Moorish mirror to see if she matched. On a whim, she tossed the shirt back and slipped off her breeches. Instead, she slipped into a long purple sleeveless dress, featuring a bib placket decorated with embroidered plant life, grape vines and blooming Yarrow. Rather than her usual braids, she opted to leave her thick hair down, folding a long black scarf to use as a headband. Earrings made of iridescent breast feathers off a wild Turkey she'd shot and ate, overlaid with the polka-dotted feathers from a hawk-killed Northern Flicker. A leather belt, if for no other reason than as a means of carrying her knife. Elk hide moccasins that she only wore to town or for special ceremonies, not wanting to ruin them at home when it snowed, and preferring to remain barefoot nearly every day that it didn't.

Within minutes she was back out the door, which she never bothered to lock. The people she shared the valley with were, almost to a person, honest, and the rare hunters were the only outsiders that ever came through. Besides, if someone wanted entry bad enough, all they'd have to do would be to break a window, and she figured that replacing expensive glass could only add to her loss. She decided to take Poetry, the roan Filly, too young for heavy work, but just right for a spirited midday ride. It would be all Omen could do to hold her to a trot. Tossing her black mane, Poetry immediately broke for the river, then splashed through without even pausing to drink. She knew her first stop was always Ramon's, and that Ramon always had a carrot or apple waiting, ready to trade for a Horse's sweet kiss.

"Where have you been, *Auguria*? How come you never come see us?"

"You know I hate to leave home."

"There's a lot to see out here," he kidded her, meaning not the occasional chili picnic or children's rodeo so much as the big cities on the other side of the mountains.

"There's a lot I'll never fully see if I give my whole life to it," she answered with a smile, "within three miles of my house!"

Ramon could see there was no point in inviting her to visit on the porch, and that she wasn't even going to get down. The short man with the huge heart gave Poetry the expected treat, patted her fuzzy reddish forehead and stood back.

"I was wondering," she began, and Ramon waited for the usual and expected barrage of words.

Instead, she stopped mid-sentence, groping for the right way to say it. I was wondering, she thought, if you'd seen that boy. No, make that, if you've seen that man. That Anglo. That *vato*, from the day of the Pig roast.

"And just what is it that you are wondering, my friend?"

"If... if you had any *cajeta*. I can always use a little more sweetness in my life."

Cajeta was a sweet buttery caramel that Ramon's wife often made from Goat milk. The grandkids, and the great-grandkids all loved it. So did Omen.

"You bet I do!"

"I'll pick it up on my way back home, and give you whatever you need for it."

166

"Just a hello once in awhile is payment enough for me," he said, watching one of his favorite people as she rode off towards the village.

How, she wondered, was she going to find out anything about him, if she was too embarrassed to ask? But it was more than embarrassment about revealing her romantic interests or surging emotions. More difficult would be the exposure of a silly but substantial mistake. Besides, she saw her life as a series of magical moments, taking place among privileged participants, not as something she could adequately describe to those who weren't there.

Awful pretty dress she was wearin', Ramon thought, just for a trip to town.

Poetry had just barely gotten her to town when a car pulled out of the fuel station in front of them, heading back the way she'd came. Omen noticed right away that there was something unusual about it, shimmering like an August mirage as she squinted to see it better. It appeared to glide more than roll, taking a strangely long time to close the short distance between them. For a moment she couldn't see anything at all, as if it were suddenly midnight instead of early afternoon. The sun disappeared from view when she closed her eyes. When she opened them back up, in its place, she stared into the glowing features of that man Eland's face. His left elbow hung over the door, and she could see his mouth move as he passed her, silent as if in a dream. While she heard no voice come out, she knew by the shaping of his lips and the look in his eyes that what he had tried to say was Omen.

So he wasn't out of the area yet, after all. Her mind raced, unprepared for the sudden appearance of exactly that which she sought. How dare he stay around, anyway, when she had told him to leave? The men that scared her most were always the ones who wouldn't take no for an answer. And what could she say to him that wouldn't make her look like a cheap or desperate woman, racing in on a hunch, overdressing to make an impression? Or look foolish for misinterpreting his intentions, and then rushing out to try and get him back. Nervous and confused, she looked back forward, the horse's hooves growing muted, the noise of the vehicle's engine subsumed by an internal wind's roar.

Eland continued easing forward, not knowing what else he could do. "Omen," he said aloud again, even though she was already several yards back. And in the way that he spoke that single word, what was imparted was more like Dear Omen. Precious Omen. Amazing Omen. Enchanted, Essential Omen. Irreplaceable Omen. And in its quaking timbre, he communicated hope, need, devotion and destiny. She was already a couple of hundred feet away by the time she heard him, louder than the Ravens whose clucks and caws seemed to suddenly erupt overhead, louder than the sound of his automobile exhaust and the noisy pound and clatter of her prancing Horse's hooves. She heard her name, Omen, as though it were a shout from some mountaintop in her mind. And within it, she heard not only the expected You Are Mine, but also I Am Yours, for what was surely the very first time. She instantly reined hard to the left, and spun around after him.

Ramon was in his front yard watching for Omen, when he saw them both go back by. His little Ursa, no longer making a small mouth and sour face, the tails of her headband blowing in the breeze, as she alternately led, circled, and galloped next to the slowly rolling car. And that dust-covered convertible, driven by what looked to be the happiest man in the world. A man who would that very night be invited, and accept, an invitation to stay forever with her in her special canyon. A young woman at the start of a year and a half of incomparable bliss, before that sad Fall day when he'd leave.

Ramon waved excitedly, then shook his head from side to side. The little man put down the gift-wrapped jar of *cajeta*, with what could only be described as a bittersweet smile.

Chapter 21

THE GRAFTING TAKES:
Bliss & Blister:

Omen watched as Eland brought his motorcar to a stop and set the hand brake with an audible clack-clack-clacking.

"I wouldn't leave it so close to the river if I was you," she remarked with a toss of her hair. "It could end up in Arizona if the water comes up."

Rivers in the Southwest were like that, narrowing to a veritable trickle in the dry seasons, but always with the potential to grow quickly into a roaring flood whenever there was a downpour near their mountainous headwaters. Calm, and then roiled. Turgid and impenetrable one moment, clear and inviting the next. A high Rio Frisco would strip the banks of their soil one time, and deposit a rich layer of plant-friendly earth the next. Like the God of the Bible, the river "both giveth and taketh away".

"Hop on," Omen said, and Eland unhesitatingly swung up behind her. She found the feel of his arms around her intoxicating as she trotted through the river, and loved how they grasped her even tighter as she urged Poetry into a run.

This time, she found she couldn't stop watching: watching the way he leapt down and grasped her horse's bridle to steady it while she dismounted. Watching the bounce of that increasingly outrageous mustache, and watching the expressions in his eyes every moment that he wasn't looking back into hers. She watched the flexing of his arms as he lifted off her heavy saddle, and the motions of his hands as he brushed Poetry's sweaty back, simultaneously bringing pleasure to both her horse and herself. Watched as he seemed hesitant to open the door to her enchanted *casa*, even after she had motioned for him to go in.

Omen followed him in, a few steps behind him, and watched as he bent to slip his dust-laden boots off. As he slowly turned to take in the sight of her home's every furnishing and decoration. As he smiled at the medicine bottles with the childlike plant drawings on their labels, paused to ponder the telltale photos of Hannah and Moonheart, and slowly ran his writer's fingers through the soft nap of her fox fur hat. She watched for him to move last to the *hornacina* in her wall – *hueco o nicho en forma de arco* – as she was sure he would. Watched as he fingered the Devil's Claw seed pods and glistening Bear teeth, the pieces of common ruddy lava as well as the beadwork that signified her onetime ritual transition into womanhood. Watched as he let loose a tear at the sight of the wood bound book he had made for her, featured as a component of her most venerated *retablo*. She watched every second... until the one where he turned and caught her eye.

Omen quickly looked away, the twitching of her sweetly short fingers betraying her nervousness. It was as if she'd been caught spying on the skinny-dipping boys at Green Gate swim hole, or had just beheld some object or event truly sacred. It was indeed both, after all, a perceiving of spirit and flesh, *materia* and *mágico* as unified and inseparable. And it was her experience of this unity of hungers that caused her to avert her eyes, not just her self-recognized fear of what he might see there inside.

It was not so easy to resist, however, his palms cupping her cheeks, gentle again as they lifted her downturned face up to his. She saw in those probing orbs a deep liquid pooling of meaning and feeling, that she now sensed herself falling forward into. Temporarily absent was the appearance of control that she said kept her sane, absent the constant muscle tension and overt reticence that she imagined was all that held her back from plummeting into the abyss where her mother had already fallen. But fall Omen did: she fell from the ramparts of her fortress, and fell out of her protective habits, at least for that first night. Fell through space and time, fell blind and smiling downward through his skin and into his both highly strange and oddly familiar being. Fell, as they say, in love.

She'd thought she would postpone any advances on his part, resist her passions and his in the interest of slowly getting to know him. But now she saw herself lighting the candle by the bed, even before the closing day had turned completely dark, and lighting a bowl of dried White Fir leaves for the transportive aroma its smoke gave off, saw herself grasping his forearms, easing down onto the bed and then pulling him on top of her.

She who had been closed off for so long, now lay opened and receptive. But now the man she had fallen for made no moves to take things farther, remaining dressed as he held her in a nightlong caress.

Was he possibly setting his lust aside to demonstrate that he desired more than just her body? Or was there something the matter with her, she wondered, that he didn't push for more?

The answer was there, if she could just accept it... evidenced in how he lightly stroked her hair, taking in her scent, and in the way he held her so tight, through her customary nightmares, until the morning's first light.

It wouldn't be easy for them that first year together, but they would one day look back at it as blessings as much as struggle.

Omen was giddy with excitement whenever she didn't find some reason to be mad, and she found in his recognition of her the soil for her growth. And Eland was driven to confront all his contradictions by the woman he gave himself to. It hurt, even during those initial weeks when he felt she had projected the evils of her abusers on the man devoted to her healing. He too was elated whenever not feeling chewed on or aggrieved, sated even while sad. He felt ever more enthralled, even after discovering her problems with accepting affection, and her stubborn reluctance to admit a weakness or need. Even after facing the frustration and rage that would sometimes emerge, triggered by insecurities and fears arising from a childhood of seldom feeling adequate. The quick shifts from pleased to perturbed, and the way her dark moods could seem to blot out the sun.

Eland suffered a nagging sense of being called away to some urgent service, a need to define and succeed at some special mission, to fulfill a particular destined purpose. But there was certainly nothing about Omen that could drive him to leave this destined woman or newfound canyon home, not the heated arguments that alternated with the soothing waters of a fantasy love, not its heady blend of bliss and blister. After all, he expected there to be problems settling down with Omen... accepted them, even, as having come with the territory.

As every settler in the wild Gila new, Bears could be hard to live with.

VALENTINE GREETINGS

You're just my style—
O, please do
smile!
Here on my
bended knee,
I offer you,
A heart most true
And 'tis the heart
of me.

PART IV

Chapter 22

NO HERBAL REMEDY:
Insistence & Entreaty

It must be told that it wasn't Omen's wounds or even the dysfunction they engendered that worked to pull the two lovers apart, for what would be some of the darkest and most anguishing minutes, hours, days and weeks of their lives.

It was from Omen that Eland had learned to see his own birth and death in the plants' seasonal cycling, his own unending dreaming and awakening. He would forevermore recognize the need to root in place, in the living soil that is home, and to build natural, symbiotic relationships there. And he, likewise, seemed to recognize his angst and urge to be constantly moving, the aching stretch and tilt towards an unreachable sun. Even as he was handing her the sweetest imaginable Valentine, something from afar seemed to be vying for his attention.

Omen wasn't the least bit surprised, then, when shortly after breakfast Eland again brought up going to Mexico.

"It's something I can't shake," he told her. "A revolution is moving towards its fateful conclusion, not more than two days' ride away."

Omen never even turned around, nor did she disrupt for a moment her steady reaching down from the chair she stood on for her bundles of fresh herbs, lifting them up to hooks spaced in rows the length of the ceiling *vigas* to slow dry.

"We've got to talk about it," Eland insisted.

Silence. *A sweep of Skullcap, good for anxiety. A swirl of Yarrow, but only effective for immunity if you take it ahead of time. Cottonwood or Willow when the headache is too great.*

"History is in the making," he added, in that timbre she'd grown to love. "The frontier is coming to a close. Everything has been spinning madly for a while, and right now the spindle it whirls around is the struggle down south. In another few months it could be Europe, and a chance lost."

A gesturing of Pennyroyal, to bring on menses. A flourish of Poleo, the only Mint native to North America, and soothing to the belly.

For Omen, a more significant loss would be a single night spent without Eland, without his hungering hands and the sure warmth of his skin. Let alone if he were to be hurt or detained, she thought, or possibly even killed.

"This is a time like no other," he calmly insisted, rising from his chair. He loved to see her like this, first bending like the graces bestowing their blessings, and then stretching tippy-toe on a pedestal of love. He liked to be there whenever there were plants to be hung, standing at the feet of his miracle, nose high to the curves of her ruby red skirt.

A swoosh of Goldenrod, the sure remedy for allergies. A spray of Oregano de la Sierra, known to work wonders when one had congestion from a cold. Nettle tinctures for rheumatism, ointments for flaking skin.

177

There were herbs said to aid a failing memory, but only dreaded Opium to help one forget. And all Eland could see was that there was no cure for an entire age quickly coming to its dramatic end. Craftsmanship was dying at the hands of soulless corporate industrialism, as he'd both remarked about and written on. Art was being shredded by the forces of the market and the low standards of contemporary culture, deconstructed into pandered commercial products and the absurdity of objectionist Dada. Forests were falling, and then insanely, the resource shipped out of state. He saw the agrarian way of life under threat like never before. Small communities appeared to have little chance under the law, especially as compared to the centers of power back East. Indeed, the contrasts had never been greater, with the majority of the wealth lining the vaults of a tiny and inordinately influential minority. The skies of the northern hemisphere were host to the towering smokestacks of flourishing factories and the buzz of bi-winged aircraft, while poverty threatened the very lives of those consigned by fate to the colonized south. What better symbol could there be, he thought, for the dashing of compassion and sentiment against the unyielding rock shore of this new way... than the Harper's Journal engraving of the valiant but asinine charge of plume-helmeted Polish cavalry, riding their horses into an impenetrable embrasure of hot flying lead spat out by the German machine guns.

Worse even than the global devastation or the Great War, was the rapid, painful, and ignoble transformation engulfing – like an unchecked forest fire – his precious, treasured West. Surely Omen knew they stood at the precipice, the end of the frontier, a frontier that had survived in New Mexico long past the gentrification of the coasts and the taming of the Midwest. Eland's home state had been both the holdout, refusing to give in... and the last kid picked for the team. Generations of resistant natives, determined Hispanics and recalcitrant Anglos had worked to hold onto the pace, the sensibility, the sentience and magic of New Mexico, and it helped that the rest of the country assumed it contained nothing that they'd wanted. For this reason, when Eland described his homeland in articles he wrote for national publications, he made it a point to include not only the majesty and mystery, but also the deprivations and hostilities – relentless sun and deadly scorpions.

Now it seemed for naught. The best one could do, Eland decided, was to position oneself in the flux and thicket of things, in the stir of the cauldron, in the crucible, at the exact point where the hammer struck the iron. If it were to be the end of anything, he wanted to be an honest witness to it. And more than that, he felt compelled to record in poem or prose the full, wondrous, heinous and glorious truth of the West's unfolding story.

"This is what great literature is made of," he told her. "It's not about the ink, or even about the author. It's not about me, can't you see?"

Omen ignored his proffered arm and got down herself, without comment. From where he stood she appeared a majestic but grievous goddess, the sacred She who gives, and hence She who could take away. The cream colored wall was the canvas upon which she seemed painted, the outline of her thick hair and rounded shoulders, the aggravation in her narrowed eyes that made her more stunning but no less attractive, an image of breathing, needing, speaking art.

"I don't want you to go," were all the words he heard. If there was more, it was expressed in a certain tilt of the head, pronounced in the trembling of her lower lip, communicated as an upswelling from the heart of Omen directly into the hearing heart of her lover. The uncomprehending pleas of ancient queens and courtesans, cast upon an already armored warrior on his way to war. The romance of the venerated Twain's Tom and Betsy, hidden away from what pestered them in the bosom of a mammoth cave. And the draw of the hearth, the ever beckoning hearth-beat of home.

Home for them both was more than a shelter from the weather in a place of convenience, more than shelves for hand-carved Kachina dolls and a Chief National wood stove to cook their meals. More even than their tools and clothes, more than the memorabilia and books that filled it. It was the soil that sprouted with the foods and medicines they needed, the forest that suspended them, the river that impelled their desire and purpose. It was cacti and flower, the burnt orange rocks spewed from dispassionate volcanoes, the Mountain Lion, speckled Gila Woodpecker, Rock Squirrel, Badger, and Black Bear. The camaraderie of like-minded recluses and raconteurs, subsistence hunters and plant gatherers. Its complexion was adobe, its mood shifting according to whim and event, its messages to the seeker delivered in an accent as old as the mountains themselves.

Truly, home was where they could best feel the soul and spirit of the world, and where it seemed to feel them in turn. It was the place of rooting for sure, and of unbreakable commitments, even for Eland. And for Omen, it was the place where her body connected to the greater body of Earth. She knew the wisdom of making yourself at home wherever you are, but for her, now, no other place would do. The *Cañon del Frisco* had proved to be, like Omen, Eland's salvation… and reclamation. But it was a food he believed he could carry with him on his travels, a binding cord, an umbilical, a lifeline he trusted would not be broken. While for Omen, to leave felt like death.

Eland leaned forward, his hands gripping her sides, and placed on unyielding lips the most gentle kiss. He didn't want anything to change, any more than Omen could bear the dying back of the flowers and the shedding of golden Cottonwood leaves every intensely gorgeous Fall.

"I don't have to go without you," he pleaded. "You can go with me."

He said this in spite of his fierce instinct to protect her, to keep her from those places and occurrences that could hurt her heart as well as anything that might sacrifice her physical safety. As he thought he would die for the sacred canyons of the Saliz, he would gladly die for her. Eland lowered one arm, sliding the back of his hand into the crease where her thigh and torso met, pleasuring in the way it grasped and held his fingers. Omen couldn't help remembering when she thought she didn't like it, when it had made her think she was too fat. Now it touched her deeper than the penetration of sex, tickled her in ways that forced the corners of her mouth into a smile. And her smile was to Eland as a lover, returned after years of being lost. Yes, it was as water to one dying of thirst, but also something that meant far more than the mere extension of his mortal existence.

"I can't," she answered, her hand no longer obedient at her side, first moving to describe long unspoken arguments and prayers, followed by a frantic waving in the air, then beating ever so softly on his strong willing chest. The wind picked up at that moment, rattling the thin glass panes. Eland imagined he could feel the Woodbine just outside, rushing, straining, in what could be its last day of growth. And the restless vine coiled like a spring inside him.

"I can't," he heard her repeat, with a crack in her voice, his eyes closed as she tightly hugged him before turning back to her plants.

Sage, to clear and cleanse. Crane's Bill and fragrant pink Mimosa, just the thing for a broken heart.

Chapter 23

AUTUMNAL:
A Last Impassioned Night Together

Fall is more than what passes,
more than the beauty of fracture and crumble,
the flaming colors of decomposition's heat.
More than a passing nod
to the season of returns,
the days of the harvest.

Fall is the first cold winds knocking the limbs from the trees,
forcing us to remember that we too
are but a force of nature in transition—
> > *deciduous, quaking,*
ever believing
in a reawakening.
> > > -Eland Howell, <u>Autumnal</u>

The day Eland and Omen parted ways started out nothing at all like it ended. If at its close the plants around their house appeared wilted from the icy touch of Fall, at its onset it seemed a world in bloom. Sprays of Purple Sticky Aster, the yellow New Mexico Groundsel and golden Snakebrush. The orange Scarlet Globemallow with their green centers, called Sore Eye Poppy by the locals. The clusters of tiny white blossoms on the winged Buckwheat and Yarrow, and the pink Mock Pennyroyal. And the ghostly trumpet-shaped Datura, its seeds long eaten by primitive shamans and healers seeking connection with the divine, some claiming it was the ingredient witches spread on their brooms to make them fly. He awoke, as he so often did, to the sounds of wild turkeys on the river and the buzz of hovering hummingbirds, the view from their bedroom window trimmed with tattered ivory lace. Eland turned to behold what he considered the most beautiful flower of all, his Omen's shining face.

Eland remained lying on his side for a considerable time, watching the heart and center of his world as she slowly breathed in and out, in and out. When at last she stirred and opened her eyes, he in turn closed his, securing indelibly the vision of her loving him and the dimples as she smiled. Then with his lids tightly shut, he traced her every feature with his fingertips, exhibiting both the curiosity and patience of the blind. First, across the strong brow that somehow reminded him of a Bear, moving from the bridge of her nose outwards along the ridge above each eye. Then down behind her ears, taking in their shape and measure, following the inner channels like a holy labyrinth or Merlin's maze. Lingering for a moment on the soft bottom lobes. He next followed the wide and pronounced cheekbones down to the jaw line, resolving in circle around the chin he loved so much. Lastly, Eland dragged two fingers down the sides of her nose, before setting them down lightly on her small mouth and those damp, full lips.

When she pulled him on top of her it was sudden and forceful, the mark of a creature that knows what it wants. Eland then entered her as meticulously as she had been urgent and quick, relishing the ever so slow sheathing of his desire. The first lift of his hips was barely perceptible, seemingly centuries worth of withdrawing from something within which an important part of him would forever be left behind. Gradually the tempo progressed, like the music of the mariachis of Socorro, like Mountain Lions picking up speed before the pounce, or the accelerated pounding of a skyward Eagle's wings. He was a man surrendered, not to the power or seductions of another, but to the pull and sway of the wordless now. As in Omen's sacred sweat lodge, and as on the mountain tops where it was impossible to think or write, in her embrace he found himself delivered into an eternal present... freed of abstraction and witty commentary, filled with the deepest awareness of and appreciation for the five senses. For the smells of their union, ancient seas and floral pollen. The graze and scratch, thrust and grasp of touch. No suggestive sound was shameful or ignored, not a single growl or moan missed. Fully conscious of the way the dawn light brought out the red highlights in her black hair, accentuating her wide, heaving hips.

Not even his graphic and overactive imagination ever stood a chance against that degree of intensity and presence, no pictures could be seen but the art housed in the soft curve of her upper arm, the exposition of strong, taut legs in the air. Only when she at last clutched him closer, her entire body gasping and contracting, did he succumb to the explosive conclusion of that sacred animal dance. Eland dissolved not into nothing but into the everything, while she shuddered beneath him, repeatedly speaking his name.

Alder Roots

Chapter 24

ALDER MEDICINE:
Connected By A Rio

Omen stirred just as the sun rose over the canyon walls, and went to swing her leg over Eland only to find his place in her bed emptied and barren. Bolting upright, it took some seconds for her to remember he'd said he was leaving before the light, and some minutes more before the tears slowed down enough for her to notice the gift he left on a nearby table. Omen walked over and picked the heavy brass object up, a mortar and pestle tarnished with the patina of age, etched with Greek Cyrillic and dressed up in a green silk ribbon. Inside she discovered a small card, but a large one would not have served any better, for all it read was "All-ways Yours"... with the first letter of each word constructed with actual stalks, leaves and branches pressed and glued. Omen stood holding both mortar and letter, naked and barefoot on the cold flagstone floor, as Eland rode a buckboard wagon directly into a shivering dawn wind already some twenty or so miles to the south.

Omen had always had special connection to the river Alders, with their twisting exposed roots gripping the shore and rock, and dipping directly into the flowing waters... and it was to them she now ran. She ran open mouthed and silent across the ruddy ground in front of their cabin, now bathed in the red glow of a rising sun. She ran with her head back and her hair trailing behind her, darting around any clumps of brush in her way, instinctively leaping over the Scarlet Hedgehog Cactus nested low and inconspicuous. She ran not to escape her feelings or fears, not to escape anything at all, but rather to recover some thread of what had been lost.

Whereas most Alder trunks were a blotched brownish-red in color, Omen's were dressed in an almost metallic, silvery bark glinting like foil in the early light. While so fearlessly and lovingly grounded, they seemed almost celestial as well, a bridge connecting stone and star, Earth and sky. What all temples aspire to communicate, these stood and spoke for oneness. The inseparability of body and spirit. The unity of the created, and all that creates. And they spoke of sustenance and salvation, for in the arid Southwest to find Alders was to have discovered a life giving spring, stream or river. A rare and vital fluid in a land where it is easy to die of thirst, and also a moving body of spirit that Omen found every bit as essential – a living metaphor for the endless cycles of giving, passing away, and being replenished. Always flowing, it was never the same water that one returned to, nor was one ever exactly the same person each time they came back to its healing waters. River as healer, with every drop an anointing. River as resource, and recourse. It was an opportunity for a daily baptism into something truly immense... and, Omen felt, immensely holy. And most of all, for someone suffering great loss, the river seemed something unending.

The sun had just begun to reach the canyon bottom as Omen hurtled across the last open stretch, crashing through the tangle of slender Willow stalks to get to the *rio's* bank, collapsing at the Alders' rooted feet.

Alders too, were medicine for the body. Omen had learned from the Doña that the bark helps with fungal infections and could also be used for sore throats and scraped skin. She had watched her brew up concoctions with it for diarrhea, or internal bleeding. She'd seen it poulticed for eczema, rashes and sores with miraculous effect. For perhaps thousands of years, Alder stem-bark tea had been used to ease headaches and deaden pain. But for Omen, in this moment, it could offer only communion, not relief.

Omen had grown to love how Eland read passages out loud to her, often choosing from among the several botany and mythology books he brought her. Even those facts she already knew by heart carried new resonance when delivered from his loving lips. Paragraphs about the Greek hero Heracles, or Hercules, who was cremated on an Alder-wood pyre, and whose remains were floated away down a sacred river in a boat made of Alder. Sentences devoted to some blonde-haired natives from Scandinavia called the Sami, who joined the ancient Celts and Native Americans in associating this tree with fire. She especially liked to hear that their word for Alder was the same as for both Bear blood, and a woman's menstrual flow. That the Sami wives chewed the bark, and then used their saliva to paint sacred designs in red on the leather they sewed for their loves. That they believed the first woman had been carved out of a sacred Alder trunk. And how she had loved his pronunciation of *Speculum Mundi, 1635*, and the tone and pace he used when reading from it – about how one who has lost their true love needed to wear a garland of Willow and Alder. There was a stirring of wind followed by the peals of far off thunder, as a blessing of yellowing leaves drifted down onto her bowed head and shoulders.

Only then did she make a sound, not so such a normal maiden's weeping as a high-pitched, child-like howl. Followed in time by a low, guttural animal moan, her lips nearly pressed to the ground. She cried for hours into what felt like a receptive hollow in the earth, as when she had tasted Eland's breath, and breathed out into his mouth. And the wind seemed to breathe with her, and with each gentle exhale even more leaves were dislodged and settled on and about her, a blanket of caring from the Great Mother, a welcoming as sweet as the brief sweep of rain.

Omen rose up onto her elbows in a shedding of tears and leaves, walked on her knees the last couple of steps to the river and rolled into the lower than usual waters. It was, she believed, very nearly the time when Eland would be crossing to the east side of this same river, where it spilled out of the canyon on its journey to Arizona. The river was always a conduit, connecting mountain and desert, desert and ocean, past and future. But at that moment it was more like a lifeline connecting her to the things that mattered most. She stood there in the shifting sands and cold water for close to an hour, shivering, imagining that she would know the exact moment when Eland rode across in his buggy, and sure he'd stop to drink, splash his face, and think about home and her. Imagining that when his hands dipped into the water she would feel it the way a spider senses when something touches any part of its web... and that when she tugged at her end of the tether, it was not the current but Eland she felt tugging back.

Chapter 25

THE FAR END OF THE TETHER:
Asunder For The Great Story

"Just think about the adventure ahead," he kept telling himself. "Keep your eyes on the work, the goal, the mission. You'll be home again soon."

A large part of Eland's motivation had always been to write the great story, as full of character and distinction, and the twists of human nature as those bigger than life personalities and landscapes that he worked so hard to describe. It could be a collection of sensuous or sinewy essays, incontrovertibly exposing the bowels of previously untouchable beasts. Or a novel, with sharp-edged reality posing as fiction, accumulating readers by affording them a reasonable opportunity to disassociate or deny. It could even be a collection of romantic short stories, if created with the same ultimate degree of sensibility and intent that went into the carving of the mountains, and the iridescent scales of the splashing Gila Trout... seducing the separative mind with the alluring unitive body, heightening awareness through the titillation of the senses, cracking open the heart and then riding its spilling crimson rivers to the pain and bliss of the entire world.

He would have preferred the agency of poetry – language pared down to its most essential, and said in the most beautiful and powerful of ways. Poetry shattered pretense and scattered irrelevancy and superficiality to the wind. Poetry was a sculptor's knife carving away everything from the Ironwood block but the inner essence and its most graceful, evocative form. The knife that then carved away itself, and then the sculptor, until there was no observer and observed left, no maker and made. Only art. And only now.

Eland travelled faster than a caring person should push a horse pulling a four-wheeled buggy, having wisely chosen to leave his automobile in the states and with Omen. He'd kept up the pace for the nearly three hour ride to where the hard dirt road cut back across his *Rio Frisco*, his Sweet Medicine River, for the last time of the trip. Positioning the Horse and buggy down-current where the buckskin gelding could drink, he walked upriver a ways in the reddening glow of the day, then knelt down next to the melodious flow, thrusting both his arms in to the elbows. These were currents that had earlier passed by his home, he knew, their little house and the wondrous cliffs that rose behind it. Before getting to this point, they had first tickled the gravel where he and Omen played and swam. Titillated the quavering Watercress she stooped to pick. Massaged the throne of Alder roots she leaned against whenever lying in the river. And just as Omen was visualizing Eland, he was imagining her, feeling the persistent push of the current as his dear Omen trying to get his attention. He lifted his dripping hands to his face, sensing himself physically as well as spiritually or magically connected to his love by their beloved *rio*, before determinedly climbing back onto the buckboard for the next leg of his trip.

Marigolds

Chapter 26

GARLANDS OF MARIGOLDS:
In Route To A Revolution

On into the night Eland rode, trying to ignore the beast that gnawed at his guts, and the spot on his shoulder where every night her head had lain. To keep his composure, he focused on what was close at hand. The rhythm of hooves on baked ground. The steady vibration felt through the thinly padded seat. The occasional jarring bump. The brush and rock that flew past underneath. And the taste of road dust in his throat. He found no solace in distant sights, no pleasure in the purple Rhyolite spires that marked the entrance to Mogollon and its hard rock gold mines, and no comfort in the receding peaks he left behind. Distant was the impact he hoped to make. Distant, the place he loved the most. Distant, the woman he was given to, as distant as she'd felt when he had tried to explain. He was the funereal Datura blossom closing at the break of day, the Morning Glories giving it up at the onset of night, the overextended vine at the end of its life.

How appropriate, he thought, to be embarking on the eve of the Spanish *La Dia de la Muerte*, the final day of October and beginning of the new year. Halloween it was called in the states now, an innocuous and nearly meaningless day followed by a night of fearless partying and feigned fright. But Eland realized that it hadn't always been so. Once known by his pre-Christian, Pagan ancestors as Samhain, it was the time when the crack between the worlds, between death and life, opened largest, with spirits of every type passing through to freely roam the Earth. The hundreds of individual fires in the community would be extinguished, all except for a single great bonfire, from which brands would be taken to rekindle every hearth anew. There would be mead drunk shouts heard over the din of the public feasting – "From the one, many!" Necks would be draped with strings of brilliant orange Marigold blossoms, so that even blind among the departed can follow their scent to this reunion. Candles would be lit and placed in windows, not to frighten away the spirits but to welcome them... and to help them find their way home.

On Eland's calendar, too, it was the end of a year. The conclusion of what had been the most incredible four seasons of his entire life. And the cold and brittle beginnings of yet another cycle, deepened by the death the first freeze wrought. Omen wouldn't need to light a beeswax taper to call him back once he completed his self made assignment, for she herself was the burning flame that beckoned, visible across any number of miles, shining clear through the back of his head even as he rode away. Wherever she stood was the window through which he one day would – *must* – reenter.

All that kept him from turning around and going back, each second, was the goal of the story, the overpowering urge not just to witness, record and comment on world changing events, but to experience the reality, tumult and drama first hand. Tumult, provided in this case by the flamboyant visionary peasant leader known as Pancho Villa. Villa the bandit and murderer. Villa the dedicated revolutionary and hope of his people. There was really no one quite like him, Eland realized, none better to embody both the best and the worst of what humanity could be. Known to personally shoot the entire families of soldiers who betrayed him, he also set up schools and credible health care for the first time ever in the territories he conquered. Pancho, who held a gun to a priest's head to make him confess to getting a village girl pregnant, and to promise to support her. Some had said he turned to banditry after killing a *ranchero rico* who had dishonored his sister, but likely his lust for adventure, notoriety and personal liberty was motivation and pretext enough. Villa embodied the contest or pairing of good and evil, the unresolvable twists that constitute real life and the best of literature.

The Mexican Revolution was a lot like the Greek tragedies, Eland had tried to explain to Omen, a moment in history that brought out all the contradictions of human kind and social institutions and thus an opportunity to open hearts and eyes if not minds. It was this he wanted to capture -- the intrigue and the battles of the soul as much as any combat on the field. Right there below the border with Mexico was a stage upon which a universal drama would be enacted, and it was here that a writer could help America understand the choices that a generation always has to make – the complexity of being and doing right, the costs of ignorant allegiance and irreparable mistakes. The war continued in part with the support and encouragement of the United States, supporting first one faction and then another, while always keeping the financial interests of U.S. investors like the colonizing oil tycoon Edward Doheny in mind. Even that gutsy leftist newspaper fellow, John Reed, was "purely deluded" in his naive glorifications, Eland had decided. There were no unblemished heroes, he'd written in one particularly pithy piece, and nothing was ever as simple as black and white. There were no strictly good and bad sides to line up behind, and the contest between compassion and evil played out in the corridors of conscience in each and every person.

Already, twice as many people had died in the Mexican revolution as had fallen in the War Between The States, uncivil as that conflict of forty years earlier had been. But for Eland, the ongoing conflagration was less a set of particulars to report on, than the flames that would illuminate truths as ancient as Earth's crust and as universal as hope… the most important insights and lessons ever told.

He was fine with leaving anything less comprehensive, less instigative, to the journalists who were already swarming like flies on the festering wounds of a nation. Journalism wasn't really writing, Eland figured, any more than were the printed instructions that came with an Edison phonograph. It was, he felt, the flux and wonder of the English language stripped of all its fine native nuance, its color and rhythm, reduced to an artless exposition of absurd or self-serving opinion. Reporting was a form of advertising in which a paper's financial backers and influential advertisers determined what was and wasn't news, and how it should be covered. What they were selling was not newsprint, he'd told Omen, as much as a program that everyone was expected to sign up to. Some day the same cabal would own all the papers in the world, he worried, with maybe just enough variation in opinion to make it look like there was still a free exchange of ideas. As if the citizens still had a voice, and a choice. Of course they really would, at the deepest levels anyway, always have a say. This would remain true no matter how biased the newspaper coverage, how repressive the government or stacked the election ballot… so long as they could holler, and so long as what they hollered was "no." Or even "hell no!"

"Hell no, we won't settle for a world of control and manipulation, injustice and hypocrisy," Eland muttered under his breath. The wagon creaked and bumped on the worsening road, the further south he went.

"Hell no," he said a little louder, thinking about the destruction of the Indian tribes, the cutting of all the trees above his childhood home in Santa Fe, the way children are often treated by pushy parents, the treatment of a hungering and hard working underclass, the racism and demagoguery. "Hell no," to the way doctors and agencies were increasingly poisoning their patients with isolated chemicals while disenfranchising, and even demonizing, village herbalists like... Omen.

Like Omen.

Like Omen, his love.

"Omen," he said out loud, almost pleading.

Chapter 27

A LANGUAGE OF PLACE & NEED

"Omen," she thought she heard, though no one was around. Just two syllables, together making the sounds she most often answered to.

She'd actually answered to a number of names over the years, each reflecting her complex character and early interests, her mixed blood, the dreams that foretold her birth, and the Medicine Bear that was said to live inside of her. She's also earned the right to be called by the Apache name Shik'isn Shash, sister and ally to the spear-toothed denizens that so often haunted the dreams of her childhood friends, those unbowed beasts known to the Anglo cattlemen as the "Grissly", or Grizzly. These same recent immigrants had given her the nickname "Trouble" when she responded to neither their clumsy seductions nor their plaited quirts, while those who'd tasted and then lost her love were likely to call her something worse. In keeping with the wine-red Latin *sangre* that steamed and thundered in her veins, she was *Flora Negra*, the improbable ebony bloom that many considered a harbinger of future events. As a teen it seemed she'd always make an appearance right before something really big happened, and when she was still a little cub, her mother Moonheart would read the drifting clouds in her eyes like the Tea leaves in some fortune teller's cups. Late at night, after a day of holding it so well that hardly no one even knew she was drinking, after an evening of terrorizing all the carousing males in town, back home and unable to escape her visions and regrets, Moon might call out for her Baby. But to everyone else, she remained Omen. As in, "Ain't that Omen somethin'." And "Omen will know what kind of plant to put on that wound."

Of course, anyone who'd ever read a bible by candlelight, or had one quoted to them at great length, was well aware of what the word meant. But when most folks say a name casual-like enough times, it can start to shed its meaning. No one thinks of grinding flour anymore when they meet someone named Miller. And long before she was old enough to comprehend the buzz going around, there was nothing left of Omen but the sound. It was possible to repeat even wonderful words like river, or love, or tree, she realized... and in the process forget the very heart and flesh of them, forget how very magical such things can be. To the degree she distrusted language, it wasn't simply out of distaste for the common shallow tone, nor the way it distracted from deep thought. The problem, to hear her tell it, was that the noise interfered with her noticing the tender touch of the wind, the song of the plaintive Poor-Wills and the sound of a Mountain Lion and her cubs padding through the Willows, and in this way language could be an impediment to what she considered true communication.

It didn't help that no matter how clearly she spoke her heart and mind, no matter how artfully her rapid hand movements traced and danced her concepts in the air, it seemed that no one really understood her, not the visiting Eastern businessman or local Goat herder, the Spanish-speaking cousin from Socorro nor her great-aunt on the *rez*. All too often they would stand there staring, disoriented, disapproving, or handicapped by disbelief. It was as if her stories, as lyric and powerful as if composed for the ears of Spirit itself, were delivered in an unintelligible language from a far away land. But hers was the language of place, not of aliens, tourists, or guests. The language of now, too filled with color and information, too dependent on context and present tense to survive being written on paper. Like a butterfly, she once said, pin the stories to paper and they'll fade and die. Her story -- the story that described her being, that expressed her protests, entreaties and gifts, that painted her soul with plant dyes and canyon tones -- was alive. And she didn't see how, like an azure butterfly in flight, they could fail to see the truth of her standing before their very eyes.

For as long as she could recollect, she had felt lonelier in crowds than walking by herself across the mesa, and more comforted by the company of wild plants and instructed by the example of wise and honest critters. What she hungered for from her own kind was no more complicated, and no more likely, than true recognition.

And the only one who had ever seen her fully, her needs as well as strengths... the only man who had ever walked hand in hand with her through both the light and dark places in her mind, was gone.

As gone as state's rights. As her mother, inaccessible behind an alcoholic cloud. As the native Merriam's Elk, all shot out. As the Bison. The free ranging Apache. Codes of honor. The unfenced range.

Omen clutched the Bear claw around her neck, the one Eland had given her, and closed her eyes.

Columbus, NM - 1916

PART V

Chapter 28

WORLDS APART:
The Town Of Columbus, Newspapers,
& Being Consoled By A Mission

It was near dusk again by the time Eland was close enough to see the lights of his next stop, Columbus. They had only recently installed the first gasoline powered electric generator in the region, and the half a dozen electric lights could be seen across many more miles of desert than the conventional kerosene lanterns which used to dangle from some of the home and store fronts. He covered those last miles in time to get a meal and room at Sam Ravel's Commercial Hotel on the main drag, a three block long stretch of businesses in the center of the dusty town.

Carrying his gear into his room, Eland patted the small wool bag that hung across his blowzy muslin pullover. It had been gifted to him by an old Hopi woman the Summer he spent on Third Mesa, writing poetry and doing his best to comprehend her spiritual ways. And it held some of the things he valued most, the means for not only personal expression but a meaningful livelihood independent of his father's always conditional help. Every man worth his salt had to have a trade, it was said, and with each trade came an emblematic set of tools. The carpenter, his plane and saw. The farrier's rasp, horseshoes and flat shanked nails. The mechanic's box of wrenches. The writer's tools, in comparison, were few, and fit neatly in a pouch. A set of Cherry wood pens with extra nibs. A bottle of India ink. And a handsome notebook full of paper.

Paper was nothing to take for granted, he felt, not even in Santa Fe where one could purchase such items at any store, and especially not out "in the sticks" where a careless accident or lost ream could mean scratching one's tales on chunks of old barn wood. And he knew what it took to create it. He never laid pen to paper without acknowledging the trees that grew and died and gave their only flesh so that his words might live. And he'd watched for hours while the sisters of Cañoncito Parish took turns pounding pulp, in order to hand-make the pages on which a visionary of the church could write down his holy revelations. Eland had his own so-called revelings to give voice to, as well as the powerful poetry of his longing for Omen. And he needed this means for exploring his contradictory needs, for showing the world hat he was not nearly as conflicted and confounded, self-possessed and self-sabotaged as he often felt. He needed to show to himself that he had a worthy gift and purpose, and to that, he would show the world.

But that wasn't all that Eland meant to inscribe and share, he was also committed to recording in this notebook the details of unfolding events, the texture of life itself and the particulars of the landscape he found himself traveling through. On one page he'd noted that most of the area around Columbus was "tortilla flat," with only a few seductive hillocks to break the monotony. To the south of town stood a five strand barbwire fence, stretched tight across miles of white sand speckled with Cholla, Prickly Pear, Snakeweed, and Rabbit Brush. Sticker-laden Coyotes chased bug-eyed Jackrabbits back and forth beneath the wire, under the watchful eyes of circling raptors. Temporal and permeable, it nonetheless clearly signaled where one government's dominion ended, and another's began.

The town had been founded as an official crossing and stop on the El Paso & Southwestern rail line. It was named after Christopher Columbus, the deluded Italian fortune hunter who in 1492 first laid eyes on the American continent, imagining that he was in India. It was obviously the hope of the town's promoters and developers that an increasing number of "explorers and discoverers" would drop both their anchors and their dollars in this driest of ports.

"Town property in Columbus is one of the best possible investments," asserted a McClughlan & Dexter Realty ad. "See Columbus before going elsewhere!"

"Elsewhere," in the first two decades of the 20th Century, was worlds apart. While the people of New Mexico continued with their largely frontier lives, surrounded by what appeared to be vast and incorruptible space, society at large was remaking itself faster than ever before. Cultural traditions and technological innovations that once took hundreds of years were now being transformed in a single generation. This was the year that kids in New York or Boston who were nostalgic for the romantic West, got to play for the first time with a new toy called Lincoln Logs. The Santa Fe New Mexican covered not only the local boring issues such as weddings, continuing state government corruption or the price of beef... but they'd also managed to amaze Eland with stories of something called a New Theory of Relativity posited by a dropout named Albert Einstein, a story about Germany using helium-filled Zeppelins to firebomb French cities, and the controversial rise of racy jazz music in old New Orleans. Folks who still passed more Horses and wagons on the roads than they

208

did automobiles were likely amazed to read about a race driver named Gil Anderson setting a new land speed record, going an amazing 102.6 miles per hour in a suped-up Stutz. Not so many months before they'd run a column on Margaret Sanger, arrested for handing out pamphlets on birth control somewhere back East, and he smiled remembering how it had sent Omen into a full ten minute rant. Women needing to take responsibility, it said, for how many lives they bring into this crazy world. Women deciding what kind and quality of life they wanted for themselves.

Over the past two years, of course, the bulk of the front page had been taken up by reports from the front lines of the war in Europe. Editorials decried the use of American ships to transport war materials, in the belief that that could lead to deeper involvement or even the deploying of U.S. troops. For all the savagery of Germany's attacks, it appeared to many here as an internecine struggle between the kinds of haughty, colonial, old-world regimes this country had sought and fought to distance itself from, a family affair in which we no longer had any relatives to side with or save. Eland tended to agree with the so-called isolationists, not in proclaiming we had no moral calling, but that our primary obligations lay at home. He reasoned that his country could not possibly serve as the arbitrator of right and wrong for the entire world, imposing our understandings and ways on cultures with thousands of years more antecedence than his own. Nor did it seem possible to police the world, when the home territories featured as many dishonest sheriffs as honest ones, and with speculators and thieves far outnumbering both.

In his first two months there, the only newspapers Eland ever saw in Columbus were day-late editions of the Deming Headlight and the El Paso Times. He didn't know if it was due to prevailing prejudice against Jews or the man's questionable ways of dealing, but both the hotel owner, Sam, and his brother had a reputation as being more than just a little bit shady. Nevertheless, they were nice enough to Eland, and he hadn't had to worry about a long line at the registration desk. Of course, the wait was never long anywhere, even at the nearby cafe with its red checked tablecloths and praiseworthy biscuits. Even counting the army camp, he guessed there were never more than four hundred or so residents of the town at any one time. Some were resilient Anglos, white folk homesteading a ragged section, or working on the huge lowland ranches. Many were Mexican or Mexican-American, recent immigrants in search of better paying work. Other Latinos were the descendants of families that had lived there for hundreds of years, in what was an extended relationship with unforgiving land.

All more or less adhered to the same standards of hard work and hearty play, of necessity and fairness, and of "do unto others as you'd have them do unto you." They flourished like cactus in the harsh environment, unconcerned with the trends of modernity, generally seeking no one's help but their own. Most had liked Eland well enough from the time he first rode in over a month before. It didn't matter that he dressed "a mite fancy." Border folk were used to seeing characters with panache, the huge sombreros, fancy engraved sidearms, the brilliant scarlet sashes that tie on the side. And he'd never tried to impress them with his education. He'd come to write their story, or the story that this life inspired in him. They were, after all, the kind of people that he'd abandoned Santa Fe to meet. As authentic as rock. As real as the love that would never fade, no matter how many months or years he was away.

For all his ambivalence on the subject of newspapers, Eland nonetheless read every one that he could get hold of, and regardless of their source or date. He did so not as a gullible and malleable audience, but as a miner of information, sifting through the angled press for straight facts that he could then reconfigure into a picture that made sense. Every detail of every event was worked into the whole, with nothing disconnected, nothing totally irrelevant. Into this composite, this weaving, he added threads of natural and human history, science and technology, politics and personal interest. News of tragedies. The labor strike in Colorado in which state militia and paid strike breakers killed twenty-one, including three women and eleven children. Suffragettes being arrested and hosed on the streets, imprisoned and engaging in hunger strikes. The 1913 federal income tax act, in which for the first time Americans had part of the money they made seized, rather than only paying a tax on their purchases. The introduction of the crossword puzzle. Ford producing his one-millionth car with the labor of a regimented and mechanized workforce, and funding a "Peace Ship" on an anti-war cruise to England. James Joyce and what Eland considered to be his undisciplined drivel, and the fawning over the facile works of Charles Sandberg and Edna Ferber. The formidable novelist Jack London dying, allegedly imagining that he had transformed into a wild wolf, and subsisting entirely on suppers of raw meat. The horrific use of poison gas by the Germans, and its rapid adoption by the various countries they fought. Montana sending the first woman, Jeanette Rankin, to Congress, while women could only vote in a dozen of the states.

Most enlightening were the deceptions revealed between the lines, the brokering of various financial and political elements for the opinion and support of the public. Always the maneuvering was at the expense of the common folk, with public opinion manipulated behind the scenes by those who really held the reins. Only a year before, the Lusitania had been sent to the bottom of the Atlantic Sea, a British passenger ship carrying arms and munitions to embroiled England in violation of America's professed neutrality. It was exactly what the faction in the United States favoring intervention had planned for, knowing that it would galvanize support for the war if the Germans sunk a ship with so many civilians aboard. Twelve hundred people died as the pawns of secret policies, 128 of whom were U.S. born.

Eland wondered if government wasn't both necessarily and inherently dishonest, the contentment and cooperation of its constituents dependent upon being told what they wanted to hear. And he wondered if perhaps every man didn't also have a lie of his own, to tend and to cling to, one that they insisted on telling themselves over and over in spite of all evidence to the contrary. The only survivor of a disaster, who escaped his guilt by believing it was God's will and choice that all the others died. The apprehensive banker, who tried to convince himself that his disinterested wife married him for his heart rather than his money. A socialist, whose grip on reality depended on the impossible goal of complete equality. An aging creator of some dubious invention, sure that one day he'd be able to sell it. Generals and warmongers betting they still had that ticket to heaven. The unchallenged and untested, oddly certain of their courage. The callous, fooling themselves into thinking they care.

Eland's redeeming mission, as he saw it, was to somehow be one of the people to make a difference, writing stories that might function as an antidote to the toxicity of the modern order, the artifice, the delusion, distraction and destruction. He believed that from the detritus of resilient earth and poetic effort something real and good could sprout... something more honest and authentic, focused and caring. Believed that if he could just describe the many sides of a truth clearly and beautifully enough, it would have more power and pull than the most clever fabrication, false promise or attractive ruse. Believed that there could be an idea, a book, a passage even that could become the mantra that halted the insane rush towards worldwide war and a potential apocalypse. His manuscripts would be the foundations on which genuine community could be built, the ingredients of a meal to feed hungry souls, a wilder crop's fertile seeds, the glad compost for a garden whose fruits he himself would never see.

At the very least, he insisted, he could use his thwarted passion and unflagging focus to fuel the friction of change, authoring a fairy tale that could lead its mass of readers to reconsider their numbing ways, to begin better noticing and acknowledging their wives and husbands, the land that provided for them, the woodpeckers rattling to get their attention, the children trying to teach them to play, their own unmet needs and repressed hungers, the swift passage of nights and days. That he could help them all, before they died, to wholly, truly live. Here, he sensed, was a word-lined way as sure as Spring, leading back to an earlier sensibility as well as forward to the best that could possibly be, a path as green as the Willow and Alder that continued to burst forth no matter how many times they were harvested by the village basket makers, grazed down by hungry cattle or blackened by a forest – or a world – aflame.

Chapter 29

SHASH:

It Wasn't Me Who Killed You

Omen loved the Apache creation story, no matter how times she heard it. She loved the way it sounded when her grandmother told it, and she loved the part with the Bear best.

When the great floodwater had gone, Grandmother would say, the Earth was left bare and flat. It looked forlorn, with nothing growing there. The Spirits built mountains, and on them Aspen and Spruce and Pine started to grow. Bear felt sorry for the naked humans, and gave them seeds to plant, including Willow, Cottonwood, *Tc'ilxe*, Pines, Junipers, Manzanitas, Oaks, all the kinds. And Bear gave them the *Dasinexuc* Cactus, the *Nadalbai* and other Mescals we still eat, Grandmother would add... and the medicines we still use to treat ourselves when we're sick.

Omen came to appreciate all of the creation stories Eland had read to her, and always it was those that referenced and revered the Bear that she enjoyed the most. And she loved hearing and speaking the many other names for Shash that she had heard. To the Ainu of northernmost Japan, the Bear was The Divine One Who Rules The Mountains. To the Cree, Bear was the Angry One and Chief's Daughter. To the tribal Sami of Norway, it was Old Man With Fur Clothes, while the nearby Finns would say Old Lightfoot, Honey-Paw or Pride Of The Woods. Most often, wherever they were found, the People Of The Land respectfully called the Bear Grandmother and Grandfather. They revered them, and indeed the Bear was central to the earliest of all human religions.

The first physical evidence of human reverence for animal spirits had been recently unearthed in grottoes high in the mountains of Franconia, Switzerland and Germany. Along with various prehistoric artifacts, they'd discovered collections of Cave Bear skulls stacked purposefully on altar-like shelves, alarming with their hollow eyes and long pointed teeth. Some of these were found encircled by formations of small rocks, while another held a leg bone in its mouth. Here were not only the tools for killing and fleshing these powerful animals, but evidence of their veneration. It seemed that from earliest times the Bear was seen as the Animal Master, the strongest and wisest of all.

For years, hundreds of ancient terra-cotta Bear Nurses had been turning up in excavated Neolithic sites overseas, reported in the scientific journals that Eland loved to peruse. Many of these were described as enthroned female Bears, or women with Bear masks on, and most were nursing a cub. A primordial Great Mother, it was this nurturing Bear that gave birth to the new gods and goddesses of vegetation and agriculture, such as Zeus, Zalmoxis, Dionysus, and Omen's favorite, Artemis. Artemis grew into the Lady of the Beasts, the Lady of Wild Nature, Priestess of the Moon. She was also known as Diana, the huntress who also served as the defender of wildlife. She was the protectress of thieves, slaves and outlaws... at once the destructive, all consuming Terrible Mother, and the Defender of the Children. The guardian spirit of all pregnant women and the Opener of the Womb. Her constant companion was a Bear, and together they ruled the plant kingdom and thus determined feast or fast. Artemis was the archetype of the elusive and capable Wild Woman of the Woods. If only, Omen thought, the unapproachable goddess could have allowed herself to be overtaken by her five senses, and taken by love.

The earliest villagers of both North America and Eurasia watched the Bear go into its den every Winter, and emerge the following Spring. This was seen as an obvious herald of rebirth, the return of life to a hungry land and people. In England they honored what they called the Strawbear, while in Germany he was called the *Fastnachtshar,* a man dressed up in a straw Bear costume who would be led in early Spring to each house of the village. There the man-Bear would dance with all the women. The more enthusiastically they danced, the richer they could expect the coming crops to be. And pieces of the straw costume would be snatched by the young girls and placed beneath their pillows to insure fertility, or left in the nests of their Chickens to encourage the laying of eggs.

For pre- and post-agricultural peoples, entering into an initiation rite was often like the Bear going into a cave for the Winter, with the initiate placed in the darkness and isolation of a secluded hut or pit. They might further be wrapped up, blindfolded, or otherwise have their senses and mobility limited, as it would be in the womb. The initiate would seem to die while inside, giving up one persona and climbing out in a new, empowered form. For this reason, the Dakota referred to a boy's rite of passage as Making a Bear. The coastal Pomo included both boys and girls in a ritual where the children were symbolically killed by the Kuksu Spirit, with the help of a costumed Grizzly. They were then removed to the forest for four days and nights. When they were reborn into the tribe, they brought with them the secret medicine songs and plant knowledge learned in their travels to the middle world. No matter what race or tribe one was from, if they killed a Bear, as sometimes they had to, they said prayers for the spirit of the animal and pleaded for its forgiveness.

"Don't think poorly of me," a hunter might say. "I am hungry and in need of your flesh. I have been cold, and will praise you every time I wear the warm coat of your hide."

Or they'd try a different approach.

"It wasn't me who killed you," they might say, before blaming it on an enemy, or on another tribe. "It was the white man who shot you," a successful Apache hunter might claim.

Omen knew the traditional reverence for the great Bear was matched by, if not in part inspired by unease, trepidation, fear and respect. And reasonably so. The Mountain Lion was seldom a danger to people, and Wolves only to livestock, but the Grizzly could and sometimes would put an end to some unfortunate woman or man. Other than certain insects and the Polar Bears of the Far North, they were the only predator in North America believed to ever actually hunt humans. Others might kill in defense, consequentially or by mistake, but the Grizzly could make it deliberate... whether because they saw people as a source of easy protein, or simply ate rather than waste what they'd killed out of territorial imperative or simple aggravation. Worse perhaps, most people found them both incomprehensible and unpredictable. Word was you could walk within sight of them time and again without them caring in the least, and then another day have those same animals suddenly running at you at forty miles per hour with frothing mouths and lethal intent.

No wonder, Omen thought, that healers and Bears not only fascinated people, but typically made them uncomfortable. No wonder the Bear Spirit was considered to be the ally of the Shaman, while making so many others uneasy. Like the Shaman or Medicine Woman, the Bear had the ability to wound as well as heal. Both were inherently solitary travelers who gathered up their power from the lessons of nature, the instruction of the spirit world, and the crucible of solitude.

Omen had always treasured her time away from the bustle and bother of crowds, always proudly claimed the mantle of the solitary. But with Eland, she had for the first time been able to be with someone intimately and still feel like herself, undivided, undiluted, uncompromised. As something more in his presence, instead of less. Not distracted, but more focused. Not toned down, but amplified, enlivened, enhanced.

Since she was very young, Omen had mixed feelings about her bruin-ness. In some ways, she proudly swelled with the Bear that grew inside her, while at the same time she hated how anything and anybody associated with Bears were automatically considered to be fat and uncomely by societal standards. She didn't like that Bears were stereotyped as always being grumpy, when she knew her own grumpiness was more a defense mechanism against being picked on. And the widely proclaimed resilience attributed to the Bear could be a bit much to live up to by a woman whose feelings were really so easily hurt. And now she felt like cutting herself open and spilling out her beloved beast, clawing the fur from her head and then busting off her claws... if doing without Eland was what it took to be a Bear.

Omen had no problem with being alone. None at all. What she could barely live with was living without her man. Her match. Her mate.

"It wasn't me who killed you," she quoted, aloud and to herself.

"It wasn't me who sent you away."

Chapter 30

CHAUTAUQUA & SNAKE OIL:
Nothing Holds You Back But You

Eland watched from his hotel window as small groups of people proceeded one after the other down the street and boardwalks and in the direction of the huge tent set up by the advance men for the Redpath Chatauqua. While first intending to stay in and write, he instead closed the curtain, walked down the Oak stairs and out into the New Mexico night.

Columbus townsfolk and soldiers found little entertainment in their village beyond the saloon, three hard working prostitutes ,and games of jack-knife mumbly-peg, and the occasional Horse race or Cock fight for money. El Paso was the closest real nightlife, and was a stopover for traveling acts from music bands and sports teams to Wild West Shows, dramatic plays and the odd one-ring circus. Few such enterprises ever made it so far off the beaten track, but when they did they could expect a near one hundred percent turnout, along with an attentive Wire Haired Terrier from Camp Furlong and however many Mexicans came over the fence to watch. It didn't matter that they couldn't speak English, seeing every showman as a mime whose movements and expressions told the tale's plot and resolution.

Posters had gone up a month or more before, announcing what was expected to be the most important cultural event of the entire year. "Family entertainment," the posters said." Inspiration for all ages! Seen by over forty million Americans a year, in over ten thousand cities and towns! Only twenty-five cents. Children under ten, free".

And how provocative, the poster photos: A busty opera singer in an elaborate French gown with a long hanging train. A still from a play in which a distressed maiden was seen trying to save her unconscious father from the evils of alcohol. A promotional portrait of Walter Eccles & The Four College Girls marketing innocence and good cheer. A trick drummer enthusiastically playing his drum while standing on his head. Authentic looking Geisha girls promising to tell the secrets of properly loving and serving a man. The Crooners of Waikiki, whose plaintive voices and ukuleles they claimed evoked the sounds of murmuring waves lapping against a tropical beach. And a Gypsy violinist dressed up in the costume of a fortune-telling lady's man, yet somehow still free of the stain of carnality.

Paying for his ticket, Eland noticed that, almost without exception, the women wore white dresses, with nearly a third of the men in matching white suits. Most likely they were church clothes, selected to symbolize cleanliness and a purity of spirit. While the Chatauqua was not a religious event per se, it tended to make of a religion of a wholesome lifestyle and the pursuit of riches and fortune. Many of the speakers were in fact ex-preachers, who put their oratory skill and practiced fervor to work in the cause of personal success.

Colonel Slocum, camp commander, took a seat near the middle among his officers and staff. Eland sat four rows back, next to an aisle as though to make a quick exit easier. There was no real reason to expect violence this night, however, with so many gray-bearded grandfathers and white-stockinged granddaughters in attendance. And Columbus had never known the numbers of fistfights and shootouts once typical of nearby communities like El Paso, Tucson or Tombstone. If there were any whiskey or weapons among those filling the tent, they were well concealed in shoulder holsters or steel pocket-flasks. It was not a night to dwell on disagreement or trouble, but an evening to escape. Into pleasant distraction, philosophy and humor. Into idealized cultures and the common values of the day. Into fields of promise, and songs of hope.

The show had started dramatically enough with that rousing old tune "The Boys Of The Old Brigade," performed by the immaculately attired White Hussars. The men of the 13th Cavalry smiled and tapped their feet as the band played there before them, resplendent in their white felt Cossack hats, kid boots, and fancy uniforms elaborately trimmed with shiny gold braid. The popular Hussars were followed by a skilled Master of Ceremonies, and then a dozen different speakers and acts in quick succession. Two sisters, each wearing a dress made to represent half of the American flag, reciting a stirring poem about mom, God and apple pie. A troop of singing children. A heartfelt speech about graham flour and the road to health. A sleight of hand magician with a toothbrush mustache, whose introduction stated he was a Christian man and not to be feared. And a fellow with the features of an eastern Cherokee, wearing a cloth tie and marketing the patent nostrums of the enterprising Anglo, was presented as "The Kickapoo Doctor" to an audience more familiar with the features of the Yaqui and Apache, Pima and Papago. He held aloft glass bottles of "world famous" Kickapoo nostrums, while cautioning about unhealthy modern lifestyles and lauding the clean, pure ways that the Indian lived.

"Who but nature could know better about how to cure the natural body?" he asked the audience. "With this here Kickapoo tonic, no less than fifteen different plants combine to assist digestion, increase mother's milk, and even restore male virility to the standards of every man's glory days!"

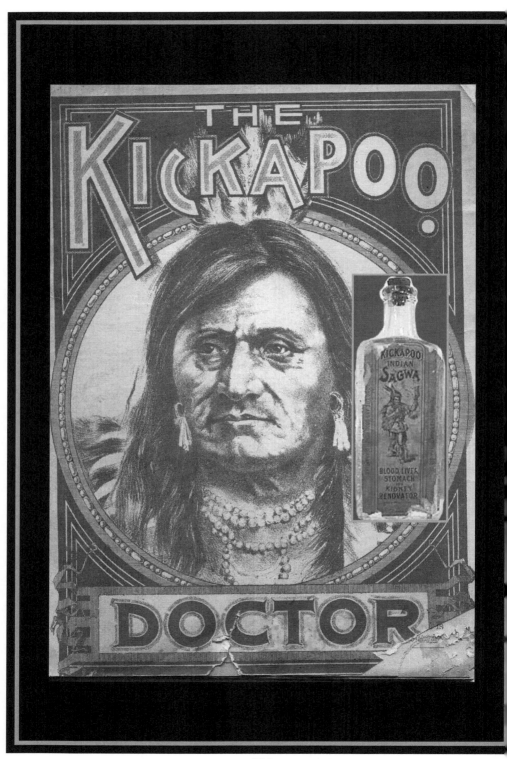

Sure, Eland thought, most of the plants are common bitters known for settling a stomach but it was the main ingredient – the highest proof alcohol – that had the folks waving their money for the bottles of snake oil the ushers carried down the aisles. It was the questionable content of just such preparations that was rousing the medical establishment against community herbalists and other non-certified practitioners. Eland shifted his weight from one foot to the other, in anticipation of making a break, when the announcer called out onto the stage the nationally celebrated motivational speaker, Harry "Gatling Gun" Fogelman, immediately launching his empowering message at an advertised three hundred words per minute.

"I have one thing to offer you tonight, ladies and gentlemen, it is the power of positive thinking. As we think so do we do. A negative thought is a poison to soul and deed, as deadly as arsenic." Fogelman stalked the stage for ten minutes without a pause for breath, most of his pronouncements and encouragement focused on the benefits of progress and his countrymen's destiny to succeed. "I say you ought to be rich. And I would take that a step farther. You have no right to be poor!"

Eland wondered what the impoverished children of local Hispanics and unemployed freighters might make of that, unable to afford the quarter admission, trying to lift the tent's heavy canvas wall for a peek.

"Tell me what you want in this world, and I tell you that you can have it!" proclaimed Fogelman.

The crowd responded energetically, shouting out their desires one after the other.

"Money!", a young man yelled out.

"Of course," he replied, with sympathetic eyes.

"A new home," a hopeful-eyed woman was heard to say.

"Then envision it, and you can make it yours!"

"Travel," a couple spoke up together.

"Yes, go for it! Nothing holds you back, but you!"

"A new dress!", came a voice from far in the back.

"Easy!"

"My youth!", grumbled someone's grandfather, bent over an antler-headed cane.

"Think young, my good man, and you will feel younger."

"Good health," a woman implored, while hurriedly mopping her brow with a lavender scented kerchief.

"God's gift to you," Fogelman insisted, looking her straight in the eye, "a gift that only you can squander! Think health, with your every breath, and the body will conform to the mind!"

"Love," a woman near the back asked, losing her straw hat in the process. "What about true love?"

"Love has not left you, m' dear. It is pounding on the gates of your heart, and you have only to unbar them. You may sight true love on the next ridge over. Or you may find it, the day that you look to see what you've left behind."

"What was left behind," Eland repeated in his mind. And with those few words, what had until then been but farcical entertainment had suddenly cut him to the bone. The force of them scraped the scab off what remained an unhealed wound, heightened the torment of hungers that had already been haunting him. Every humorous line, he'd wished Omen could have laughed at with him. When the most inane acts came on, he'd wished he had her there to exchange a knowing glance. The choir of little girls, he imagined she would have enjoyed even more than him. And now the rattling of Gatling Gun faded into the far-off background, allowing different sounds and images to emerge and come forward. The serenade of river, with Omen walking alongside it, bending over in a never-ending search for healing herbs and heart shaped rocks. The melodious winds of the canyon, and the way Omen smelled when she had been walking through patches of Clover and Mint.

"There is nothing you can't have," Fogelman said, "if you want it badly enough. All the riches are yours for the taking. Every dream can come true, so be careful what you dream for."

Still lost in his reverie and longing, the only words Eland heard were the warning. Be careful what you dream for. A dream had taken him hundreds of miles to the raw edge of a vast conflict, and an unforgiving desert. But then, maybe it was a dream that would guide him back.

"Always set your sights high to avoid settling for too little," the Gatling Gun exhorted, punching his fist in the air. "Your future is a blank canvas, and you have in your own hands the pastels with which to color it. Make it anything you want! This is America, and America means possibility. Nothing– oh, but nothing– is impossible! Picture the greatest end, I tell you, getting up every morning with a spry step and glad spirit... and then move, with your head up, inexorably, confidently in its direction!"

But what direction, Eland questioned. Finding and following the purpose that would define him. Or following his spirit even now stretching north towards the Saliz Mountains and the woman who felt like home.

"You are the only obstacle to your own fulfillment," the speaker said, pointing accusingly. "Leap over," he said, leaping fully three feet in the air and landing with a loud thud on the stage. "Move on," he added, wiggling his knees as if his legs couldn't wait to run, "and with each and every step you take, say to yourself this:"

Fogelman stomped his feet as if marching, chanting his mantra of positivity: "Yes!" (stomp) "I!" (stomp) "Can!" (stomp) "Do it!"

Eland got up to leave ahead of the crowd, focused on the ground ahead of him, imagining Omen's wide little feet walking beside him.

Yes... I... *can.*

Chapter 31

FRAGILE MINT LEAF
& TOUGHENED MESQUITE THORN:
Axis Of The Needle

Eland took off his black hat first, careful not to grab and possibly bend the flattened five-inch brim, depositing it on the rack provided. He next slipped off his silver buttoned coat and draped it on a hanger he got out of the closet, then pulled out the revolver and sat it next to the bible in the hotel nightstand. Next he pulled off his shoulder bag, removing from it the bags and bottles of herbal preparation that he'd promised Omen he'd carry. Lastly, he pulled out his journal, opened it to the first empty page, and began to write.

> *I call up a vast separateness around me,*
> *invoke clouds to smother starlight,*
> *dance in ever tightening circles*
> *inside myself,*
> *howl your essence on naked winds.*

He was struggling to come to terms, by making his being without Omen even more deliberate, more magical... and less mundane, less mistake. If he was to be without her even for a few months, he wanted to be this painfully alone, this unknown. If he had to do without her light, he would embrace the dark.

> *A great suppressed suffering*
> *rises unbearably in my chest.*
> *It escapes my throat in unfamiliar,*

dinosauric sounds,
like the most elusive bird's call.

He had surprised himself with the strange and pitiful little noises
that slipped out the corners of his trembling mouth. It was a small
and helpless creature he didn't recognize. A lost child, waiting for
Eland to take him by the hand and lead him back to where he was
loved and cared for.

> *You had only to slow down*
> *or to look away*
> *in order to leave me.*

He needed to believe he hadn't abandoned her, that somehow by
not coming with him it was she who had gone.

> *I scream for you*
> *in a tone none else can hear...*
> *spiraling backwards in pain*
> *to the arresting dawn,*
> *simultaneously plummeting forward*
> *through miraculous eternity again.*

Eland rose slowly from the table and tucked his journal and pen
back in its bag. He threw himself down hard on the squeaky bed,
then yanked his boots off before lying down. The only window in
the room opened to the south, away from home and Omen. And
as soon as he realized that, Eland rolled over onto his other side,
spending the entire night facing the wall... and towards his true
love, resting or sleeping far to its other side.

If only, he thought, he could do what he needed to out here during
the day, then be miraculously transported by flying carpet back to
her arms at night. Or better yet, that he could somehow be both
places at once. It hurt to be without her when he rode the lonely

trail, when funny lines came into his head and she wasn't there to hear them, snicker or approve. When he saw a Kestrel kill and feed on a Gambel Quail, without her there to take it all in with him. And when he ate his steak dinner, longing all the while to give her bites. But the worst were the nights, with no distractions other than his own strained breathing, the persistent memories, worrying if she was alright. He felt his lust for her, for the pounding, snuggling, and fusing of bodies, but that was a little thing compared to his need to be able to watch her in the increasing moonlight, as she contentedly slipped off into sleep.

So many people, he realized, lived with somebody they loved but weren't in love with, staying together because of the financial security, or deluding themselves that it was somehow or other best for their kids to see them feign affection and set aside their dreams. Some worked jobs they tolerated, but that did nothing to nourish their souls, their gifts or hopes. They made choices based on what they called the lesser of two evils, rather than co-creating the reality that they most wanted and needed.

Omen was, in the flesh, everything that Eland ever tried to write about. The beauty and challenge of life was in her. The wildness of the mountains, the sensuality of the creature world, the magic of plants. Fragile Mint leaf and toughened Mesquite thorn. Impetuous youth and wise old age. Desert storms and winds that embrace. The tears and laughter of countless generations, tumbling in their time from the precipice of their imagined isolation into the one. One spirit. One composted mantle of soil reaching around the molten Earth like a hug. The fires of creation and destruction. The absolute contentment of a placid lake mirroring the deer and Bear that drink from it. She fed rather than crushed in him the native bloom of curiosity, the inexplicable urge to defy convention, the Dandelion spark of revolution, the wholly human call to distinguish and excel.

It was crazy, being without her. Worse than any insanity he would have suffered had he squelched this urge, this assignment, and stayed. She was not, however, the compass that would always point home, as once he'd thought. Omen was the axis on which its needle – and his very life – now whirled and spun.

Pulling out a blank sheet of paper, Eland leaned forward to write.

My Dearest, Lovely Omen, he began. I know you can't read this, and I well remember you growling about how a letter would be a sad-ass substitute for my being there. But I have to try to get this to you. I have to. Besides, I know someone will read this aloud to you if you want to hear what I have to say badly enough.

Eland paused, looking over what he'd written, hoping to ensure that his words would be cause for her to feel wanted in his absence, rather than their making her feel guilty for not coming along. And to see that they didn't make him sound pitiful, especially when Omen would hear them spill from the mouth of her closest friend and neighbor. He was uncertain what to say, being too far into his quest to turn around, and knowing he'd forever resent her if he had to sacrifice his purpose, his calling, and mission. With no idea when he'd be able to leave, simply repeating his pledge to return would sound not only redundant but hollow, serving only to remind her of her wait. That is, if she would indeed wait for him as he hoped and prayed. As a result, he wrote instead about the local flora he knew she'd want described, the color and shape of the rock he'd brought back to the room that day, and the weather over the seven week period that he'd been gone. About how he found himself imagining the smell of her neck whenever he caught scent of distant mountain rain, and oddly scanning the dirt streets of Columbus for her familiar barefoot tracks.

More than anything else, I'm writing to assure you that I remain completely, irrevocably yours. I knew that from the second that we met. I no longer can feel myself without you, and whatever I might accomplish out here will only be the result of what we are together. Oh darling, I will be back. Soon!

He wrote the last word quickly, before any second thoughts might force their say. Unlike pencil, there was no way to erase that which was rendered in ink, and that's one of the things Eland loved most about pens. The bold, sharply demarcated lines, yes... but also their indelible nature, and the commitment in him that they inspired. If he wrote soon, then soon it would have to be. Soon wading the coursing river to get to her enchanted adobe house. Soon knocking on the hand made door, or calling for her to open it. Soon holding her in his arms, as if all that mattered could be contained there, and nothing outside that arc and grasp could possibly matter.

I'll be heading back in a couple days, he concluded. There's nothing happening here anytime soon, and my story from now on is my story with you.

Eland signed his name with a flourish. He then drew a simple picture of a man and woman beneath what could be construed as an Alder tree – a figure of himself reciting from a book while that of Omen happily listens. Finally, true to his oft noted verbosity, he added the postscript below.

You had me promise to write you a poem, one that would never be put to paper. One worthy of being committed to memory, one too personal for anyone else's ears. And so now I promise this, too: that nothing but death itself could keep me from riding home, and personally reciting it to you.

GRAL FRANCICCO VILLA

Chapter 32

PUTOS Y HUEVOS:
The Pancho Villa Vendetta

As Eland and most of the town had watched the conclusion of the entertainment, Pancho Villa led his soldiers and their wives and camp followers steadfastly in the direction of the border. As tired and saddle worn as Villa was, he still had that characteristic look of poise and confidence. Villa needed no motivational speech to bolster his courage, he had a belief in himself and in the dignity and necessity of his cause... and he had drive, motivated now not only by the aims of his revolution but also by his burning need for vengeance. Vengeance, but against no fellow Mexicano no matter how they may have hurt him. Vengeance against the lying, conniving, two-faced gringo government of *Los Estados Unidos*.

It was not the usual imposition of inequities that weighed on him so and kept him awake late into the nights. Not the colonization, exploitation and impoverishment of his country by American as well as European companies, nor redress for the stealing away of *Tejas* from Mexico so many years before. It was more personal than that. It was that *puto Presidente* Woodrow Wilson, who chose another elitist revolutionary faction to support instead of his populist movement, selling U.S. made guns and ammo to his competitors while he had to make do with antique arms and defective ammunition purchased from Sam Ravel, the controversial Columbus hotel owner and marketeer.

The last straw had come only a short while before, at the battle for the Arizona border town Agua Prietta. Wilson had not only denied assistance to the Villistas, but had actually transported the opposing troops on American trains, on the American side! Villa and his patriots arrived worn out and hungry after a long and hard march, only to find their enemies already positioned behind fortifications in the town, well rested from their U.S. paid train ride. Were that not enough, when Villa launched his attack that night, his men were first blinded by high powered search lights from the American side of the border, and then mowed down by American bullets fired by American-favored Mexicans.

There was plenty about Villa for Eland not to like, including his fits of anger and acts of brutality. But he couldn't help but appreciate his welcoming of armed female *soldaderas* into his ranks. And just the fact that he was willing to stand up to the leaders of the most powerful country in the world, with barefoot Indian blooded peasants armed with Old West Winchesters, surplus Mausers and bows and arrows – was enough to earn him some respect.

No one had ever had to tell Pancho Villa "You can do it." He had (to borrow the regional expression) the *huevos* to again and again attempt the impossible, and be willing to die trying.

If the rumors Eland had been hearing all week were true, Villa would prove the power of his positive thinking by sending forth what was left of his bedraggled Army Of The North in the first invasion of the United States by a foreign army since the War of 1812.

Colonel Slocum was still insisting Villa would never try such a thing, disregarding a number of ominous reports. Eland couldn't figure out if this was pure stupidity on the camp commander's part, or if he was deliberately quashing those reports in order to ensure the attack and therefore precipitate the long desired war. Many saw what they later called the approach of storm clouds.

THE ILLUSTRATED
LONDON NEWS.

No. 1767.—VOL. LXIII.

SATURDAY, JULY 12, 1873.

WITH
EXTRA SUPPLEMENT

SIXPENCE
By Post, 6½d.

The Herbalist Knows The World Through Her Nose

Omen learns to read...

Chapter 33

STRUGGLING THROUGH
AN UNFAMILIAR FOREST OF WORDS

Omen stood in the post office staring at the unopened envelope, with a tremble in her grip. It had been made out to her personally, one of the only pieces of mail so addressed that she had received in the nearly four years she'd been there. Sure, there was always the annual tax bill, already a ridiculously high six dollars a year, with increases expected. But the word Omen seldom appeared in writing otherwise, and this time it held extra significance. These were the same letters, penned in exactly the same way, as the dedication on the first page of the book that her love had made for her.

"Eland," she thought, picturing his long tousled hair, his understanding eyes.

She took note of the small three-cent stamp in the top right corner. It featured a steaming locomotive, its cars undoubtedly filled with the benefits of progress, easily charging over and past any resistance on its one-way trip from what was to what would be.

Omen stepped outside, holding the letter up to the sun to see what she might be able to make out of its contents, slow to chance opening its Pandora's box. Inside could be seen a folded piece of paper filled with what looked to be not longhand but carefully printed words. Like a rustling in the underbrush, it brought with it a message for which she could as yet attach little meaning or intent. It could have been something hurtful, like a snake that had been stepped on. Or as harmless as some small mammal, lost and searching for its home, its mate, its burrow.

Omen slid her boot into the stirrup, swung herself up into her roan's saddle and rode straight back home, ignoring the friendly locals who tried to wave her down, and forgetting about the things she needed to buy from the general store. She was without a doubt thrilled to have heard from the man she loved... and yet, equally furious with that same fellow for the absence that necessitated a letter, as well as for another unappreciated reminder of her practiced illiteracy. Eland had managed to teach her the sounds of most of the letters, but it still seemed as if they tumbled randomly onto the page, rather than being paired and sequenced to easily evoke for her the words for things.

Reading, for Omen, was like an anxious struggle through an unfamiliar forest.

She regarded words as iconic and aural representatives of ideas, feelings and beings, not so different in that way from the green beings and their poignant communications. But they were species she was unfamiliar with, not knowing their energetics or effects, unable to discern the edible, poisonous and medicinal. And there were simply too many of them, forming not a forest like her beloved Southwest with welcoming spaces between the trees to meander through, but a mass of obstructive intertwining foliage such as those rainforest jungles she had heard of but never seen.

Omen pulled up to the cabin at a trot, and quickly unsaddled. So forcefully did she swing the door open that the breeze it created set all the bundled herbs hanging from the ceiling *vigas* to swaying back and forth. Plopping into the nearest chair, she reached for the mother-of-pearl handled letter opener and carefully slit the back of the envelope. From it she pulled a five peso bill, money printed by Villa to help his people while governor of

Chihuahua ...and a single folded sheet of note paper, dried rose petals spilling onto her lap as she unfolded it.

"M-y D-e-a-r-e-s-t," she began. sounding out each letter over and over again until a word at last started to make sense. "De-ar? Dea-rest! Dearest!" And on it went, for a painful number of hours. She was not only a sensitive person, but also tuned in to Eland as if to a single favored radio station in a band of static. And so she smiled as she read where he quoted her "sad-ass substitute" comment. She grew hopeful upon recognizing his words "I-will-be-back," and too excited to stay seated when she imagined him saying "Soon!"

Likewise, she felt alarmed when she deciphered the word "death" in his final line, just to imagine that it could now or ever get between them as these miles and months had.

Omen sat his letter on the stack of field guides, Harper's Weekly magazines and The Illustrated London news, publications she was determined to learn how to read. From a nearby shelf she removed a tablet of paper, set it down in front of herself, and picked up an already sharpened pencil.

PART VI

Chapter 34

FLESH & BARK:
Eland's Last Desert Walk

Eland had made up his mind to leave the next day. He would sell the horses and buggy to help buy another auto -- maybe a pickup truck that could be used to transport firewood back on the land.

He decided on this moment to leave, not for lack of a building story, but in spite of his being witness to one of the biggest stories of the year. There was much intrigue to cover, if his main goal was to expose the intrigues and betrayals of government, a touching tale of social inequality and the crushing of rural lifestyles under the hard heels of an ever more urban and industrial continent. There was poetry in the juxtaposition of forces and fates, philosophy in the reasons for each person or agency's acts, psychology in their insecurities and violent need to either lash out or control. The tale of progress, subsuming the past, and with it the community values, traditional healing systems, spiritual beliefs and indigenous languages of the people, and the biodiversity of the land. It was true that nothing terribly exciting had happened near his Columbus base, but any number of history changing events could unfold within a few days' ride from where he stayed, in the course of the next few months, if not weeks.

Eland felt sad and elated, derailed and revived, all at the same time. He had much to think about, feel, and get over, and he knew the best way to accomplish that would be to forgo an evening of celebration and goodbyes, and take a lengthy walk into the moonlit desert night.

Strangely, he hadn't missed the fascinating social events he was used to participating in, not during the entire year that he had stayed with Omen in the canyon. Getting to know, courting, playing with, sensing, and savoring each other had splendidly filled the hours, as it filled a need in him that no number of other people or activities could ever have hoped to do. And now in Columbus, when he could have most used the salve of entertainment, it felt somehow disingenuous. When he had enough wine in him to enjoy a good show, he ended up feeling sad that she had not shared the pleasure with him. If the event was boring, on the other hand, he reproached himself for having wasted mortal moments that could have been better given to thoughts of Omen, to what he was there on the Mexican border to learn or do, to his writing, or to walking the land. Increasingly he had chosen to go immediately from dinner to the desert, and sometimes he wouldn't be back before sunup. The ground stretched out much the same in every direction, largely indistinguishable, but what he was really exploring was the inner terrain, the terrain of a man's heart and soul.

Slipping on his shoulder bag, Eland was reassured to feel the familiar shapes within. He sometimes called it his "survival bag" because of its aesthetic as well as the practical necessities it contained for his wellbeing. This included his journal and pens. An old stone Bear fetish he'd bought from a collector to give to

Omen when he got back. The powdered Yarrow and Mugwort that she had insisted he take with him, each wrapped in wax paper and attractively tied with plant fibers. A tin of *Estafiate* ointment to treat any abrasions or burns. Extra ammunition, just in case. And matches for the same reason. But then again, he knew that what he really needed to survive would not fit in any bag, and that if she were small enough to carry, he would surely carry her not in some bag but in a vest pocket instead, positioned directly over his heart.

For the last time, Eland locked the door to his Commercial Hotel room, descended its creaking carpeted stairs, through the lobby and out the door to the street.

The main drag ran east and west, and it was towards the west he decided to walk this time, squinting from the red glare of a setting sun. He pursued it to the edge of town, just as it dropped out of sight, passing between the Custom House and the quarters of Lieutenants Benson and Lucas before skirting the base of Coots Hill. It was always a temptation on these nightly walks to climb to its summit, the only high landform for many miles around. And he wondered how, given the rumors about Villa, there were still no army lookouts posted on top.

The sounds of the town grew progressively quieter as he continued his wandering, even as the volume of the thoughts in his head dropped to a hushed whisper, and finally to nothing at all. Taking the place of motor rumblings, dog barks and internal commentary, was not silence but a complex melodic symphony of life forms, a rustling, hooting and howling of grazing, swooping and stalking creatures. It was an affair that started up on time every dusk with or without human audience, while the townsfolk were busy dining, talking, tending to their children or carousing in the saloon.

At the base of Coots Hill, he thought he heard something entirely different within the increasing roar of the wind, first a slow thumping that he might have thought horse hooves if not for their low muffled tone like a chorus of heartbeats. Then what he was sure were human voices for a minute, unintelligible but sonorous and paced like conversation, but the harder he sought to hold his breath and strain to hear, the more it seemed to be only an overtone of the wind itself as it funneled through the Creosote Bush and Russian Thistle, perhaps a mournful production of a saddened landscape.

It seemed to Eland, at least in part, to be a landscape of not only beauty but of grief, and none of it impersonal: grief over his father and their limited relationship. Over his least meaningful writing being that which made the most money. Over being a poet who hoped to awaken the senses and conscience, engagement and responsibility, in an era when fear seemed to be causing an entire society to seek distraction, illusion and escape. Grief over all the children in the world without mothers, and mothers that never took the time to love themselves. Over the European war that threatened to involve the entire planet, and the convoluted revolution that continued to bleed Mexico dry. Over the fact that the Southwest had gotten so overrun with homesteaders since 1905, that even Mule Deer were getting scarce in the mountains, and he might never live to see one of the last of the Grizzlies. And somehow every bit of grief over his life or the world existed within and took the form of his grief over his no longer bearable separation from Omen, his love.

Eland grieved not only being apart from her now, but also the years between when they were born and when they finally met. He grieved the trauma of Omen's early days, and the effect they still had on her emotions and attitude. The struggles and tense exchanges in that first year together, and how little he imagined he had helped her. He grieved her unwillingness to either come with him, or ask him to stay. He grieved what he saw as his failure not just to maintain, improve or extend a promising relationship, but to serve and further something essential, pure, wild, destined. Something truly magical, as magical as Merlin's quests, or Quetzalcoatl's return. He regretted having said the wrong things, aggravating when he meant to humor and stretch, enlighten and encourage, tease, and teach her. And Eland was sad not to have done enough to preserve that covenant and alliance of love against their inner learned demons and worst habits, as well as against the collective influences, resistance and destruction, delusion, and disbelief of an entire culture and time. Theirs, he was sure, was a partnership meant to outlast the falling away of flesh from bone, to survive being reconstituted again and again into new forms... forms that must each time go to great lengths to find one another, and in the process, rediscover themselves.

For all this grief, however, there was an equal and growing sense of hope and excitement, the righting of mistakes, the healing back together of that which had been torn and rendered. He would bind the wounded stalk of his being to hers, and watch as time and love caused their flesh and bark to be one again.

Chapter 35

OMEN'S DREAM:
What We Can & Cannot Know

"Of prophecy, I believe and understand. Of the decisions now before me, I can never see clearly enough."
  -Eland Howell, in a letter to his father

Omen's nightmare began innocently enough, in those wee hours of the morning when she was most likely to dream. It started with the bright colors of the river, inspired perhaps by the sound of the winds picking up outside. These swirled and shifted and finally began to separate. The browns that were river rock, distorted by a fluid lens of coursing water, dropped low into the shapes of mountain moraines and canyon cliffs. The vibrant greens of aquatic plant life spread out to become grassy meadow and Fir forest, while the diamond blues mixed with hopeful sunshine, rising to the top of her imagination and spreading out wide... to become the western sky. It became first an impressionist painting, then photorealism, then a movie to which she was an objective observer. It was a scene she did not realize she was a part of until she felt the pebbles on the trail rolling beneath her feet.

At first everything seemed wondrous in its unfamiliarity, a landscape of freeform sculpture and unchecked creativity. Then, first one recognizable feature appeared, and then another. A mountain spire that she used to orient herself on her walks down the canyon. A favorite bend in the river. An alpine meadow where she gathered Yarrow. Soon everything appeared as recognizable as an old friend, though not in the same juxtaposition as before. A certain Clover-filled dip existed where a special knoll usually stood. A Nettle patch where she would have expected to see a small spring and well used Fox den. Even the river she knew like the back of her hand seemed to somehow flow gradually uphill now, instead of down, and the path home that should get easier and easier, just got harder and harder.

It didn't matter though, because at that moment she realized her Eland was walking there beside her. The black hat with the rounded crown and flat brim. The jacquard vest and shoulder bag. The bare feet eager for each massaging of the land. The bouncy stride and constantly swiveling head, taking in everything around him. She wondered how could she have failed to notice, even for a second, the presence of the man who seemed as much a part of her as her own aching, pleasuring flesh. This seemed to her like the key to some important-to-solve problem, that she had simply not seen him fully for what he was, where he was, forever beside her. Even more so, at the core was the fact that she had not allowed herself to believe. In the Eland that loved. In the Omen that deserved that love. In them together. No devoted hero, no true happiness, no magical fairytale could survive such disbelief. If he was ever gone from her, she decided, it was only because she had not been able to trust that he was really there.

Omen dreamed herself smiling, and smiled in fact as she slept. She dreamt her smile was the lure sure to make any fish rise. That it was a bloom on her face that he would have to stop to smell and taste. That when he turned her way again, he would see the look on her face and know for once that she was truly happy. That because she appeared so happy, he would be all the more pleased that he had never left.

It was disappointing, then, for her to see him in her dream looking in her direction unmoved, continuing to scan without a pause to take her in. He slowed to investigate the Javelina tracks in the sand, grinned at a pair of courting white butterflies tumbling through the air, and narrowed his eyes to better make out the Redtail Hawk calling from a distant Pine tree. But as for Omen, he gave no sign that he even knew she was there.

"Eland," she said finally, though he made no response. Then she dreamed she said "Eland" more loudly, and had anyone been there in her house, they would have surely been awakened by the calls for him coming from her bed.

Omen thought to reach out and take hold of him, to take him by the ears and point his face at hers... and she was angry with herself for not doing just that. Instead, she followed quietly behind him, as the path gradually became less and less familiar again. She watched as the cliffs became progressively shorter, as the river got both shallower and narrower until it eventually disappeared altogether underground. The further they went, the smaller the rocks got until they were as sand. The few plants were all of a single species, more grey than green, and she felt disproportionately disturbed not to know its name. A few more steps, and she realized they were both approaching some undefined danger. Worse still, for every hurried step that she took to catch up, it seemed that he had somehow taken two, until he was too far ahead for her to possibly be of any help.

Whatever form it would assume, whatever particular language of negation or absorption it spoke, she knew the force that they approached to be none other than death itself. Not that it was necessarily ill-intended or malicious, likely taking no pleasure in the taking of life, somehow making things intimate without making them personal. But what he was about to walk into was terrifying nonetheless, terrifying in its completeness, its finality, its irreversibility.

"Eland!" she shouted, but the winds swallowed the sound of her voice. She tried to run, but her legs felt heavy and slow.

If only, she thought, I would have given more. If only I had not waited for him to reach across the miles, and had reached out and given to him instead. If I would have admitted my needs when I craved, rubbed him even when I was tired or feeling bad. If I had done these things, he would slow down so I could catch him. He would be able to hear me, even over the crash and roar of a storm. He would always be able to see me. And he would never step into the jaws of destruction without me.

"Eland! Eland! *Eland!*" she yelled out, until she finally woke herself up with her cries.

Omen pulled back the covers and stood up naked in the dark. Feeling the pressure in her bladder, she hurried outside with nothing on but the slip-on boots that she kept by the door. What little moon there was flew hidden behind a thick layer of clouds. She was surprised by the sprinkling of an early snow that met her, tiny spongy flakes that adhered to her hair. But it felt good at first, blowing against her feverish skin as she walked to the appointed spot, squatted in the blackness and peed. It was only when she stood up again that she began to feel the gripping cold, each rush of canyon wind sucking from her body another portion of that heat it needed to survive.

Omen turned and walked slowly back towards the cabin, hugging herself with both arms in order to better shelter from the unexpected gusts and snow... shivering from the cold, shaken by the implications of all that she did – and could not hope to – know.

Villistas - 1916

Chapter 36

A CLOCK STOPPED:
A Battle Begun

Columbus, New Mexico – March 1916

It was at that second that all hell broke loose in the town of
Columbus. A few of the Camp Furlong sentries had already been
dispatched, silently, by the hand forged knives of the *Indios*
Villistas, but not before an alert soldier was able to get off a shot
that brought down one of the stealth attackers. At the sound, one
after another soldier and townsfolk awoke to seek out boots and
pants, dresses and children, guns and ammunition, and with one
unanimous assumption on their minds. The rumors had been true
after all. The United States had been invaded, not just raided by
opportunistic robbers but by an armed force purporting to
represent the authority and interests of another country. Under
Pancho Villa's orders, his close subordinate Colonel Beltran had
crossed the border with close to two hundred barefoot fighters at
midnight, and was now pressing on to the planned objectives.

His first stop was the train station office where advanced elements
of his command had already shot and killed the stationmaster and
taken over the tracks. The Colonel paused a few moments in the
depot doorway, smelling the mix of blood, oil lamps and rail yard
grease, listening to the tick-tock of the office wall clock. The
longer he lingered, the louder it seemed to get, like the machines
of the factories in which he as a boy had worked. Like the
pounding of nails into the lid of a coffin. The coffin that was his
country. Beltran tripped on the head of a Bear rug, then angrily

silenced the offending timepiece with a single pistol bullet in its numeral laden face. 4:11 it would always say, in mute but dignified testimony to the sole invasion of U.S. soil since the British had burned the White House one hundred and four years before.

Lt. Lucas hadn't been asleep for more than an hour before he'd been awakened by the sound of Beltran's few mounted cavalry clopping past his bedroom window. He slid the pistol from its holster hanging near his head, then sat up ever so slowly so as not to make the noisy bed-springs squeak. Looking out the crack between the curtains, he could see the black silhouettes of four mounted men in large sombreros walking past.

"Greasers," he thought. "I knew it!"

Easing down onto the floor, Lucas sat back against the wall and rested the now cocked .45 automatic rifle on the tops of his bended knees. He kept it pointed at his door, sure that once they broke through he'd be able to take down at least a few. The Colt held seven rounds that would chamber and fire as fast as he pulled the trigger, and each with enough power for a one shot kill. The lieutenant worked to steady his breathing, although he imagined that it was still loud enough to be heard by the bandits on the other side of the thin wood walls. He was scared, but not nearly as frightened as he was excited. He felt more awake than he had in his twenty-four years on the planet, more alert, more present. He had prayed for some action, and now it seemed his prayers had been answered.

Almost as soon as they'd passed his quarters, Lucas rushed outside in his stockinged feet... happy to have gone to bed dressed, yet furious that he couldn't find his boots. Hopping and cussing from innumerable sand burrs and cactus spines, he made his way to the main barracks, where he called on his men to get

*Permanently Stopped –
the Columbus Train Station Clock 1916*

their gear and catch up with him. Then Lucas grabbed Corporal Harry Wisweel, the troop Horseshoer with the strong New York accent, and the two of them rushed to the guard tent where the arms were kept.

"Goddam it," he complained, seeing that the machine gun cases were locked tight and the sergeant with the key nowhere to be found.

The Colonel had ordered the fully automatic Benet-Mercers locked up after one was pilfered and sold on the black market, but now there was an urgent need. Lucas was disgusted with his superiors for being so concerned with making things secure that they reduced the options– and hamstrung the responses– of the thinking, fighting man.

"I'll take care of it," Corporal Wiswell said with a grin, pulling a chisel and mallet from the leather tool belt around his waist. Lucas relished their getting to bust the locks off the gun cases, smashing in his mind all the inane restrictions that they had come to represent. There was nothing more absurd, he felt, than sending men into harm's way and then handicapping their ability to carry out their appointed mission.

By then, several of the other enlisted men had caught up. Hearing a fresh exchange of fire coming from town, they all exited the tent and moved off towards the tracks, carrying with them two of the machine guns and several crates of the special ammo that they required. They could hear a second front warming up to the south of the base, near the stables, and still more firing from somewhere near the train depot. It was to the latter, that Lucas decided to head.

He and his men were rounding the corner of a building at a trot when they came face to face with a youthful foot soldier, already aiming a Mauser rifle in their general direction. Its long barrel wavered as if the *Villista* were hesitant to take a life, or else simply unsure which of the gringos he should shoot first. And he still had not picked out his target, or else resolved to commit his first murder. Lucas felt no such inclination to hesitate. This is what he had joined the army for, what the recruiters had promised, and what he had feared Columbus could never provide. In seconds he had pulled out his service pistol, and sent three heavy slugs into the peasant's boyish chest and abdomen.

"Number one," he said proudly, beginning his count... while wondering what to notch.

Chapter 37

LITTLE RED FLOWERS

Eland heard the first shot of the battle clearly enough, even being nearly half a mile away. Whatever thoughts he'd been thinking were instantly concluded, replaced by the animal like responses of heightened awareness and considerations of attack or escape. At first, the urge to get to the town in time to warn any who might still be sleeping to get up before they were killed in their too soft beds, but then the realization hit that it would be totally overrun long before he could get there with his little pistol and bag of journals and herbs. Worse, the Mexicans he knew of did not seem any less in need of and perhaps even deserving of some warning of the dangers that awaited them. He couldn't help but wish that he could convince them to go back, and not to try and pit the enthusiasm of young conscripts and the patriotism of old men against the most modern army on the planet. He would have liked to say, "yes, struggle for your ages-old rights, struggle to be treated right and have a dignified life, but do not throw your lives away."

His second response was a jolt of fear, not for his own safety so much as the possibility that anything could stand between him and the woman he was returning to. Quickly ascending Coots Hill, he found it strangely empty of soldiers from either side of the struggle. Always seize the high ground is the wisdom Eland had garnered from the history books he'd read, but no American privates kept watch from its top, and no *Villistas* had hauled cannon there to shower destruction on Columbus. Only a boisterous Screech Owl, all the unheard and unseen... and a prominence from where he could measure the tide of the battle below.

The early rifle shots had appeared defined and distinct, but now with the raising of dust, the edges of the staccato flashes appeared softened, the blinking of musket fire billowing like flowers. *Salvia henryi*, he thought, when the flashes looked small as that Sage's tiny crimson blossoms. Larger flashes reminded him of Omen's much-loved Scarlet Penstemon and Red Cinquefoil. A volley of shots, like strings of brilliant Sunset Hyssops and Indian Paintbrush. There were no botanical allegories, however, for what he heard and saw next, multiple rounds being fired so fast they seemed to create a single wall of sound, and a bigger and steadily growing red glow emanating from the center of this village named after one of the continent's first civilized exploiters.

Eland surveyed a route in the general direction of the town, one creased with shallow gullies pointing the way to what now appeared to be a burning town, ravines offering at least a minimum of concealment and protection. He would get as near as he dared, in hopes of being at least of some help to any citizen in need.

Chapter 38

AN OMINOUS GLOW:
Machine Guns vs Bows & Arrows

The orange glow from the middle of town looked utterly ominous to Lt. Lucas. Clearly arsonists were at work, and just as clearly it seemed up to him to deal with it. There was no major to tell him otherwise, and certainly no colonel to urge caution or restraint. He was the authority of the moment, even as each man or woman was in truth the only authority over him or herself. The prohibitions of gods and people were set aside as they always were during times of war. Killing was not murder now, but a duty... a duty to put down the attack. And to preserve the lives, the possessions, the honor of the American people.

Lucas, still as barefoot as most of the Mexicans he fought, led his squad northwards across empty lots littered with bodies.

Sixteen, seventeen, eighteen he counted in the dark, and there had to be more that they couldn't see in the first glow of dawn. Any enemy combatants who still moved were dispatched by the soldiers with rifle butts or pistol shots. Even those with their hands in the air were summarily blasted after one of Lucas' men was wounded by a Mexican pretending to surrender.

Stepping out onto the street they could see a large group of raiders, some with torches held high, others going in and out of various businesses whose goods tempted them. The light from the burning hotel and other buildings competed with the advancing dawn, and for the first time the enemy could be distinctly made out. They were no longer faceless demons of the shadows, but real and villainous human beings with cotton pants and serapes, felt fedoras, and straw sombreros. Some were tall and thin, a couple heavy, and some short enough to be children. A few appeared bent over with age, but most walked with the spry steps typical of extreme youth.

As Lucas surveyed the street, his men set up their two Mercer machine guns. First the folding tripods had to be spread open, then the arm fixed to its cradle. The bullet-filled magazines were inserted in the top behind the breech and snapped into place. The bolt had to be grasped firmly, pulled back against the pressure of its mainspring, then released sharply to feed the first round into the chamber. Lucas stood watching the Mexicans mill around as each gunner seated the wooden butt firmly against his shoulder, grasped the handles with both hands, and lined up the crude sites. At fifty yards, there would be no need to hold them over the target, so they rested them somewhere between the average neck and belt line.

"Get ready," Lucas barked, as one man could be seen torching the curtains in a store's busted out window. As two raiders wrestled and squealed like toddlers gleefully playing in the road. As one in particular seemed to have turned, staring intently in their direction in an attempt to discern who or what might exist there beyond their spreading circle of light.

"Let 'em have it!"

The first storm of bullets caught the man that was so intently looking their way, hitting him in the chest and face: number nineteen. Flattened the torchbearer so that he fell atop his own blazing wand: twenty. And ended the roughhousing games of two teenage privates from Sonora: twenty-two and counting. As soon as one thirty round clip was emptied, a nearby loader would snap another one in. The Mercers were like noisy, stuttering twins, unleashing a living hell on the unfortunate invaders.

Number thirty-three or four was a soldier walking backwards out of the hardware store with the end of a rope in his hands, evidently trying to unroll the coveted prize from its spool. Two Mexicans who one after the other picked up the dropped rope, became thirty-four and five. Sgt. Cardenas made number thirty-six or seven, even as his friend Carreon shouted at him to get his fat ass out of the street. He had made the mistake of carrying several boxes of new shoes out into the firelight in order to pick out his size. The first few pairs were either too big or too small. The last pair he tried on his feet, some fine leather oxfords, fit just right.

"Damnit, Cervando," Sgt. Carreon said, after running through the flying bullets to see his already deceased friend. As rounds from the Mercers struck the ground in front and around him, Carreron caressed the fallen face. Then from the big man's pocket, he pulled out a red toy truck that he had pillaged for his son. Carreron then stood up slowly and began to back up down the nearly emptied street, holding the truck in his left hand, firing his revolver ineffectively from the hip with his right until emptied. He next picked up a bow and quiver full of arrows that one of Villa's intrepid Indian warriors had fearlessly if foolishly employed in this fight against machine guns.

Continuing to stumble backwards, and with rounds steadily biting into the walls and ground all around him, he notched a single feathered arrow and sent it wobbling in the direction of Lucas and his guns, arcing ever so defiantly through the smoke and glare of Columbus' pre-dawn air.

Guadalupe — Nuestra Señora de las Yerbas

Chapter 39

TENDING THE WOUNDED,
& TENDING HIS WOUND

Walking cautiously and stopping every few yards to listen, Eland was still only halfway to town when he ventured upon a man groaning in pain. Pulling his revolver and moving closer, he could see in the growing dawn's light that there was nobody else close by, and that the grievously wounded man was Mexican and not Anglo.

As soon as their eyes met, it no longer mattered the color of skin or flag, and Eland immediately kneeled to determine his condition. A nasty hole through his upper chest made its own breathing sounds with every inhale, indicating that a bullet had penetrated a lung. There was no way for him to even know whether the *Villista* would live or not, but he could staunch the bleeding, assist clotting and apply antibacterial herbs that could lessen the chance of a deadly infection, but survival would still depend upon how quickly he could get seen by a doctor or Medicine Woman. If only Omen was there, she'd know what more to do.

It seemed to Eland that even God or the Great Spirit, by any and every name, either couldn't or chose not to interfere in the internecine conflicts and seemingly senseless bloodletting of mankind. Clearly it appeared the intention of the Great Mystery that people make their own decisions and face the consequences for what they did and did not do. It seemed willing to watch humanity do the wrong things sometimes rather than intercede and rob them of the onus for their mistakes, and of the wisdom that should follow them... rather than strip people of the credit for what they do right, and the satisfaction that comes with it.

Nor was the Mother Nature he often retreated to that much more accommodating. She provided insight and opportunity but not forgiveness or consolation. Connection and belonging but not solution, or at least not always the solution that Eland might have liked. Nature worked tirelessly in pursuit of balance, but that was not the same thing as fairness. Life was seldom fair, he thought. Over the course of the previous fifty years, many of the forests of the Northwest had been stripped of their trees, with no consideration of the forests' needs. Entire tribes had paid the price for the resistance put up by a relatively small number of its members. He knew that the slaves had been freed not so much out of a change of heart as to increase pressure on an unbowed Confederacy. That little boys were sometimes punished for the deeds of their clever older brothers. That mothers suffered the sins of their boys. That it was the common soldier who paid for the choices of the generals, the politicians, the industrial magnates. That the well meaning citizens of Columbus were that very second paying for a history of exploitation by a small handful of influential *Americanos*, as well as their government's betrayal of Villa at Agua Prieta. And apparently, that this bloodied *Villista* had been shot by his own compatriots, either as a deserter, or at least as a shirker looking to avoid getting into the fight.

It wasn't fair, and he'd come to accept that fair just didn't exist. It was not fair that the Mexicans were at the mercy of the North, or that the people of this border town were at the mercy of both these avenging raiders and the authorities that controlled without protecting. Nor had it been fair to Omen for him to expect her to heal her troubled soul overnight. To think she would come with him when home meant so much to her. To insist on going on this trip when she had no sane option but to stay. That he had ever caused her any pain. He felt sorry for a lot of things and apologetic to all the many people that he had ever hurt. To his parents, his ex-girlfriends, and that Mexican still moaning in the dirt... but it was to Omen in particular that he apologized. He apologized to her on his own behalf, but also for every evil act and omission in the world.

"I'm sorry, Omen," he said as stood back up. "I am so very, very, very sorry."

It was a time for tending the wounded. And for tending his wounds.

Eland walked on to the still burning section of town, backlit by its flames even as an equally ruddy sun began to raise its head over the eastern horizon.

The wind that had been still since dusk now picked up again. And the way it pressed against him reminded him of Omen, stepping up behind him as she liked to do, wrapping her arms around his belly and pulling herself tightly against his butt and back.

Chapter 40

THE ALWAYS & FOREVER WATCH:
Foreboding & Need

Omen flipped open the case on her watch. It was still another hour or so until dawn, but she knew further sleep would be impossible after awaking from such a dream. She could feel her hard beating heart, like a Bear in her chest anxiously pacing back and forth, stomping its feet, straining to burst out of its rib laced cage. The nightmare was over but its effects remained. She could still taste the metallic flavor of adrenalin on her tongue. Her throat felt cracked and swollen as if from yelling. Her legs were sore as if they had not spent the night in bed, but running instead. And she shivered in her sleeveless nightgown although the room was not what she normally would have considered cold. For once, she felt more like bone than padding -- bloodless, brittle and exposed, wind whipped and rattling.

"I've got to pull myself together," Omen scolded.

Snapping closed the watch case, she stopped to admire its inscription. There, inscribed by hand into its thin gold plating, were some of the first words she had ever learned to read, and they were still some of her favorites.

"Always & Forever," it said, with the stylized ampersand at its center, and the A and the F done up in extra fancy scroll. The sentence was redundant, but it served to emphasize something that she highly valued: the lasting. The changing but continuous. The threads connecting all the forms, all the ages, creating a fabric that somehow remained intact through the endless transitions. It was something that both she and Eland treasured about their relationship, the sense that they were bound by more than circumstance and desire, that with sufficient devotion and focus, with a tight enough and loving enough grip they could remain partnered in passion and purpose forever. Through wearisome tedium, distracting victories and crushing defeats. In the face of all that would distract them and those who would try to forcibly tear them apart, their loyalty repeatedly tested. Through all the spinning and twisting. Through so many times of being squeezed from wombs, stretched by growth, addled by adolescence, weakened by disease, then covered with palls or sheets... or left open-eyed and mouth ajar in forest duff or desert dust.

And he could, she thought, be that very minute laid low in some undistinguished stretch of late night sands. She knew that it was as important to heed such dreams as it was to listen and respond to her feelings and intuitions. Experience had shown that even if the images were not true in the literal sense, they still represented a significant truth, something that needed tending to. While Eland may not have been confronted by death, there was undoubtedly something powerful that he had just felt or faced. If not guns and bullets, then perhaps an accident on horseback, a Rattler bite, a disastrous theft by an unscrupulous burglar, a traumatic loss of faith. Besides, it would have been impossible for her to get the images out of her mind even if she wanted to... the imminence of mortal danger followed by an unresponsive Eland acting strangely, as if he couldn't hear her, acting as if she wasn't even there. And of course, she was not. She was right there in their home in the canyon, in the arms of her solitary magic.

Omen pulled a black crocheted shawl on over her bare shoulders and stepped into her sheepskin slippers. She took a match to the oil lamp by her altar, raised the wick to light it, then lowered it again before putting its glass chimney back on. She wanted to be able to see the items arrayed there, but did not want to ruin the mystique of the morning. She had always loved the early hours, sitting with a steaming cup of Red Clover tea in the quiet chill, her sleepy eyes gradually widening as the sky slowly turned from black, to grey, to blue. It was the enchanted time, along with sundown, when it was easiest to commune with one's ancestors or the precious departed. When the ancients could be felt moving through the thin mountain air. And in other countries when Leprechauns and Sprites, Pucks and Fairies came out of hiding. When *Usen* – God or the Great Spirit – seemed to share the same room as man, inhabiting not just the heart but the hearth, the kitchen, the warming tea. Too bright a lamp might break such a spell, send the enchanted ones scattering, remove her from the company of the eternal. All the more important now when she wanted – needed – to reach out and make contact with her so-loved man, to know whether or not he still breathed.

Helpful in this regard were all those things he had brought into their lives, such as the beautiful old bookcases and his seductive but incomprehensible books. Others he had purchased for her as gifts, like the artist's easel and the stud earrings with amber cabochons set into a motif of leaves. Knowing how much she adored containers, he had provided glass jars of every size and shape, most of which were filled with her favorite tinctures or oils. A small wooden box from Russia inlaid with a carved amber heart that could only be opened if you knew its secret. A silver jewelry box from India inset with polished camel bone. A musical gourd shaker featuring a hollow handle where she stored some of the prehistoric beads she had found. Honoring her love of plants, he had gathered the seeds of a fragrant *Salvia* and planted them in the pot by the window, the one shaped like a nesting swan with its neck curled back. He had bought her many plant identification books that, nearly every night, he had sat and read to her like fairytales to a hungry-to-learn child. Because of this, and because of her connection to the Bears, her shelves included a pottery sculpture of a Bear Mother telling improbable stories to twelve or more disproportionately tiny kids affixed to her lap. A black clay pot with a simple Bear design on its side, burnished smooth and signed on the bottom by a friend of Eland's at the San Ildefonso Pueblo named Maria, was arranged next to that heavy brass mortar and pestle from the 1700s that he'd somehow found for her. A hand painted plaster statue of Guadalupe, not unlike the Doña's. And most meaningful to her of all, the wood covered journal with the Grizzly he had carved himself, now partly filled with her fanciful plant drawings.

Omen touched the sculpted Bear on the book cover, then nervously checked the watch again. Her eyes pooled with tears that she could not yet let go of. She did not know why she was crying, whether it was from what she would consider to be shameful fear, or an appropriate honoring of his unique place in her life. If it was regret for having let him get away from her... or perhaps, the mourning of her lover's untimely demise.

Chapter 41

PREPARATIONS TO LEAVE:
An Unexpected Letter, Unseemly Displays

As physically and emotionally exhausted as he was, Eland spent the morning assisting the only doctor in town as he patched up a line of wounded soldiers and locals. There were no more *Villistas* to treat, however. How odd that all died and none had been merely incapacitated. The doc talked about revenge killings on the part of American soldiers, and Eland imagined how the entire country would feel vengeful enough to accept a presidential decision to invade Mexico in turn. Come afternoon, he broke away to survey the rest of Columbus.

Eland could see the camp with dozens of dead horses lying in front of the cavalry stables, likely an attempt by the attackers to slow pursuit. "There has been no sign of camp commander Slocum since before the battle," one old man told him, and while folks praised Lt. Lucas and others for their courageous defense, the Colonel was lambasted for apparently having hid until the danger was over.

Eland crossed over one street to inquire of the Commercial Hotel, not a board of which remained, and therefore nothing of Eland's belongings besides what he carried in his bag and wore on his back. Word was that the *Villistas* had specifically sought out its owner, Sam Ravel, to get even with him for having sold them faulty ammunition that cost many Mexican soldiers' lives, but Sam had been fortunate to be partying in El Paso instead of in his bed at the hotel.

Every window of the town's new telephone company office had been shot out, with the intrepid operator courageously continuing to make calls for help even as the Mauser and Winchester rounds ripped through the air above her head and tore the plaster from the walls. With so many structures made of adobe, less than a block had burned, but the smell of the still smoldering wood permeated the air. The bodies of the raiders had been gathered and piled in giant heaps inside a vacant lot.

"They had it coming," Eland heard one fellow say to his wife as he edged closer to the crowd busy appraising and berating the fallen enemy.

The dead were mostly shirtless and shoeless, just as they had been most of their lives. They were the lower middle-class and the poor, the kind of men making up the front ranks of armies everywhere. Lack of opportunity was what swelled the ranks of all the Villas, Napoleans and Washingtons of the world, and what always had.

And, Eland noted, the bodies all looked Indian, as Indian as the women and kids massacred in Black Kettle's camp by Col. Chivington a thousand miles north of there, or as Victorio and Naiche, the Apache war chiefs. The peoples and armies of Mexico carried in them the genetics as well as spirit and attitude of what were often called "redskins." The night before, he realized, could well be the final organized battle between Indian forces and the U.S. Cavalry ever. He may have just witnessed from the sidelines a last battle of the Indian wars, and thus very possibly the end of that era already being eulogized as the Old or Wild West. Not the capture and deportation of angry Geronimo, and not the one-sided confrontation at Wounded Knee in 1890... but Columbus, now, March of 1916.

So too were they the bodies of the very old and very young, eliciting at least a degree of shame or regret in even the most hardened of the victimized American civilians. The smooth-faced soldiers, on the other hand, seemed to be making a lark of it. Their crude levity and disrespect for the dead could be explained as letting off steam, or as a means of feeling empowered after having been so scared. Or perhaps it was something less seemly as well, not just arrogance but a disconnection between the head and the heart. Whatever the motivating psychology, an army photographer soon arrived, set up a tripod, and began taking photographs of the clowning men that they could take home as souvenirs. And not, Eland figured, the kind of pictures that would endear American armed forces to the world, were they ever to hit the newspapers.

As Eland watched aghast, several soldiers took turns posing with the severed head of one of the raiders, pushing a lit *cigarro* into its mouth. Others posed smiling with their arms around the shoulders of stiffened corpses, their campaign hats tilted jauntily to the side. One sergeant preferred to have pictures of himself standing on the very top of the largest of the human piles with a knee lifted and a foot resting on the head of a trophy.

The Hispanics among the onlookers went from somber witnesses to raving zealots when they saw the photographer packing up as one of the sergeants unscrewed the cap on a steel can full of kerosene. The raiders were almost entirely Catholics, and deserved a Catholic burial. Burning them would be sacrilege, a dishonor not only to their race but their religion.

"That'll teach those brown devils," said a bandaged soldier as he struck and tossed a match.

"*Diablos*," one Spanish speaking resident whispered, her breath a scorching desert wind.

Eland turned away in disgust, moving on to the Columbus post office, a building left mostly undamaged. The postmaster sat outside next to a canvas bag containing the mail that had come in the day before. A young woman had just received a package from him, and now hurried away to open it.

"Only one letter for you today," he said, recognizing Eland.

The envelope was hand printed and barely legible, as if it had been made out by somebody's little child.

"Nothing else, are you sure?"

"Why, 'specting something?"

"Hoping for lots," he answered. "Expecting nothing."

"Where are you going to be staying, now?"

"I'm not concerned about staying," Eland said. "I'm looking to buy a truck to leave in."

"Can't say as I blame you," the postmaster added wistfully, as though imagining a city he would never visit, tropical isles he would never see, or mountains he would never climb.

Eland walked over to the nearby boardwalk steps and sat there, carefully opening the envelope, sniffing at its contents like a perfume tester, and pulling out its sheet of fancy paper.

"*My Deer Eland,*" it read, in large letters squeezed between hand-drawn lines. "*I need yu.*",mwhereupon he felt the tears starting to well again.

"*Plees,*" she wrote. "*Com home.*"

PART VII

Chapter 42

Trunks & Limbs Rejoined

Omen caught a breath and felt her heart beginning to race. She had just ridden into the village when she heard someone shouting "Columbus attacked yesterday, the U.S. invaded!" It seemed to be her dream come true, and all her reasons for worry borne out. "Seven soldiers and as many as a dozen civilians dead," was the report, causing her to step away and look off to the South in an effort to reach out across the miles and feel for herself if he was still alive.

The newspapers always arrived a day or two late, and even then would not include the names of the slain for another issue or two. Yet even if they had listed an Eland Howell among the casualties, she would not have believed it. If the authorities were to drive up with a casket in their truck bed, she would in her fashion assume that it was no more than a terrible case of mistaken identity, and expect upon lifting the lid open to behold a stranger. As strongly as Omen had felt Eland in danger, she now sensed that he was alright. And even more: that he was perhaps at that very moment working his way back to her side.

The second she'd written and mailed her first ever letter, Omen had begun to prepare for a reunion, making the bed for the first time in several days. Getting out a second pillow, and putting them both in matching pillow cases. Straightening the tincture cabinet as she had long been wanting to do, and cutting Spring flowers with which to garnish its shelves. Then she burned twists of Sage to cleanse and bless the house.

When Omen was done, she started gathering things she might want for an extended stay outside. Her favorite purple dress, short-sleeved and laced up the front. A colorful blanket that she spread near the river crossing under the shade of Alders. A handmade reed basket into which she put plates and silverware, a package of Ramon's smoked turkey, a chunk of cheese, and half-loaf of Sunflower-seed bread. Candles in case she decided to read after dark, and extra blankets to help keep her warm through the night or nights. Even if Eland had left Columbus immediately after the raid, she realized, and even if were coming straight to the canyon, it would still be two more days before he could reasonably get all the way there in a buggy.

It was not a buggy he travelled in, of course, and the only horses it employed paced under his new truck's piano-hinged hood. As she hurried back and forth to the river with the canyon wind in her , he was racing at upwards of forty-five miles an hour on the long stretch to Silver City, his mustache whipping around in the topless roadster. As he stopped to pour water in a hissing and sputtering radiator, she was settling down on the grass and pouring herself some steaming tea. While he swayed first one way and then the other, through the hairpin turns of the Saliz Mountains, she sat on her blanket. Facing the road across the river with a tentative little smile on her face. Gently rocking from side to side.

They would never be able to say who saw whom first. Or if, being equally intent, they might have seen each other at exactly the same time. What was a rather rattly old brown pickup truck sped around the last turn and into view of the canyon mouth, the Frisco River swollen with snow-melt, and the woman standing to greet its breathless driver.

"Omen!" he yelled. They rushed to the edge of their respective side of the roiling river and she made a quick motion with her hand to indicate that the water was running fully waist-high. Then, as if in answer, as if there were someone drowning in its chocolate swirls, as if there were no time to spare, the two long separated lovers simultaneously jumped in. They met in the middle with their clothes still on, throwing their arms around each other, bracing their feet in the shifting sands while a cold, persuasive current pulled at their clothes.

For the craziest amount of time they stayed there, their trunks and limbs rejoined, their roots as well as hearts again intertwined.

Chapter 43

PLANT EROTICA
& CREATURE SENSATIONS

They stepped out of the water to the tune of a circling raven chortling, clicking and cawing, its wings making a loud rhythmic whoosh with every downstroke... and to the performances of thrush, robin, and bluebird, their notes sounding not so much like whistles as a carillon of tuned glass bells, struck by clappers of excitement, joy and caprice. Logically, they could not have been celebrating anything but their own Spring courtship, but to Eland and Omen it was like a composition written and performed just for them. It felt as if the entire canyon had been waiting, instruments in hand, for this fated reunion. The cliffs with their tube and crevice flutes. The river reeds, and the oboe wind that would set them to vibrating. Loose mountainside rocks ready for the Javelina or Mule Deer to send on a tumbling drum-roll to the bottom. The castanets of bright new leaves in the hands of the Cottonwood and Alder trees.

Once to the blanket, Eland took his arm from around her, grasped her hand, and stood back far enough to get a good look at his love. She appeared to him backlit by an aura of verdant green foliage, framed by bright orange cliffs, topped by sails of white clouds slicing through aqua sky. Her purple dress, wet nearly up to her breasts, clung like a second skin to the exacting contours of her belly, her groin, her hips and legs. In her face he saw the familiar strength and pride, exaggerated by her wide cheekbones and untamed eyes. But he also saw a softness such as she had seldom shown outside of the bed. And the shyness of a young woman who had allowed herself to write the word "Need," and then allowed it to be read.

"I..." he started to say, but she shushed him before he could finish. I love you, were some of the words that wanted to escape. I'm sorry, he hungered to say, for his having been so bullheaded, single minded and unwilling to reconsider. For having stretched her until she was frightened, teased her until she cried. For his attachment to being right. For leaving his destined sweetheart standing at the threshold as he rode off into the morning.

And I missed you, he was thinking, just as he had felt that he had known and missed her even before their first meeting.

"Shhh," she said again, perhaps hoping to quiet his mind.

There were plenty of things she wanted to express as much as he, including apologies for always resisting giving in, and for having had to struggle to give. For at first having taken as her own without crediting what were gifts sent by Spirit through Eland. For the harsh stances she had sometimes made in order to appear substantial and significant, and the tenderness and vulnerability that she had often been afraid to express. For having confused sweetness with weakness, and independence with strength. But today she was dedicating to reality, to a shared awareness and presence unfiltered and unobstructed by language. After nearly three months of trying every day to learn how to read, she wisely concluded it was time for the parlance of sight and scent, sound and touch.

Eland responded by reaching out to take in his hands, not her breasts as she might have expected, but one of her tight braids. Somehow it gave her the shivers to feel him slide the leather tie off its end, wriggle his fingertips into its plaits, and gently separate the threesome strands. Before he finished undoing the second one, Omen was herself undone.

Omen, in turn, released the brass buckle holding together his belt, sending his pants falling to his ankles. She then wriggled the still dripping dress off over her head, squatting down and pulling him on top of her.

Their kisses were alternately soft and hard, sometimes full mouthed and other times just a grasping of the corners, with sweet moments of attending to the top or bottom lip only. And when she was ready for him, she rolled over and got on top, seating herself on his firm desire. She began by bending forward to rub noses and gaze into his eyes, then bowed backwards so that her hair cascaded behind, her breasts nuzzling the sky. Omen planted him deeply in the ground of her being and in turn she found her roots in Eland.

She moved fast and then slow, in spirals and waves, rising sometimes high on her knees in order to better plunge back into sensation and hope again. When the sun took time to rest, they were still making love, the canyon still busy delivering its blessing song.

Theirs was a decade when much of society argued bitterly over whether humankind was a result of organic evolution or divine creation, and how closely people were or were not related to what was called the Animal Kingdom. Those insisting that they were cut from an entirely different cloth might have reconsidered their position upon hearing the sounds of the man and woman now coming from the woods. Sounds like a rhythmic pounding of hooves on the drumhead ground. Like a dry flapping of wings, followed by the squish and slosh of some purposeful being perhaps entering or exiting its watery domain. Avian cooing and primate yowls. The roar and the moan. The grunt of Ursus. The

Coyote's tearful opera. Had they been willing to cross the river to satisfy either their prudish curiosity or prurient interest, they could have beheld Eland grazing on her ear like a tender-lipped eater of grass, as well as thrusting hard like a carnivore. They might have turned away in embarrassment, at Omen nuzzling into Eland's chest like a Rock Dove wriggling her beak through a lover's breast feathers. Or else have become riveted on them... on their alternately rolling and hopping, pawing and clawing. On their excitedly tasting the sweetness of their beloved, like Bears licking the berry juice off one another's mouths. Chewing on the nape of the neck like Lions. Running to their mate's deepest core, like Wolves, down corridors of each other's scent. Sliding sensuously against one another like Serpents entwined, knotting and releasing again, and again, and again.

To a witness more familiar with and allied to the natural world, the couple's ways of loving could have additionally evoked the spirit of plants within. Rooted in present time and potent place. Coiling like Bindweed, blanketing like Clover. Tendrils that sought out the silky crevices and welcoming vessels of the so sought other. Pistils growing and then shrinking, stalks rising and lowering. Flowers opening and closing, reddening with the flush of each coital Spring. Bright colors and seductive shapes to attract the eye. Special perfumes to win over the nose. Swollen petals that rub against beak and bug, parting their pouting blossom lips under each heavy showering of pollen.

If the observer were a Wise Man or an unashamed Medicine Woman, she would likely also sense Omen's subterranean potentials pushing their way up like new sprouts through a hardened crust. Eland, no longer sending out runners in every direction but curling back and committing to his fertile berth instead. And then Omen as a predator, no longer as afraid of scarcity, of a loss of self or a decrease in respect when open and sharing. And Eland as a sparkling Salmon, having first left the river in search of the sea, and then having turned around and pushed upstream against the flow... a wild-eyed fish with rips and gashes in his skin who had climbed over innumerable natural and self-made obstacles in order to return to where his heart was spawned, to his final destination, to where he would... once more... begin.

Omen

Chapter 44

APOLOGIA:
Reinhabiting A Life Together

"Te amo," he said, gazing into her eyes when they first woke up. *"Mi querida,"* he said in her ear as she stood chopping the Watercress for a salad later that afternoon. *"Mon amor,"* was how he had put it a few days earlier and *"Ich liebe dich"* the day before that. She understood the Spanish words, the meaning of the others she inferred: he loved her, and he would say it in a million ways.

"Sheth she' zho'n," he told her, impressing Omen with how much trouble he must have gone to in order to come up with an approximate rendition in Apache.

And besides different languages, he expressed himself in a wide range of styles and tones. He whispered I Love You, so quietly she could barely hear, to see if she would look up from the plant book she was trying to read. Shouted it across the river to her where the water passed over a cloister of rocks and thus sang its loudest and most zealous. The words would alternately hum and hurry, rumble and relax. Sometimes teasing, sometimes reassuring. All one note, or three different notes forming a subtle sensuous scale. He professed his affection with a nervous jumbled gushing, then with a simple head motion and grunt, or a bedroom growl. When no sound at all came out, he described his adoration, his passion, his respect, all with the nuzzling of his nose. Or a look in his eyes. She could not have been more sure even if he had written an entire book about her... when he woke her up from her continuing nightmares and evoked pages of promised love with the way his fingers stroked her hurting head.

When she replied, it was often in dramatic comparisons such as, "I love you more than the Alders love the river. More than the flower loves the Sun. More than the Bear loves its warm coat of fur and cherishes its solitude. I will love you deeper than any ocean, deep as the fires they say burn at the center of the world. I will love you longer than the river runs that returns unto itself. Longer than there is an Earth hugged by a sky."

Since she had started writing, everything she wrote had begun to take the form of a poem. The short angry paragraphs that she intended as essays. The descriptions of plants she recorded. Even the instructions on the labels of her tinctures and the monthly grocery list all became colorful and fluid, metaphoric and full of implied meaning. The words stood for themselves, but they also spoke something more. And while they spoke for Omen, they also spoke for the awakened heart of humankind, whether anyone knew it or not. Like an undiscovered treasure, it required either a desire or knack on the part of the reader to uncover the hidden symbols within her revealing lyric maps.

They both wrote with their bodies in similar ways, in expressions of posture, motion and nuance. As hidden as the text of her being had seemed to others, to Eland it was as clear as words on paper. He could, to borrow a cliché of the time, read her like a book. But that did not mean he was never surprised when he turned the page.

Since he had gotten back, they had found it difficult to ever be further away than they could reach with an outstretched foot... so this day they had worked side-by-side as well as equally hard. Bringing up water for the house. Preparing their food. Planting and watering the herb garden. Eland typing up a story to try and sell, while Omen tried hard to figure out each word in a plant identification book. One benefit was that whatever they were doing, he could look up and with a glance continue their conversation. When she moved a certain way, he understood it to be a statement of affection. A cocking of her eyebrows was a discernible question that he was usually proud to have the answer for. Thus the last hour had been a predictable if satisfying paragraph. The next, he would never have guessed.

"My neck hurts," she said, "and yours must too."

Eland recalled a time when she would have pulled into herself when she felt the least bit out of sorts. She would have fought to regain control over her instincts to reach out and tend to him, so as to avoid being seen as servile or labeled a typical housewife. To be sure that she was wanted, and not just wanted for what she could give and do. To make certain that every exchange was measurably equal, to keep things flat-line fair in order to prove she was on par. Instead, she reacted neither out of habit and fears, nor strictly to please. She gently but firmly laid him down on his belly and began rubbing him, not just to meet his need... but because it pleased her as well.

The heels of her hands pressed deep. Small, strong hands squeezing, pressing down, gripping and lifting. Pinching and plumping. There was no hurry to it, as might have been expected, no indication of a rush to finish, no pall of obligation or duty, no festering resentment or measured withholding. She gave, through her heart as her hands, everything she had. The neck. The shoulders. Each arm, the buttocks, and no leg left out. Every second, every touch was a focused yet relaxed, strong yet tender, therapeutic yet sensuous presentation of whole love. Whole Omen.

Eland- 1920

Eland started to protest, but realized he was setting a bad example. If he wanted her to learn to fully accept all that he and the world gave her, and to feel worthy of it, he had to prove that he could receive. Not like the male that would take for granted, resist like iron or duck and run... but like a mountain opening canyon-wide for the coursing of the rio. Like a student loving and swallowing a truth. Like volcanic soil absorbing the rain. And not like general rainfall spread promiscuously and scattered by the fickle wind, run shallow and quick to evaporate... but rather, the focused streaming of a woman's being into the targeted core of a chosen man.

Eland purred low and contentedly, his eyes half closed. Columbus had cost him a lot of money, and his articles were always written on speculation, and yet he had never felt so rich. Every stroke of her hands was priceless, beyond bid, impossible to steal. Her hugs more lush than purchased velvet. The way she wriggled and snuggled her head into his chest, worth any cost. Worth life. And there was a richness to the way they lived that life. If one could really only be said to have what they noticed, then Eland and Omen might have had more than almost anyone on the planet, for every flavor in every meal got their attention. Every scent drifting in. Every decoration, convenience or tool in the home. Every cleft and crag in the cliffs the home was built into. The transitioning insects and migrating birds, as much as the river and rock that never left. The feel of the mattress after a long day. The millionth kiss as fresh and regarded as the rest.

"It's okay, sweet Love," she said, when he was looking for the fourth time like he wanted to apologize. "You did what you felt you had to do. And maybe we couldn't have learned what we needed to otherwise."

"That doesn't change the fact that I should have made a different choice."

"I don't like the word 'should,'" she said. "I should have asked you to stay. But we've got *now*."

"It's not that I want to dwell on regrets," he replied. "I need to take responsibility for where I go wrong, if I want the credit for what I do well and right."

Eland reached up and held in his hands the face he found so beautiful.

"I apologize," he said, with a low and slow vibration.

Omen lay with her head on his chest for a long minute, taking refuge in the waves rising and falling.

"I'm sorry, too," she quietly but firmly said.

Then she resumed rubbing, now working on his front side. She shook her hair back out of her face with a toss of her head, took a finger to the corner of Eland's mouth to coax it to smile.

Atalanta

Chapter 45

ATALANTA & MEILANION

More and more, the view of the multi-hued canyon walls from their cabin was becoming for Eland what it had long been for Omen: the destination found, the place one felt best around and longed for when away. It felt wonderfully new and strange to him that he took his bearings from their evident and shining truth, that not only where he was, but what he needed to do, was somehow fed by their rise and glow.

Eland sat watching the shadows of the clouds moving dramatically across the face of the cliffs for just a little longer. Spread out on the porch were the dozens of books he'd brought back from Santa Fe after a trip to introduce Omen to his parents.

"I'm glad you are finally getting serious and settling down with somebody," his mother had said, as though any decent woman would have served her hoped-for end.

"I'm glad you waited until you found the one that was right for you," his father had said, once out of ear-shot of the mom, and before embracing Eland in a longer than usual hug. "This one," the usually tentative man added, "is what I'd call a Keeper."

Deciding which books to hang on to was proving more difficult. He liked the dull scientific ones for their facts, the novels for their insightful twists. The great writing inspired him to be as good, while the worst of the prose motivated him to prove it could be done better. From Twain to Goethe, London to Lawrence. The temptation might have been to keep them all, but it seemed to him that his power now came in tightening his focus, concentrating on the fullest experience of whatever felt most significant. He painstakingly made stacks of those they would try to find shelf space for in their little house, and and others which would either be sold or given away. His favorite volumes of poetry, reference books and field guides would have to remain. And on their way out were the obvious, the repetitious, the derivative, and the simply entertaining.

Omen watched from the woodpile where she was enjoyably sawing up pieces for the stove. She smiled as Eland opened each and every one, flicking through it if it contained any photographs or illustrations, opening to a random page and reading a few lines if not. It appeared to be a ritual honoring more than gathering new input for the selection process, as though he needed to personally shake the hand or pat the back of each volume before filing them in the casita or sending them on their way. Many of the rejected copies were full of wondrous illustrated scenes of exotic and far away countries, tribal tableaus and turbaned dancers, overgrown jungles and Saharan expanse, visions that had fed the nomadic urges of an author who had already explored most of the American Southwest.

That was part of his process now, he realized, sifting and selecting, zeroing in on the essence, the heart, the moment, rather than the thin and broad field. No longer tons of books, but a most special library. Nor many romantic interests, but rather, one devoted love. Not a thousand goals, but a handful that were becoming more and more accessible each day, tasks to excel at, deeper and more artful accomplishment. Not one-time trips to Tunisia and Sumatra, but repeat, circular loops to the always calling canyon cliffs, the woodpile, the garden, the bedroom where they made love. To the peaks from which they could see most of the purple range, the river where they gathered water and swam, and the miles of ridges where the Rocky Mountain Elk were known to drop their antlers.

Shedding, they both realized, was part of their ongoing work, part of what would make this a powerful and not just survivable marriage. And part of their becoming, their manifestation, their expression and growth. They shed like horns when the season for fighting had passed. Shed like protective layers of Winter fur in the Summer's heat. Like the discarded shells from which the Cicadas finally fly.

"Read me something," Omen said as she walked over and hung up the saw.

She pulled a chair as close to his as she could get it, knocking over a stack of collected short stories in the process. She put an arm around him and rested her head on his shoulder as the wind pitched locks of her long hair in front of her face.

"I have just the thing right here," he said, pulling out a book of myths. "It's a little on the tragic side, such as are most things Greek."

"I can handle it," she answered calmer and slower than she ever used to talk. Something had happened while he had been gone, not an end to her inner struggles, but a true equanimity and honest confidence. Poise, perhaps, at the edge of her known world. Grace displayed in the more deliberate ways her hands had begun to move, in the way she walked. Eland saw that she had been remade, not into something else or to suit someone else but rather, re-inhabiting her unimpeachable core, the joyful little girl who hugged trees when she was barely old enough to stand, the balanced giving Medicine Woman trapped too long beneath illusion, armor, doubt, or scowl... and doing the effort of such transformation first and foremost for herself. The roll-top writer's desk he brought for her was stunning because of the work she had done to remove the layers of different finishes and paints, scraping away only that which had been added, that suffocated, restrained, misrepresented or concealed. Likewise, she had painfully scraped away much of what was not the real Omen, those behavioral habits and ways of perceiving that limited, distorted and obfuscated the reality and treasure within.

"Here," he said as he opened and handed it to her.

"What are you doing?"

"You don't need me to read it to you anymore," he said, slightly wistful but wholly proud of her.

The cover was embossed leather with an attractive iconic design, and the first letter of every tale began with a special fancy script. She carefully handed it back.

"I know," she said, "but I want to hear it from you."

Eland was surprised at her, a woman who had preferred to do everything nearly perfectly so that she would never feel obliged to ask for it from others.

"Please," she said softly, snuggling back into his arm.

"Okay, I'd love to," he agreed, with one hand holding the book and other squeezing her knee. "I'll read the parts I think you would like, anyway."

"Atalanta," he began, "was born to a father who wanted only a boy, and who ordered that she be taken to the forest and abandoned there. The anguished nurse carried her as far as she could walk into the hills, leaving her on a soft bed of pine needles inside a warm, dry cave. On her way back, she prayed to the Moire and all the gods and goddesses to have pity on the child and send her some boon. It was Artemis, the wild maiden goddess of the hunt, who answered her sad plea, sending a Mother Bear to care for the helpless infant girl. The great beast nursed her on the nourishing milk of her wildness, lay between her and the cave opening to protect her from the cold night winds, and covered her with a warm furry paw while she slept."

Omen cooed, though she would not have wanted it described like that. Eland turned and kissed the top of her head, then continued the story.

"Atalanta quickly grew to be a bright and strong child, sometimes riding on her Bear-Mother's back, other times trotting along by her side or scrambling ahead to explore. She learned the ways of Gaia, the Earth Mother, including knowledge of the weather, how to get honey from a hollow log in the Summertime, and to find plants and roots to eat beneath the Winter's snow. Which flowers appeared in which month, and how dragonflies mated."

Omen bit his shoulder lightly, ensuring a dramatic pause.

"When she was deemed old enough," he went on, "Artemis sent her personal attendant Orythieia to further train her in the arts of the hunt. These included reading sign, tracking, stalking, running, and shooting the bow and arrow. Every creature of the meadows and woods were her playmates, and by the time she was in her teens she could already leap from crag to boulder like a Mountain Goat. She outran the fleet deer and outfought the mighty lion. It was her hope that she might spend the years of her mortal life free and living her ideals and desires, but it was not to be."

"What then?" Omen asked, when she thought he had been silent too long.

"She took pity on the lonely father who had left her to the fates," he answered. "Plus, thirty some years and twenty-some pages worth of difficulty, unhappiness and compromise. She finally marries the only man who could keep up with her, Meilanion, and they are heartbroken when their only child dies. It does, however, conclude with what you might consider a happy ending."

"With the loss of her son," Eland read, "an immense longing for the mountains welled up inside her, and all the weariness she had felt as a result of the constraints of court life became suddenly unbearable. Meilanion loved her so much that she was able to persuade him to give up all his habits, conveniences, comforts, obligations, titles and riches, and to return with her to where she felt strongest and best. Wherefore the bards do tell of gods who did not smote or punish, but applauded this necessary quest."

Eland closed the book, put it down and held her close.

"And then, to hear the bards and poets tell it, the two lovers walked hand-in-hand towards their now shared hopes."

Omen took a finger and wiped a grateful tear from her eye, then touched it to Eland's lips.

"And then," he said, choking up... "Artemis turned them both into Bears, which forever and together can be seen walking and playing in the forests of their wildest dreams."

Plant Gathering – 1934

Chapter 46

THE WALTZ:

Music That Only Plants, Animals, & Children Could Hear

The Canyon, New Mexico – 1926

Eland sat writing beneath a gnarly old Oak while Omen moved about gathering plants. He loved to watch her between paragraphs, stooping to converse with the various patches, determining which were sufficiently proliferating to chance harvesting from, and having a prayerful moment with each one before she trimmed its leaves, dug out a section of its root, or pulled it up out of the dirt. Sometimes she spoke a few words in Apache, either complimenting it, giving thanks, or asking it for its permission. Other times she would sing a little song, or simply sit cross-legged in front of it with her eyes closed and her palms on the ground.

She was not only taking, he knew, but also giving back, beginning with her palpable love, deference and respect. And also by carrying supplemental water to the patches, working Ramon's pig manure into the soil, spreading seeds and transplanting cuttings. Thanks to her efforts over a hundred native herbs were plentiful again, as well as uncounted varieties of reed and rush, grass and bush. The beneficiaries of her largesse included the butterflies that lapped at the burgeoning blooms, the deer that found more to browse, and the sugar-loving Black Bears who fed on the madly multiplying grapes. And because of the increase in deer, a Mountain Lion had moved back to bear her kits.

Omen's ritual gestures and caring ministrations reminded him of the Taos Medicine Man who had befriended him when he was young, the old Indian's unabashed intimacy with the natural world and the way he looked and moved his hands when he performed ceremonies in the underground kiva. It occurred to Eland that what all shamans and magicians throughout time had in common, besides their unusual degree of sensitivity, was an alliance with plants. Not just the Sacred Datura, Ayahuasca, and Peyote that they used to enter into the realms of spirits and visions, or the Comfrey and Oshá they used to heal the body, but every green being. They learned from them by adopting a shared ancient language of cell and soil. By heeding their fine example of adaptation and growth balanced with focus and rootedness. By getting near enough to blur the lines between plant and human, close enough to exchange breaths.

It seemed so sensual the way she held those she had pulled to her face to kiss and to sniff, teased a flower or stroked a stem, or how she now wriggled her hands into the ground to free a root. Eland acted engrossed in his writing as she ran over to show him what she had found, as excited as a child.

"Look," she laughingly commanded as she thrust the plant towards him.

Bits of wet sandy dirt fell off onto his paper. He felt somehow seized, clarified and transported by its intense presence and strong scent – a combination of medicinal camphor and fermenting swamp.

"I found another stand of Yerba Mansa!"

"So I see!"

"It's good for both fungus and infection," she said, with that subtle mix of accents that he found so cute. "A di-oor-retic, just what you need for mouth sores and stomach ulcers. Good for your urinary!"

Omen had picked up a lot of new medical terms since she took up reading in earnest, though she didn't always use the terms quite right.

He took it from her and held it up high so that a ray of afternoon sun streaking through a break in the Oaken foliage marvelously backlit its long shining leaves. Each leaf was laced with white veins against a shining emerald field as transparent as the stained glass of a gothic church.

Yerba Mansa only grew in the muck, the boggy saturated soils where even Cattails had trouble, and rare habitat given the narrow channels and flood cycles of Southwestern rivers. Eland admired the long twisty root, the white petals atop tall stalks like Coneflowers, and especially the vibrant green of the leaves, imagining it to be the color of Omen's equally verdant soul. Inside of each, he knew, was the stored light of the sun. And by furthering the lives of the plants, as well as by growing their gifts in herself, she was carrying that light forward.

Omen had the sudden thought that she might be expecting him to give too much attention to what she was doing, and not enough to his equally wonderful task. Now that she could read, she loved his words all the more. They were alive too, like the plants, in the microbial medium of earthen truths, bursting into blooms meant to excite the hearts and open the minds of even those too long unexcited and closed up. They too spoke of the gifting cycle, of connection and change, hard lessons and recurrent hopes. They were seeds just as sure as those she collected in the canyon, though more like those of Dandelion which are cast with no expectations into the catapulting winds. She brushed the dirt off the tablet as she picked it up, then noticed he had completed less than a page.

"Am I being too much of a distraction?"

"You're the attraction," he answered as he sat the Yerba Mansa down.

"But Baby," she said, surprising herself again by having used such a term as baby. "I want to make sure you are getting to do everything you want to."

"I may be writing fewer words some days, but they are meaning more and more."

"I know," she said, "that staying in one place as long as you have must be hard. You've only been to Santa Fe twice in two years."

"Don't worry," he replied, fully aware of how worried she must be that another urge or calling could take him away again. "I don't feel I'm doing any less. It's just a new way for me to do things."

Omen lay down on her back with her head on his lap, and her unbraided hair draped across his legs.

"You always said you feel like your life is a mission, and I wouldn't want you to try to deny that for me."

"I wouldn't do that. I still have a purpose, but I don't have to go anywhere to find it. It was right here all the time, creating a life – and affecting the world in our small ways – with you."

Unlike those beleaguered immigrants, they had joined a union that required they leave none of themselves behind, a committed combining where they felt more themselves, not less, fed by the variations and differences and affirmed by their similarities. She had not given up her power, but instead, they were both more powerful when they were together.

And Eland didn't leave his writing to be with her. He had, as he put it, come home to his story.

He closed his eyes and ran his fingers over her temples and brow.

"Besides," he added, "whatever purpose or mission had ever called to me, I wouldn't have wanted to do it without you."

He meant it too. Not painting a masterpiece without her to inspire him, suggest colors and sit at his side. Not exploring the Arctic vastness without her to share the glorious sight of the Northern Lights with, without her there at night needing his characteristic warmth. Not making money unless he had her to spend it with and on. Amidst the whirlwind of global change, they pledged their love would outlast every trial. And so it would be.

Eland opened his eyes, and found her looking up at him. It had been weeks since he had made up his mind to ask her, and now he was just waiting for the right time. He hesitated not because of any ambivalence or lack of confidence in his feelings and cause, but because he feared with her need to feel independent and in control she might say no. He didn't worry she would ever break up with him, but that the formality of the commitment might just be too much. He was close to saying the words when Omen raised herself up and kissed the top of the nose he sometimes thought too large in profile. He, in turn, bent down to kiss the belly she sometimes wished was smaller. There were no parts

unloved. No shadows un-embraced. No gifts unacknowledged.
And no opportunity for either difficulty or bliss ignored.

"Will you marry me?" She asked, taking him completely by
surprise.

Of course, he thought, as tears welled up in his eyes. To protect
and cherish, to help flourish and grow. Rooted like the plants in
the ground of shared being. Side by side seats at the premier of
unfolding reality. Stretched between the stars.

"You read my mind," he said, lifting her the rest of the way up
and then slowly rocking and shuffling in a circle.

"Oh god, yes," he answered, as they held each other even tighter...
dancing to a kind of magical waltz that it was said only plants,
animals, and very special children could usually hear.

Chapter 47

THE NEW WOMAN OF THE '30S:
Lots To Celebrate

The release of Eland's second work of fiction was considered sufficient excuse for a party by both is wife, Omen and much of the village. "The Heart Of Kokopelli" had been reviewed and lauded in The New Mexican as "the finest of recent expressions of the ever questing male soul, his emphasis on the burden basket meant to serve as a lesson in conscious choice, satisfying fulfillment, and gladdening hope." To his eccentric artist and theatrical friends from Santa Fe and Taos, it was worth the drive to the remote Southwest corner of the state to be near the inspiration that fed Eland. To his Hispanic and cowboy *compañeros*, there could be nothing more entertaining than ogling these oddly dressed pilgrims from the city.

It was a diverse tableau for sure, typical only of a boundless imagination and those rare and timeless nexuses hidden away among the jagged mountains and high desert valleys of places like enchanted New Mexico. The honored couple walked through the yard hand in hand, with one of Hannah's wild-haired daughters riding high on Eland's shoulders. There they were greeted by chile farmers and publicists, a horseshoer, a screenwriter, the town's school bus driver, and a flamenco dancer in full costume. Looking around, they acknowledged the presence of a Persian rug dealer with some highly expensive wine, and the young cowboy paupers with rodeo buckles willing to help him drink it. *Nuevo* gypsies cautiously staying within sight of their shiny new 1933 Harley Davidson motorcycles. A man who owned an old barn working out a deal with a sash wearing painter who made his own barn-wood frames. A film director talking to a local mentally handicapped man, seemingly oblivious to the fact that the conversation made no sense. Eland seemed to have just the right words for every one of them, the twist of phrase that made each feel genuinely recognized and more alive.

"Well if it isn't the famous author," Ramon said to Eland as they walked up to his house. "The old man and The New Woman Of The 30's," he added to Omen, enjoying quoting the front cover of the lifestyle magazine lying face up on the picnic table.

"Not hardly," Omen replied with a deliberate frown and barely suppressed grin. "Maybe you mean women IN their thirties."

Omen admired the many potted flowers Ramon had lined up inside a small fenced area, tended by a man now dependent on a wheelchair. She felt more wonderfully herself than she ever had, steadily expanding what she knew and cared about while moving ever closer to the core, the essence of what she called her true Omen-ness. The last thing that she wanted to be compared to were what she considered the vacant-headed followers of herd fashion, even if the latest marketing icon was the so-called liberated woman. She resented that the advertisers used the fact of feminine spunk as an image to try and sell them cars.

"Okay," Ramon said with a gesture of defeat, "you're incorrigibly old fashioned."

Omen laughed, though not entirely sure she liked that assessment any better. It was true that she often wore dress styles for the 1800's, or even from the time of the Renaissance, that her hair hung past her waist now, and that she stubbornly insisted on their living simply. But in other ways she did indeed embody the traits such sensationalized articles described: self directed and ambitious. Competent and assured. Strong and sexually realized while also being conscious of her clothes. Willing and able to fill careers generally claimed by men, yet committed to fun. Acting on her beliefs and values. And balancing responsibilities with desires.

Yet, as Omen would explain, none of the vast range of womanly characteristics and traits could be considered unique to the era. She would be the first to point out the continuing percentage of women who preferred to exploit the status quo, and then complain about it later. The indentured and those bound only by habit. Those whose complacency indicated a tragic and lingering lack of self-love. And those who were too doubtful to take chances or too frightened to move.

Likewise, as Omen claimed, there had always been and would likely always be people of the female gender who broke the rules and created their own roles. Women who were at home in their bodies, in touch with their lust, in tune with their gifts, and talented at both giving and receiving. Women who spoke their minds, knew their needs and sought to meet them wholly so that they might better give to the world. Who trusted their instincts and insights, and the special messages few others discern. Who committed much and kept their pledges. They weren't just transatlantic aviators but social activists, field biologists, and politicized poets. The women running for high office and those locking themselves in protest to the gates. They could be found in the more conventional positions and trades as well, being the most inspired and engaged of the librarians and nurses, secretaries and grade-school teachers. They were also that portion of housewives whose every seemingly mundane act was filled with satisfaction or joy, personality and pride, pleasure and purpose, compassion and grace. They both held together and helped form the world in the often quiet heroics of their touch and care, the fiercely loving heroines of the everyday.

Eland - 1932

"How about it, Eland," Ramon asked. "You read the papers. It's getting really crazy out there isn't it?"

Eland smiled and nodded, opening the old man's beer for him.

"Seems like people are always trying to do two things at once," Ramon said. "Keep things they care about from ever changing, while changing everything and everybody else as fast as they can."

Eland thought about it and decided that Ramon was right. He was simultaneously excited about the new scientific discoveries, and saddened by the course of events. But for now at least, it seemed to him any efforts at holding onto things, whether a tradition or language or piece of land, were far outstripped by the forces of change. Even in the isolated town of Lower Frisco, minds were filled with the fact and fancy of modernity. Filled with flash card images of Shirley Temple, synthetic rubber, and Salvador Dali. Of modern tractors and combines, juxtaposed next to malnourished children. Social Darwinism, as it was called, was being used to justify the accumulation of riches by a minority of power brokers, and art and literature were expected to keep up with the times. This love of all things modern was resulting in an obsession with the future. Eland's paean to the power of mythos and prehistory would have to compete with the sensational reporting of Sinclair Lewis' It Can't Happen Here and Huxley's ominous Brave New World. As well as that Englishman H.G. Wells' effort, whose title pondered The Shape Of Things To Come.

In the past couple years, the Star Spangled Banner had been made the official national anthem while jazz had turned to swing with the healthy doubt of "It Ain't Necessarily So" and the hedonism of "Anything Goes". Depression era songs like "Minnie The Moocher" and "Brother, Can You Spare A Dime?" had given up their positions on the charts to an upbeat version of "I'm An Old

Cowhand On The Rio Grande". A car named Bluebird had been driven at 276 miles per hour. The 21st Amendment had put an end to that ill-fated experiment, Prohibition, and a new agency had been organized called The Federal Bureau of Narcotics. Books by non-German authors had been burned in Germany just as volumes by Germans were being burned in the States. The first of many concentration camps were being built within sight of international observers by the National Socialist Party, also called the Nazis. Assyrian Christians had been massacred in Iraq while the British and Americans were opening the first pipelines meant to transport Iraqi oil to their floating tankers.

"I'm not against change," Eland finally answered. "I just wish I had a little more influence on the direction it's taking."

Omen put an arm around him, proud of her husband and sharing his concerns, including about the old man's apparently worsening health.

"Tell us the truth about how you're doing, Ramon," Omen prodded. Their patron sat his bottle of beer down on the nearest flower-box as the most precocious of Hannah's daughters jumped down from her adopted papa and hurried off to play.

"The important thing isn't how long you live," Ramon replied, winking and clipping a blood red rose for each of them. "It's what you do with it, and how much you enjoy it. And being true to yourself and honest with others with every breath you take."

"Now come here," Ramon said, motioning Omen closer. "I have something for you."

Omen walked over to him, curious what he was up to.

"Your mother left it with me," he went on, "after she tried to find you two on her way north with that new feller she latched onto. I hear you will be driving a load of her stuff up there yourself in a day or so."

"True enough," she answered, though she had no interest in going on about it. She was here now and wanted to enjoy the sweetness of the moment. When it came time to make the round trip, she would try to be just as intensely and openly there.

Omen took the small package in both hands. It was a handkerchief embroidered with wildflowers that had once belonged to her grandmother, folded and tied with string. She slipped the cord off without untying it, and then amazed herself by pulling out a beautiful piece of ceremonial art.

"Wow," Eland said, as the sun glinted off the abalone inlays on what was a tortoise shell hairpiece. It featured a crown of bright green Quetzal plumage, and one side of it was carved into a likeness of an Aztec goddess. Xochiquetzal was her name, as she suddenly remembered.

"There's a note with it," Eland said.

It was from the now fifty-eight year old Doña Rosa.

"Para tu journado," it said somewhat mysteriously, in finely lettered Spanish. For your journey.

"But when would have Moon seen her," Eland asked, "and how did she know that you were going anywhere?"

"Make way, make way," a young boy yelled at the top of his lungs. "Riders coming through!"

"Don't stand in the way of the race," another smaller child ordered everyone while following on the heels of the first. Most of the assembled made a wide path, but the preoccupied film director barely got out of the way in time. A pair of huge horses with tiny riders raced by with a very recognizable girl in the lead. They passed so closely that the flowerpots rattled and Ramon's half-full beer tipped over onto the ground.

"Don't worry yourself," he said as Omen rushed to pick it up. "All things fall. Even the leaves of those trees you love so much."

Then the old man called over to someone to bring him another.

"Wait," he shouted over the noise. "Make it three!"

"My friends and I," Ramon said as though to himself, "have lots we want to celebrate."

Chapter 48

XOCHIQUETZAL
& THE GRIEVOUS ROAD

Albuquerque, New Mexico – September, 1940

Omen squeezed one last item into the trailer, then joined Eland in lashing down her load. The field around them and leading up to the road was completely filled with the golden blossoms of September, species that she collectively called Those Darn Yellow Flowers With Sticky Leaves because they were so hard to tell apart. As the wind bent and folded them, it seemed to Omen that they formed patterns not unlike letters of an unspoken language... and that those letters stood for rooting Willows, expressive sighs, and running deer. That when read together, they became words such as Omen, and home. The taste of Wild Grapes, the smell of Sand Sage, and the breath of Bears. Like rockslides and bird chirps. And like Eland, the way he would always say...

"I love you so-o-o much, Omen."

"I love you so much, too," she responded, as she had thousands of times before. "More than the Alder loves the river..."

Before she could complete that mutually cherished litany, Eland pulled her close for a long, hard kiss.

"Are you going to be alright?" she asked.

"Nothing is ever completely all right, but I'll be okay. I'll be there with you, every step, every moment, if you will reach for me. Just make the most of your trip, be careful, and hurry back to me."

"Oh, sweetie..."

"Let's pick some flowers for the road," Eland said, by way of changing the subject. Eland kept hold of her with one hand, and started gently gathering with the other.

She could see that he was taking it hard. She'd never been so far nor gone so long without him, since his return from Columbus so many years before, but she was a good driver, he made sure the spare tire had air in it, and he knew she was a damn good shot with that little five-shot Smith & Wesson .38. she'd tucked underneath the seat for protection. As always, he wanted to empower her, and he put that empowerment over his own need to have her ever close... but there was no escaping the sad ache beneath his strained composure. She could hear the little boy in him crying out for her to stay, no matter how much he insisted otherwise, no matter how loud the smile. It wasn't an insecure mind that hated to watch her leave, but a body that had been grafted to hers, and a commingled spirit. Nor did he feel any desire to control, but only to accompany and assist. His need was for proximity and synergy... and being – like that very minute – always close enough to reach out and touch the top of her bare foot with his.

"Are you going to make sure you eat? And take your herbs at night?"

"I'll try to remember," he said in a not so reassuring tone.

Part of him wanted to tend and nourish himself while she was gone as a way to honor her and what they both believed. Another part wanted to wait like a vision quester baking in the sun, indulging in neither food nor pleasure until she returned to share life with him again.

"It might only be two nights," she pointed out in an effort to comfort him.

"Two nights can feel like two decades without you," Eland answered, unconsoled. "Give your mother my best."

Omen fired up the Oldsmobile, shifted into first gear, then pulled out towards the road. In the rear view mirror she saw the trailer full of Moonheart's belongings, many of which she remembered from her childhood, following her like the ghosts of her past. And behind that, she could see their house in the distance and an image of Eland and the river waving at her. She waved back out the window until she'd gone around the first corner and was well out of sight. She knew in her heart that he hadn't moved yet, that he wouldn't stop until he could no longer hold his arm up.

It was hard for her, winding her way out of the twists and forest near Aragon and into the flat stretches by Horse Springs. Harder still past Datil and Magdalena, spiraling down into Socorro and onto the highway. The mountain ranges of the Gila – the Saliz, the San Francisco, The Mogollon, the Datil – got larger and larger in her mind as they got smaller and smaller in the mirror. She was one hundred and thirty miles north before they disappeared from view, by which time they had grown in her imagination into giants larger than the sky.

Omen had affixed to the center of the dash the ceremonial Aztec comb given to her by Doña, and now she arranged the blooms Eland had picked like sacred offerings around its base.

"Route 66 Motel, $4 Night, 30 Miles Ahead," a billboard said. Soon she came upon another, advertising a bank with the line "Put Your Trust In Us." That was asking a lot, she thought, given the way the economy had been dragging since the stock market crash in '28. She turned the metal knob on the A.M. radio to see if she was near enough to a transmitter for daytime reception. The first one she found had an announcer talking in Spanish about what he was calling "Revolutionary Prices." The only other she could pick up was playing popular hits, beginning with a gut wrenching number by a soulful black heroin addict by the name of Billie Holiday.

> *Life is bare*
> *gloom and misery everywhere*
> *Stormy weather.*

It seemed like an appropriate song even though the sky could not have been clearer, nor the day any nicer.

> *All I do is pray the lord above will let me*
> *will let me walk in the sun once more*

Everything seemed covered in a wash of grey, now that she was heading away from the canyon and Eland. And a storm would likely seem to have lifted, once she was heading back home to his arms. Omen rested her elbow on the open window and her head on her hand. She started to wish the load were lighter and that she could go just a little faster.

> *Can't go on*
> *since my man and I ain't together*
> *Stormy weather*

Omen reached over and turned the radio knob back in time to hear a mournful tenor performing a Mexican *corrido tragedia*.

Xochiquetzal

Something about the Aztec comb kept drawing her attention, and twice she had to swerve slightly to get safely back into her lane. It wasn't just how incredibly gorgeous that she found it, or how bright its emerald Quetzal feathers and refractive inlays of ocean shell were. It was, rather, an energy she believed she could feel through the darkest cloth. And the deity carved into its face: Xochiquetzal, the mother of the most-revered Quetzalcoatl, god of transformation and changing times. Her name meant Flower Feather, fitting for a goddess of flowers and herbs, of the food crops the Aztecs depended upon and the sacred dances through which they gave thanks. Of fertility and fun. Omen smiled, recalling how Xochiquetzal was also considered the *patron* or guardian of an odd company of herbalists and Curanderas, artists and craftsmen, prostitutes and pregnant women.

She was also known as Patroness of Erotic Love. Goddess of Artistry and Delight. And Goddess of the Flowering Earth. According to the stories Doña Rosa told, Xochiquetzal was attended by a retinue of singing birds and colorful butterflies everywhere that she went. She was celebrated in the Fall at a Farewell to the Flowers festival held in her honor. The people, the temples, streets and houses were all decorated with dozens of wonderful varieties of flowers. They would make merry, and make a show of intently smelling the various blossoms that would all soon wither and dry up for the season. A feast in honor of the flowers followed, which had been meticulously recreated by Doña when the then fourteen-year-old Omen last journeyed to see her.

It wasn't long after Moonheart had moved her to the canyon that Omen went through a third and final period of training with the traditional healer. When the lessons were over, she had presented her young apprentice with an elaborate *Quechquimitl* sewn and embroidered for her, alive with complex Aztec designs and a floral motif. Flowers from the garden had been potted and brought inside, and foods she had spent days preparing were spread artfully on a blanket. In the midst sat a two feet high image of Xochiquetzal crafted out of wood. Omen remembered her having the body of a young married woman dressed in a blue tunic with feathers woven into the material in the shapes of favored Mexican blooms. The deity's arms were as though dancing, braided red leather served as her hair, and a headband of Quetzal plumage rested atop her head like feathery Stag horns.

"But does she have a lover, Doña? Or is she happy by herself?"

"If she had a soul mate," she answered, "I would think it would have to be her own twin, Xochipilli, the Flower Prince, the god of positive creativity, of flowers, dancing and feasting."

Omen smiled, imagining the two frolicking together at the base of mist-laden pyramids.

"But it's also important," Doña went on, "for you to understand that Xochiquetzal is fulfilled by her aware being, her magical role, her learned and gifted skills, her special place in the universe. I'm telling you, we have to be happy by ourselves, and with ourselves, if we are ever to be happy with another. And when our tribe, our friends, or our soul mate journey without us – whether it's for a short trip to get supplies, or the final leap through the crack in the world – we have to be able to feel them within us, and continue with what must be done."

"What do you mean, what must be done?"

"That varies with every person, depending on their gifts, vision or calling. But through it all, we must embrace and help nourish the essence of life. There is an ancient Nahuatl saying: *In Xochitl, In Cuicatl*. Literally, this means The Flower, The Song, and was often used as a metaphor for poetry. The poetry of life. The most true thing on Earth."

"Why isn't she celebrated anymore?"

"The people have chosen to forget, not just Xochiquetzal but their traditions, their ways of healing with plants, even their native tongue. These days most of us speak the languages of our conquerors. But not everything has been lost. In another month it will be All Souls day again, and if you were still here you would see the ground thoroughly covered with orange and yellow Marigold blossoms in honor of the old ways. And in early prayer, for a beautiful and bountiful Spring."

"Pull over, if you can't drive any faster than that," someone yelled out their car window, breaking Omen's reverie and causing her neck to tighten.

She didn't need a fancy odometer to tell she was getting close to Albuquerque now. Whereas she had only been able to get one radio station before, now she was able to find several with a quick spin of the dial. A jazzy program with lots of Ellington, Mitch Miller, and the Andrews Sisters. A country station with Cowboy Copas singing about his "Philipino Baby," and an all news station going on and on about the terrible events overseas and the gloomy possibility of the United States being drawn into the war. How close she was to the state's largest urban center could also be measured by the steady increase in vehicles on the road, and by how much newer most of them seemed to be. Here over half were snazzy roadsters, whereas in the village of Frisco a good third of the trucks still used hand-cranks. Prior to Socorro, she had only passed four other vehicles, but now they were packed so close that it was hard to change lanes. Worse yet, the trailer made for a slow climb up the last steep hill before getting into the city, causing the radiator to blow steam and the engine to overheat. Coasting down the other side cooled it off a bit, and so she continued on through the South Valley of Albuquerque with its Hispanic barrio, bean fields and automobile salvage yards until it started to steam again. Omen took the very next turn into the downtown area in hopes of filling up with both water and gas.

"Damnit," she cussed, as the Olds abruptly choked and stalled in the middle of the first major intersection. Almost immediately, drivers began blowing their horns behind and to the side of her. One, a rude *ah-ooh-gah*. Some high pitched and repeatedly punched. Others delivered long and low like bulls bullying their harems of cows. Omen tried the electric starter button, but the engine would barely turn over. She sat leaning over the steering wheel for a moment, then opened the door to get out during the first break in the traffic.

She turned at the sound of screeching brakes in time to see the horrified look on the face of the driver as his car smashed her door closed again.

Omen had often complained to Eland about the way the rubber tires – and the times that produced them – seemed to suspend her in the air, away from her source, and apart from the source of all growing beings. Now a force more powerful in some ways than even the mighty forest or the canyon winds had thrust her back to the ground.

PART VIII

Chapter 49

BRINGING OMEN HOME

Omen never felt the impact of steel against flesh, nor did she hear the sounds that breaking bones and crushed organs could make.

When she opened her eyes it was to see a ring of distorted stranger's faces struggling to peer in at her as though through a concealing fog. At once the faces began to rotate, first a revolution to the left, then continuously to the right. They seemed to spin faster and faster, the motion of their spinning creating a wind that gradually blew the fog away. Now when she looked past her partly closed lids, she saw clearly her own legs wading through a river of red and yellow Marigolds covering the street. She watched, as though with lowered heads, the countless buds cut special for the occasion lifting, curling and cresting about her ankles as she walked, sending concentric floral ripples in the direction of sidewalk shores, and leaving an undulating wake behind. If she raised a foot quickly enough, some of the flowers would break free from the rest and float as erratically free as soap bubbles being chased by eager children.

Nothing seemed ominous to Omen, only curiously odd. Those on the walkways were not strangers but strangely familiar folk, people whose names she imagined she should know, all clothed in indigenous dresses, tunics and *huipils*. The street that they lined the sides of was cobbled rather than paved, and wound through what appeared to be an old village rather than a modern state capitol. The villagers seemed to be waiting for the arrival of some anticipated procession, and it seemed to her that she was that procession. And that she recognized a feathered headdress roughly outlined in her own midday shadow as it moved across the beauteous seethe and surface of fire-tinted blossoms.

Her mind seemed empty of thought, yet something anxiously drew and nagged at her, as if to pull her right out of her skin if she didn't hurry fast enough. She must complete the ritual quickly, she sensed, so that she could get back to the canyon and Eland. Her one overwhelming feeling was not the lightning pain of firing nerves in damaged limbs, but the lingering and growing ache that comes from an essential unmet need, an urgent impulse to find her way to the end of the village and across however many miles of deserts and sierras to her mate and her home.

"You can't just let her go," she heard someone say through the returning haze of the operating room.

Omen understood none of it, and it was only at the most instinctual level that she was able to sense that this was no one she knew... and they were talking about her.

"We've stopped the internal hemorrhaging," another answered.

"There's nothing else we can do."

Other words came in and out in a jumble, like Financial and Responsibility, that meant little by themselves and nothing at all once strung together.

"What religion is she? We'll probably want to call in a priest."

The hardest for her, as well as the most reassuring, was the sound of Eland screaming to be allowed in.

"But you *can't*, sir."

Eland had demanded her release in no uncertain terms, only a single day after the limited operation and within minutes after the doctors' hopeless prognosis. The only choice the officials had was between calling for Security and immediately signing the papers. Now Eland turned off the main highway, east and south on the ever more deserted roads, to the still little town of Frisco and the canyon not far beyond. Moon followed close behind with Hannah and two of Hannah's little girls. No one in the caravan talked, not even the children, except for Eland telling Omen every so often how sorry he was, and how incredibly much he loved her.

"More than the flower loves the sun," he said as if she were sitting up listening. "More than the Bear loves its warm coat of fur... and cherishes its damn solitude."

Eland said damn for the same reason he always had, which was to get her attention. Make her look up from her work. Provoke a sarcastic response or wry grin. He wetted his fingers and placed them by her nose to feel for the movement of air from her lungs, to be assured she was still alive and breathing.

How ironic, and how terrible, he thought... that the healer who had successfully healed so many others of so many different kinds of ailments had now run up against something she could not treat.

Nor could herbs and remedies – or even magic and prayer – be expected to repair a squashed spleen or ruptured liver.

Eland pulled off the road at last, his arm asleep from having been reaching into the backseat for Omen most of the way. The headlights of the Morgan reflected on the river crossing, sadly low for that time of the Fall. They shined on a restored riparian wildland, a river ecosystem made healthy again through the reintroduction of Cottonwoods and Willows, Cattail, and Sacaton Grass. Muskrats cavorted near the new beaver dam and fish were doubtless making love under the expanse of Great Blue Heron wings. For two decades the couple had worked to keep the free-ranging cattle fenced off the land, and with each new season increasing numbers of plants had made their way back to stay. Every Spring brought the sound of yet another species of bird that neither Eland nor Omen had ever heard. With each reintroduction the land had become more of what it once was, and in this way, more itself.

Eland realized that like the canyon, he and Omen had lost parts of themselves only to regain them through practice and prayer, personal insistence and the passage of time. Parts such as her willingness to trust and his need to settle down. His humorous side and her little girl inside. Her inclination to play and his patience to stay. The longer they had stuck close to that special place, the better able they were to hear the will and whisperings of the earth.... and the more their real selves they had become.

Eland hurt now as he never had before. It was unbearable to see her on the cot as they moved her across the water and up the trail to the house, insufferable that there was nothing in his power he could do to bring her back to life – grinding seeds in the mortar he gave her, skipping in the kitchen, filling their little house with her high energy and his being with love. It helped only a little to remember how pain made a person more aware of their bodies and feelings, more alert to the way one's chosen environs affected them. He recognized, as much as had Omen, how suffering could temper one's skills, test their resolve and strengthen their will. How debility was a teacher of humility, and how infirmity counseled patience. How the loss of one sensory organ could lead to a heightening of the others. How at its worst a deadly virus did nothing but return a person to the ground that they arose from, extended from, and then folded back into.

Eland wetted his fingertips as soon as they got her to the house and off of the army surplus stretcher. While the others watched, he held them close to Omen's nose, anxious to feel the passage of air like a whispery breeze from her mountain-grown lungs, the breath that would assure him that she was still alive.

"One is not made un-whole by death", he had once written, "but by a failure to fully live. By that which dilutes focus, weakens intention, or dishonors one's spirit. And those things that contribute to a person doubting their instincts and intuition, their significance or value. One was made un-whole," he'd explained, "by the suppression of feelings and the repression of needs. By the subjugation of one's animal being and the slow deterioration of excitement and calling, hunger, and hope." If health was wholeness, he knew they could never be healthier than since coming home to self and dream, purpose and place. She emanated a vitality that belied her stillness with something wild and able still pacing inside of her, climbing over her promontories, splashing through her waters, flying from her boughs.

In his articles and books, Eland had made clear time and again their philosophy that good health wasn't the absence of trauma or pain, but that it was the most complete embodiment of one's authentic nature. The depth of sensation, emotion, and experience. The fullness of expression and response. The fulfillment of a special passion and unique purpose, the seizing of one's destiny and the living of their dreams. Even Ramon had understood that health was a matter of how one lived, not how long. And likewise, Earth wasn't made any less – or any less healthy – by the eroding of mountain rock into fertile valley soil, the death of a Cottontail in the jaws of a Gray Fox, or the shredding of forests by an erupting volcano. Even the natural extinction of species was only a recycling of the various components into the whole, with each pruning back resulting in a new burst of growth, an enhanced opportunity for transitioning color and form.

But none of his realizations and conclusions, none of them offered any comfort. Neither myth nor truth were poultice enough to assuage the ache when the Autumn leaves wrinkled and fell. And nothing, not even the distractions of art or promises of gods could ease his pain over his Omen lying on their marriage bed like a broken song.

She was not, however, to be pitied. Yes, Omen had been a healer, but that had always been her way in, not out. Becoming a Medicine Woman, a teacher, a committed wife – had all meant more caring, more connection, more implications, more commitment, more expression for she who had been a secret, more intimacy for the woman who had once jumped whenever she was touched.

Eland led his guests to his studio where the two sleepy girls had already found beds, then returned to lay down next to Omen. Concerned that an arm or leg over her anywhere would cause her pain, he merely nudged up as close as he could, his devoted nose resting by her shoulder as though there were no other perfume than her precious scent, afraid to fall asleep and miss the sound of even a single heartbeat.

In the soft glow of the oil lamp, she looked not shattered but full... not as if she were fading, but as if finally learning to relax.

Like the Doña, Omen had become a purveyor of insights and herbs, good food and real magic, all on a quest to stay physically well and able, and to try and provide some of the same for others. But what she sought – and taught – was completeness. In the reintegrated parts of her once fractal self. In the blessed forever bond she had with Eland.

They would do their dance together for all time, as he swore once again... engaged in the endless adventure and the cyclical fulfillment of sacred deaths and awakened lives.

Chapter 50

OMEN DREAMS AGAIN:
Planting The Bones Of Bears

"Too big for a Black Bear," Carl Rice said to his brother Bo.

The tracks around the half-eaten calf were the size of frying pans, and the two ranchers from Cliff figured they had a killer Grizzly on their hands.

"Haven't seen one of those around here in ages," Bo replied.

One had been killed a couple of years earlier near Luna, or so they heard, by a Mormon fellow named Hulsey. The word was that it had been young and especially small, but that they had the head mounted anyway... since the Brown Bears had become so rare.

Meanwhile, only an hour's drive to the north of where they hunted, a stilled Omen lay dreaming. She dreamed of mountain valleys teeming with unusual and wonderful kinds of plants, each speaking of its particular gifts and needs in its own peculiar voice. Among them were a few dangerously poisonous varieties swaying in unison with the many dozens of curative species.

"They're all alike, Bears are," Carl was grumbling. "Killers, every one of them."

One moment, the scene Omen dreamed appeared like an idyllic Arcadia to her, and then the next seemed scarily wrought with danger. The birds she dreamed into existence had now grown ominously quiet, as though something worse than death might be making its way through the forest towards her, something that alarmed even the stout ridges and dense rock of the cliffs around her. It was not a presence so much as a great absence that bore down on her, a vacuum, a black hole into which everything – even memory – might disappear. Yet somehow, it seemed that in some way Omen was ready for whatever was coming, that there was something about her that the years had no claim on, that no teeth could bite down on, that not even fading memories could erase.

For a change, her nightmare did not focus on watching and waiting for Eland. She did not need to look for him in her dream because this time she could sense him right there next to her, just barely beyond the range of her peripheral vision, close enough to feel his radiating warmth on a cool evening.

"We'll be clear of them soon enough," Bo concluded. "How 'bout you get the dogs together, and I'll call for one of those fool Depredation Permits?"

Omen dreamed midnight in the middle of the day, a total eclipse of the sun, a red ring like a fiery noose dangling from the sky. Deer and elk running towards the smoke of a terrible fire from something that scared them even more. Knots of people that didn't hear the elk when they whistled, nor notice them as they pounded the earth in passage.

When the brothers finally caught up to their hounds, Carl dispatched the full-grown female Bear with a single round from his .405 Winchester. She had not tried to run away, but chose to stand her ground and box at the agitated pack instead. She had not turned from the dogs to charge them when they rode up, nor soaked up bullet after bullet in her bid to destroy her human antagonists. They, in turn, had neither walked nor ridden record miles in pursuit of their quarry. Nor had they emptied their weapons like some hunters were forced to, or been unseated from their horses and savaged by their target. And they had not been forced into a contest between bowie knives and unsheathed tooth and claw, a battle in which they'd have barely prevailed.

While the brothers stood over their fallen quarry, Omen was home dreaming heroes and heras overcoming incredible odds. Feats worthy of fables. Miraculous healings. Landscapes protected. Women liberated. Villages saved.

"We'd better get to dressing it," Carl said after letting the dogs worry the carcass a bit. "I promised the kids I'd take them to Silver City tonight to see that new Tarzan movie."

"It's not bad," Bo admitted while tying his Horse up and pulling out a skinning blade. "I liked getting to see the lions and tigers myself."

"Yeah, they're something else I'm sure," Carl concluded.

He lifted up on one heavy foreleg, while Bo made the first cut on what would turn out later to be the very last confirmed Grizzly in all of New Mexico.

And Omen dreamed the bones of mountains. The bones of ghost-Bears haunting the caves and Willow corridors of the still tribal mind. Bear bones. Pale yellow skulls prayerfully stacked in ancient caves and ingloriously nailed above log cabin doors. Tagged skulls resting on metal museum shelves and drifting like chalky specters through darkened space. Softened ribs chewed by rodents, ribcages through which flowering Mountain Nettles grew, and once stiff backbones dissolving like flesh into waiting soil. Claws that tore into the muscle of pursuing hounds, that rolled rocks down hills and marked the trunks of Alders and Aspens. Claws on hunter's watch fobs, claws dragged into a

Packrat midden, claw necklaces around the necks of Siberian Shamans and Apache Medicine Men. Hollow bone rattles – death rattles – filled with tiny crystals gleaned from river sand. And she dreamed herself taking up a bleached leg bone in her hand, pointing with it at something not yet in sight.

"Experience every Bear," Eland had once written, "as if it were the last of its kind. Notice every bee as though you might never again get to hear its buzz. Celebrate every tree as if you could wake up tomorrow to a world with neither green nor shade. Appreciate the mountain as if it could wash away before your very eyes, and your lover as though you might never see them again. Waste neither words nor silence, and savor every breath as though it were your final one."

"That'll do it," Carl said just then, as he and Bo piled just the head and hide onto the back of the wagon and prepared to head back to town.

This while Omen lay there with a sleeping Eland's head on her arm, now dreaming of planting the bones of Bears in the ground the way that she had so often planted Cottonwood Saplings along the banks of the Rio Frisco, dreaming that they sprouted fur, became engorged with blood like sap, grew flesh and hooves and paws and then set clods of dirt a-flyin' as they burst forth from the ground.

And she dreamed that she had laid down for a while a wondrous mission fulfilled, wholly given to the earth. That when she next woke and stood, Eland rose up with her.

Chapter 51

THE LAST CANDLE GOES OUT:
Our Flowers Will Stand Up In The Rain

Eland secured each candle in place, heating their bottoms first so they'd stick to the tree-root steps leading up out of the river. Then the Sacred Datura and other flowers he'd hastily picked. Then masks he had gotten in Mexico from a man who swore they were powerful guardians who could protect the true from the false, the sacred from the vile. Little silk bags of dried herbs hung by string from the branches of the sheltering Alders. Owl, Eagle, and Hawk feathers they had found on the ground over the years, set to dangle from the Wild Grape vines winding basket-like around the small round grove.

Climbing into the opening, he emptied out the remainder of the bags' contents, arranging them around and on top of the rocks near the grove's center. At their base, he placed a ten-inch high glass-front iron display case with her favorite leafen and amber earrings next to the several rings he'd bought for her, and that the hospital had eventually returned. And on the bottom shelf, some revolutionary pesos and spent cartridges from his time in Columbus away from her, symbolizing not adventure so much as realization and return.

Close by on the ground, he positioned the ancient stone *metate* that she loved to use, reducing a harvest of Nettles for drying into cakes. Next a stone Mogollon mixing bowl, its center still green from some Omen potion. Then the fired-clay Bear Mother that he'd made for her, looking as though it were telling both Omen's and the Grizzlies' stories to the clay kids affixed to her lap. The gourd rattle she'd sometimes employed when trying to help heal someone's aggravated spirit. And especially, the wood-covered plant journal that he'd carved a Bear on two decades before... the gift of heart and the surrendering that had helped him to earn her trust.

At the foot of this makeshift altar he had dug a shallow hole just the size for two people side by side. With the first few shovelfuls it had seemed to him like a growing cavity set to take her from him.

Then he came to see it as the bed that could hold close their mated bones.

Eland had washed her and clothed her in a long dress, rich forest-green linen with its breast and shoulders appliquéd with black velvet Roses. Then he spent two hours or more getting Omen the hundred yards to the river, gently dragging her on a blanket where the ground was soft and sandy, and hand carrying over the rougher sections. He didn't have too hard of a time, but then she was alarmingly lighter after seven days without nutrition, and only the water that they had dripped from rags into her parched mouth and throat. But her beauty remained, as undiminished by her condition as it would have one day been by the wrinkles and handicaps of old age. The luxurious black hair with the red highlights now fanned out against the deep purple blanket, like the dark feathers of a ceremonial headdress, like the rays of a raven sun.

Eland picked her back up in his arms when they got to the edge of thicket, the dense strip of forest and underbrush lining both sides of the river. Supple Willows with reddened stems and sage-green leaves leaned into the already narrow trail so that he had to twist sideways in order to get Omen through. In their shade grew flavorful Mountain Nettle and the Moonwort that released a strong, sweet scent when brushed with a foot. Topping them all were the *Alamos*, the Cottonwood trees on which an ambush of Kingfishers sat. And nearest the water, the Queen Alder, Omen's favorite of all the incredible trees of the truly amazing world. The Alder had, in partnership with Eland, helped her to heal her spirit. And it joined them both in healing the damage to the fragile canyon ecology, fixing the soil with crucial nitrogen and resisting erosion with an embracing net of roots.

The Alder would have felt special to Omen even if she had never learned any of its story or learned to read by studying its myths. She loved that it had been long known as the King Of The Fairies, that the faces of the Sacred Kings during the Midsummer rituals were painted with the red dye of its inner bark. That the fairies were said to use the Alder catkins to dye their clothes, thereby making themselves invisible to human eyes. That while its wood burned slow, it nevertheless made the best and hottest charcoal and had once been the choice of medieval warriors for forging their magically imbued swords. That woodsmen would sometimes strike the silvery barked trees with an axe, and then upon seeing the bright red flesh beneath be reminded of blood and rendered too sympathetic to continue an assault. For these reasons and more, the Alder was considered to embody the power of fire. And because of the way it turned water into steam, it was called "The Tree Of Resurrection" by Homer. The Alder was the botanical Phoenix, Omen had decided... the leaf-feathered firebird of rebirth.

Arriving at the river's edge, Eland lifted her up again, stepped in and began sloshing his way through. Then near the opposite side, he slipped on a submerged rock and almost fell in, jarring Omen and splashing her with the waters of the Sweet Medicine. At that second, she did what he would not have expected. She moaned, and that moan was like the most precious sound in the world to him, sweeter to his ears than if all the birds in existence came together to sing him a common song. Eland's heart sped, and hope surged through his body like the river at flood-stage, propelling them out of the river and up the root staircase into their grove. As it was nearly dark, he rushed to get some of the candles lit before putting one hand lightly on her head, and another on her heart.

"Omen, my Omen," he said in a cracked and choking voice. "Oh, please, tell me you can hear me!"

She softly moaned a second time, and slightly moved her head.

"Tell me," he pleaded, "that you can feel my love."

He watched as she opened her eyes, murky yet searching. She seemed to gradually take in where she was, and the special treasures arrayed there. Then she returned her gaze to Eland. Seeing her apparently struggling to open her mouth, Eland leaned over and lightly kissed his beloved wife, gently moistening and parting her lips with the tip of his tongue.

"Oh Eland," she said, with words that sounded like a crackling of dried leather.

"Oh god, how I love you Omen!"

Tears fell hard now, like a sun-warmed waterfall onto her chest.

"Hmmm-uch," she seemed to say. "Hahm... uch," between straining to take a deeper breath.

"What is it, Baby?"

"How much? How long?"

"I will love you," he assured her, "longer than the river runs. The river... that returns... unto itself."

She seemed to be focusing better now, locking into his adoring – and likewise adored – eyes.

"Lo-onger," he stuttered, "than there will be an Earth hugged by a Sky."

Omen ventured a tiny smile, that silently answered: Forever, and ever, and ever....

And then she began to fade.

Eland recalled that in the Teutonic countries, the spirit of the Alder was once said to carry children off to the Otherworld, a world inside of the visible physical one where another way of being became not just a condition, but a place in time. In one tale he remembered an ailing child was carried on horseback through the woods, in search of a certain healer or medicine. The child asked her papa if he could hear the Alder Queen calling her name, beckoning her to come. "No," the father assured, he heard nothing, and he insisted that she would be treated and be fine. Then looking down, he sees that she has died.

"I don't want you to go!" he pleaded desperately.

Omen shook her head as though to say: I'm not going anywhere, you silly boy.

And in many ways, he knew that was true. She would always be there, in the canyon as well as in his heart. At least in spirit.

But, Eland thought, that just wouldn't be the same as having her here in the flesh, to be able to hear her breathing, to ask her questions and listen to her smart-aleck responses. The sound of her little girl voice. The solid way she puts her feet down in the house. Even the sniffs when she has a cold, and the complaints those times when I disappoint her. How can I trade her singing, those notes that work their way out of the kitchen when she thinks no one is listening... for just spirit's whisperings? How can I live without her scent and the way she reaches out in her sleep and pins me beneath her little Bear's paw? How can I do without her help with everything I do, and the honor of helping her in turn?

The first of the candles burned out.

"I can't let you go!" he cried out in exasperation over her ever-shallower breathing.

"Then," Omen said, unbelievably slowly. "Then... don't."

It was the same with her as it was with the disappearing forests of the country, the eradication of Pancho Villa, the wild Indian and wild open spaces... the imperiled Harbinger Frogs and extirpated Grizzly: If he could not prevent their deaths, he could at least write for others the lessons of their lives, sing their songs.

Eland pulled from the jar several flowers and laid them on her chest where she could hopefully smell them, including a large white Datura blossom that the missionaries called Angel's Trumpet.

And with that, he recalled the ancient Aztec poem:

> *Here through art, I shall live forever.*
> *Who will take me, who will go with me?*

Eland reached for the inlaid hair-comb that Doña had given her and placed it beneath the blooms so that Xochiquetzal's bright green plumage became a part of the bouquet. Then he lay down next to her, and she gradually turned her head until their noses were touching, sharing the same air, with one heart echoing the other. She opened her lids halfway and held them like that, without blinking, looking directly again into Eland's candle-lit eyes.

> *Xochiquetzal and the Prince Flower gently breathe in*
> *the aroma that is us.*
> *Our flowers are uniting.*

And he was, indeed, experiencing himself falling into her, and her being pulled up into him. She would express herself through the beauty she planted, watered, and grew. And through the best of what her husband, her mate, her extension would ever do.

Yet a second candle succumbed, blown out by the increasing wind.

> *Here I am, my friends, a singer*
> *From my heart I strew my songs, my fragrant songs*
> *before the face of others.*
> *I shall leave my song-image on Earth.*
> *Xúmetl the Elder flower, and Tlapatli the Datura*
> *bless us.*
> *My heart shall live, it will come back.*
> *My memory will live.*

Everything good Eland could imagine, he imagined as a testament or monument to her: Omen Mountain, and Omen Yarrow. Ursa Meadow and Bear Rock. Healer's Point and Medicine Woman Forest. She had pressed more than seed into the earth, and it had manifest as lifelong healings and lasting art, heart-opening poems and purposeful passion with each new growing season.

> *I cry as I speak and see the root of song,*
> *let me plant it here on Earth so it may be realized.*

Eland daubed her tear from her eye and mixed it with the one sliding in a rivulet down his cheek. Thunder rumbled nearby, but she showed no sign of hearing it.

> *My song is heard and it flourishes.*
> *My planted world is sprouting,*
> *my heart shall live,*
> *our flowers stand up in the rain.*

And so it was that they would, together, persist. Even as a rain cloud blotted out the stars. Even as the first few drops fell down and the last candle melted and went out...

> *Our flowers stand up in the rain.*

...and they shall stand up
in the rain

Chapter 52

AWAKENING FROM TORPOR:
The Magic That Brings Back The Sun

"After every storm," Eland wrote, "the sun comes to drink. From sandstone cups, and the faces of Sweet Clover."

Then he closed his notebook, and took with both hands the warming cup of tea.

From his perch Eland could see clouds rising as if from the ground, their strongly defined shapes lifting and dancing like bog-ghosts at the behest of the dawn. The shallow cave provided a front row seat to all the dramas of natural life, the graze and hunt, the bloom and the wilt, death and birth. The feathered one's fussing over territories, and the vigor of creature sex. The flex of tree and bush. It was situated seventy feet up the side of the cliff above their house – directly across from the Alder thicket that concealed their hallowed grove – a concave hollow blown out of solid volcanic rock, carved by the wild little hands of wind-propelled raindrops. The gentle inward slope of its walls created what Eland considered a most marvelous effect, a natural amphitheater magnifying every sound of the animate land. When the breeze was just right, the giggling of water over river-rock filled its vessel, along with the croaks of Great Blue Herons and the contented calls of terns. They worked in concert as he sat or lay there awake. They penetrated his mind when he slept and became the many Songs Of Omen in his dreams. They had enjoyed climbing up together, and now he had made it a ritual to spend his mornings there. He had even dragged up a small cotton-filled mattress, nested out of reach of all but the most horizontal of downpours.

It had been almost two years since the accident, and since that awful night of loss when Eland hadn't cared if he lived or died. Hannah's girls had become almost daily visitors, asking him to teach them what he knew of Omen's secrets, of the responsibilities and rewards of the Medicine Woman way. They asked, too, for things he had learned from his experiences and the choices he had made... a more concrete testimonial than what he could possibly share on paper. He nevertheless continued to write for much of every day, more recently on typewriters even though he still preferred the aesthetics of pen and ink – a flowering of essays and poems, political satire and inspirational tales. Even a children's book featuring a Curandera Bear, which he was slowly finding time to illustrate. His recent work had earned him a modest income as well as invitations to various functions, a couple of which he'd attended in rapidly growing Santa Fe. He'd given scant attention to the flirting women there... not only because he had promised Omen forever, but because in his heart, mind and soul, no one else would do.

Eland climbed back down the steep trail and around to the front of the house. Opening the door, he was surprised to see that an unfortunate Hummingbird had gotten in through a rip in a window-screen. *Pochtli. Tozcatl. Da-hi-tu-hi. Colibre'. The Jeweled Sorcerer.* The one whose name meant "Life Bringer" lay inert on the floor.

"Just what do you think you are doing in here, little one?" Eland asked, with no more hope of it stirring than responding.

Attracted to any bright colors, Hummers had often zoomed in and out of the open cabin windows, poking at the beeswax candles, investigating the crimson beads on Omen's Apache necklace and being baffled by the window ornament of dried flowers mounted in beveled glass. Eland always felt a little guilty for fooling them that way, knowing they were expending their precious metabolic energy frustrated by faux flora. Today one had made it in but apparently couldn't find its way back out. It had more than likely flown its fragile body against the fixed pane of glass repeatedly, until collapsing, closing its small black eyes and ceasing to breathe. Eland gently slipped his fingers under and around the bird like a basket, carefully carrying it outside and sitting the warrior of the sun in the shade of a Juniper tree.

Eland sat down in the grass, feeling helpless and ashamed.

"It was my house that had lured it," he thought. "My glass. My illusion of freedom."

The Hummingbirds' airborne skirmishes that Eland often saw were believed by the Aztecs to be mock battles, with them practicing each day for the renewal of their war against the powers of night. According to legend, if the people ever lost the birds' alliance and help, or if the Hummingbirds were ever allowed to go extinct, the sun would no longer rise from above the mystic mountains — and humanity would be doomed to perpetually look inward through an obfuscating dark.

A story that Doña had taught Omen described an age when the Aztecs were still a nomadic people in search of a home. Their leader was a great warrior named Huitzitzil, "Shining-One-With-The-Long-Weapon", attesting to his prowess with a spear, wearing arm bands and bracelets made of iridescent green Hummingbird feathers. They soon found themselves under attack and a great battle ensued. While in time they managed to repel the much larger tribe, the great warrior had taken an arrow through his heart. Then, to everyone's amazement, a small emerald bird was seen spiraling upwards from where his body had lain. He had

Awakened from Torpor –
WoundWort –Stachys spp.)
by Jesse Wolf Hardin

taken the form of the combative little hummer, it was said, and would be known thereafter by the spirit name of Huitzitzlopochtli. From that point on, all deceased defenders of the homelands would be reborn Pochtli. They would be treated to fields of sweet, pollen-laden flowers, while preparing for dusk and the always fateful struggle with oblivion.

And now, Eland sat wondering what song to sing for it, what prayers of love and apology to say over its stilled form. Should he honor it by salvaging the plumage, or should he bury it intact with no further violation? He got up and rubbed his cramped legs in order to get the blood flowing in them again. He was on the verge of losing himself in sorrow, self-recrimination and regret, in obsessive imaginings of the irrevocable and the irreparable... when the stilled hummingbird suddenly launched into flight! Wound-up and whirring, revved-up and revived, dancing skyward again!

Eland could have dismissed it as simply a bird pulling out of torpor – the hummer's known ability to slow its metabolic rate to almost zero in response to a scarcity of food, frigid weather or deadly threat.

He preferred to think of it as a miracle instead. Recalling yet another Aztec poem, he now recited its words to himself:

> I am the Shining One — bird, warrior and wizard.
> I have no equal — not even one.
> Never in vain do I wage nightly battle —
> for mine is the magic that brings back the sun!

Pochtli, the Hummingbird, was alive.

And, thankfully, so also was Eland.

Eland Howell - 1960

...and not even death shall keep them apart

Chapter 53

FIRST NEW PLANT OF THE SEASON:
Tending The Altar

"In her I found home, and through this home, a place. To lose her, would have been to lose my way."
    –Eland Howell, <u>Memoir Of A New Mexican</u>, 1961

At sixty-nine years of age, Eland Howell still dressed dapper in his palm leaf sombrero and double breasted vests, exhibiting his characteristic zest for life, and remaining irrevocably wedded to the earth and the woman resting there in its arms. On most days, one could see the man of letters at home in the canyon tending his herb and vegetable gardens, hosting fellow writers and wits, providing a second home to a pack of increasingly feral children... and every night, hard at work on his memoirs.

This morning, as every morning, Eland began by reading his stockpile of magazines and newspapers – railing at their biases and omissions, lamenting the reported injustices, laughing at the more inane and ridiculous stories, watching trends to better predict what was coming next. Over the course of the past two years, it had been reported that the Soviet Premier Khrushchev couldn't visit Disneyland due to what were referred to as security concerns. That ten year-old Mimi Jordan had won the national hula-hoop contest, managing to twirl her hoop and drink from a container of milk at the same time without spilling a drop, and the fact that up to ten thousand babies had been born without limbs thanks to the popularity of an anti-nausea drug called thalidomide. That the pesticide DDT continued to be a commercial success, in spite of increasing reports that it was poisoning the water supply and causing a mass die-off of songbird species. That jazz singer Billie Holliday had died, and Barbie – the first mass-produced doll with breasts and mascara – had been born.

Other recent firsts that Eland took note of included the computer microchip, the bikini, and the birth control pill, the electric toothbrush and the television series "The Twilight Zone". The first spy-plane to be shot down over the Soviet Union, and the first lie that President Eisenhower had been officially caught at. Since the beginning of the year, he'd read announcements that the United States was sending the first Monkey into space... and Russia, the first man. That the Central Intelligence Agency had organized an invasion of Fidel Castro's Cuba by expatriates in Florida, only to be routed in what the headlines called the Bay Of Pigs Fiasco. That a young Jewish entertainer going by the name of Bob Dylan was getting popular singing: "And the times they are a-changin'." But as much as they were seeming to change, other things seemed to stay the same – the same kinds of conspiracies and political skullduggery, wars and the reasons given for them reappearing in the headlines every ten or so years with nearly identical casts of characters... expressed in a renewed tone of outrage and shock.

Of course, current affairs and recorded history afforded but one linear model of time and events, inevitably colored by the perspectives of those doing the telling. It seemed more accurate to say all things happened not in a line but in circles. And that each full circle was not a closure but a revolving – or evolving – out into the next larger loop. Everything in the world, he believed, progressed in just such a spiral. A spiral in time. Even the information in one's genetic code was theoretically recorded on a spiraling helix. And it was to an ancient spiral engraved in rock that he now walked.

Taking a canvas harvest-bag from the wall, Eland made his way to the giant boulder's base. It had seemed like a long Winter with little but Watercress and Dock to gather, but by now there were a number of plants coming up. Mountain Candytuft. Wild flax. Wallflower and Mallow. He planned to bring some home, but first he felt drawn to empty his hands and touch the ten-feet high rock the way he had touched his true love, slowly tracing with his fingers the spiral's deeply incised lines. Inwards, around and around to the center, going from sheer energy into matter, from air to soil, head to heart, limb to root. And then back outwards again, on and up to the next level of manifestation and possibility. In nature, these things happened simultaneously with all things circling into themselves and the earth even as they reached out to the rest of the contextual universe. Eland loved the spirals on Celtic monuments, Sumerian artifacts, and Russian tribal cloaks, but he loved the one right there in the canyon the best. It had once signaled the boundary or entrance to the ceremonial center of the early Mogollons, the Sweet Medicine People. And for Eland, it marked the opening he'd found to meaning, purpose and place. To the potential for continuity and continuance. Lineage and unbroken connection. A passing of the way and wand.

Eland got down on his knees and began gently clipping the top third off the young Mint he had known would be there.

He would not be able to tend that place himself for all that many more years, he knew. His aliveness was evident in the quickness of his eye and the ability to remember detail. In the strength with which he worked a spade, and compassion and force in his written words. In the jaunty clothes he wore, the partially unbuttoned Mexican shirt and the cloth belt from Spain wrapped twice around his waist. But so were the long years that he had lived expressed in the ashy tones of his hair and a network of wrinkles. To look into his face was to behold the twisty trails of youthful folly and vital experience, chance and mistake, risk and reward. Trails that had led through episodes of violence as well as virtue, tragedy and tenderness, resistance and rescue, damage and repair. Through mountains and valleys, and across wide deserts to another country and struggle. Trails that had led him to Omen, to home, and hence to himself. Like the high-water marks on the canyon walls, or the telltale tracks of a passing animal, they told a story. Together they chronicled feelings as well as events, the laugh and frown as well as the wear and tear, the wind and sun. Eland was incontrovertibly older, and many would say wiser... but in other ways he was as he had always been.

Likewise, Omen had changed her look, relaxing her tone and poise enough to blend with the body of the earth, smiling her way up the roots and stems of the grape vines sprouting wildly from her mound, her bed, her rest. Her spirit was now an energy that helped the plants to be happy and to grow. She was in the river when it shrunk to a sensuous trickle in the Summer, as well as when it got moody and swelled and roared in the late February rush. And in the hues of the cliffs, lending them her glint and blush. He would always be able to hear her in the canyon winds, with rhyolite consonants and sacred airy vowels, their "whooo" and "shoosh" bent into a semblance of comforting or inspiring words. In the trill of the landing Say's Phoebe and the passionate exaltations of the mama Mountain Lion. In the Black Bears that circled the kitchen, hoping for entrance. He could pick up any wondrous rock in the canyon and find Omen's heat and spark within.

Not just any fire lending its passion to the night. But *her* fire.

Eland believed that even death could only alter, not corrupt or pervert. What transformed through the coming and going of generations was primarily appearance, flavor and effect, as a particular recipe changed from hand to hand, grandmother to granddaughter, father to son, one generation to the next. And handed also, fin to paw, hoof to claw. Yet through it all, the endless pressing and chopping, mixing and stirring, folding and braiding of life – through its swelling and rising, full of itself, then through the oven's heated test – still the ingredients remained the same: incorruptible, eternal and essential elements recombined in directed beings with lasting bonds and unshakable alliances. There was, Eland felt sure, an insoluble connection between himself and Omen, as between them and the planet, as between their insistent spirits and ever more revealed purpose. A deathless intimacy in the midst of endless birthings and dyings.

Pulling a quart jar out his bag, Eland fertilized the plants he'd been harvesting from with a nutritional fermented Nettle infusion. And nearby, he pressed different kinds of seeds into the ground that he had brought for that purpose. It pleased him that when he reached down, it was as if it were Omen's arm as well as his, her small Bear paw helping him spread and tuck the seeds. It was great pleasure, as well, that the little songs and chatty praise honoring the plants felt like they came from her pretty mouth, and then through his throat. That he could sense her strong, soft warmth curled up *Ursa*-like inside of him... and feel her legs move with his as he took a roundabout way back.

Eland stopped all of a sudden, excited to see where a Bear had just recently marked an Alder. As would be expected, the deep claw scratches had exposed the bloody looking wood beneath so that the silvered tree looked scarred with living flame.

It's the Bear, Eland thought, honoring Omen.

And it was also Omen, making it a point to honor Eland and their still shared home.

She was like the bruin in the Apache tale, telling the villagers that she had smelled *Xa'itc'rgelba-ye*, the first new plant of the season,

Bear Claw Scrapes on Alder

and the proof that the much-welcomed Spring had arrived. The difference was that Omen didn't lead him to a single scent. She walked him through fields so thick with fresh blooms that he could barely avoid stepping on them. Through stickery Rosebuds as well as sweet Easter-Daisies. *Corydalis*. Pink Vervain and Pink Penstemon. Salsify and Sego Lilly. Tansy Mustard and Mallow. *Phacelia* and Evening Primrose.

Eland could still see her there, anytime he didn't stare too hard... sometimes a mischievous little girl doing cartwheels and somersaults. And sometimes a Bear-browed Medicine Woman as wrinkled as he, bending to give attention to each new blossom.

Chapter 54

THE RACING PEN

The pen in his scarred and creased hand raced unrestrained across the page. It wasn't a creature running from some foaming red-eyed predator, but rather, in determined pursuit of fleeting opportunity.

He wrote as if his were the images that could entice his kind to truly and deeply live before they died, the words that could foretell the future through a ritual revealing of the past. He wrote as if the viscous ink were the one known antidote to some venomous bite, as if it fell upon him and him alone to get it to those in need in time. As if his phrases were the hands with which he could reach the drowning and comfort the terrorized before it was too late for them. As if he had only one lifetime in which to take what mattered most and commit it to paper. To someone watching, it might appear his hand was not so much pushing as being dragged by the pen, a fuzz-headed toddler clinging desperately to the legs of his mother as she rushed like a madwoman from room to room.

For every other project he used a typewriter, albeit a slick manual Smith Corona instead of the latest IBM Selectric. But for his memoirs – the most personal of all his work – nothing could satisfy him but the intimacy of a bare hand sliding across willing paper. The scent of ink drying in his wake. The glaze of sweat that his hurrying hand left. This was to be a focusing on the innermost center as well as a spiraling, comprehensive overview, all made more powerful by the actual facts of his many decades of fully engaged existence. Of noticing and caring. It would truly be his story for once, and as such, it would also be hers. The canyon's. New Mexico's, and the West's.

Unlike Eland at work, most things in nature seemed to happen at a steady, sometimes relaxed pace, moving inexorably if sometimes imperceptibly in the direction of its personal destiny. Even the mountains that he loved so much, the ones he always depended upon to be there no matter what else in his life ever shifted or fell apart... these, too, moved, shrinking and dissolving bit by bit under the seasons' swelling ice, pounding sun and heated rain, simultaneously lifting upwards with the stiff deliberateness of old women rising from granite beds, swelling with a quiet rumbling pride while plummeting along with everyone else through the limitless reaches of space. The movements of all things seemed to occur at their own natural tempo, broken only by decomposition or sleep, and occasional necessary bursts of speed. The Sweet Medicine River flowed both gentle and constant, save for its seasonal heaving with Spring snow-melt and the rare storm flood in the Fall. The Sharp Shinned Hawk soared in even, languorous circles until that explosion of feathers that marked the flashing instant of its bloody attack. No wolf could sustain the rush of the chase. No deer could survive all day the speed of its running away. Too slow, he was sure, and life would simply keel over. Too fast and it was likely to vibrate apart.

Eland knew that their range had been formed not in a gentle wearing away of stone but in a sudden release of molten pressure, volcanic eruptions as dramatic and furious as the planet had ever seen. But soon those passions, too, had slowed, ebbed and cooled, while the ancients stood at their scorched edge in their loincloths and watched. Both flood and volcano reminded him of terrestrial musicians, picking up speed and increasing their volume at an appropriate dramatic point in the song, an evolutionary crescendo and emotional release right before dropping back down to the kind of steady rhythm that an evolving universe could dance to.

Try as hard as he might from atop the highest peak he could climb, Eland still could not see anything resembling a final end. What he saw was a progression, a dance in the direction of endless new forms, impressive new tests, and countless new beginnings.

No wonder, Eland stopped and thought, so many different belief systems spoke of rocks rolled back and bodies resurrected, glistening heavens and lusty *Folkvang*, salvation and reincarnation. What the ancestors' minds had so struggled to describe, the bones had always and intrinsically understood: a truth too large to bear a single name, more evocative than learned nightmares and more powerful than the most formidable of human fears. It hummed, howled and flared, a symphony as bright and loud as the most evocative dawn sky, an unsurpassed vista and undiminished energy vibrating at the core of everything, in the middle of the living Earth, the very center of truth and being. It was source and shift more certain than anything his mind could imagine, more than fire-torn forests stirred by amorous lightning, more than broken hearts and faltering bodies, more than defeat and dismemberment. More than the eventual disappearance of the sun predicted for some distant millennia to come.

It was this, beating in the heart of the land.

And it was Omen that beat in the heart of him.

It was her – and that center of truth and being – to which his pen so hurried. Not towards culmination and rest, but to an endless rousing and awakening. Not to the end of his tale or ours, but both backwards and forwards to the start.

The Waltz – 1966

EPILOGUE

The Canyon – September, 1966

The writer rose and carefully packed his soiled buckskin shoulder bag with a special, green Medicine Bear fetish, a particular brass mortar and pestle pulled from his collection, and that life changing letter he'd written to Omen from Columbus over four decades before. Eland was on his way to add them to a certain altar, in a certain special grove, as a certain sentimental waltz started playing in his head.

All around him were the colors of Spring... saying nothing, revealing everything.

–Finis–

Unforgettable

ILLUSTRATIONS

Part VII

Part VIII

Adelante —Jesse Wolf Hardin

ABOUT THE AUTHOR

Author Jesse Wolf Hardin is the cofounder of the acclaimed Plant Healer Magazine (www.PlantHealerMagazine.com) and the flagship event for the folk herbal resurgence, The Traditions In Western Herbalism Conference (www.TraditionsInWesternHerbalism.org), as well as cofounder of the Anima School of nature awareness and plant medicine. His hundreds of published articles and over a dozen books have helped stretch as well as entertain his readers on topics as diverse as healing and herbalism, deep ecology and natural history, sense of place and indigenous traditions, American history and contemporary politics, primitive hunting and antique firearms... always with a message such as increased awareness, sentience and aesthetics, the wisdom of the land, personal responsibility and a code of honor. Hardin's contributions have been featured in collections as diverse as The Soul Unearthed (Cass Addams,Tarcher/Putnam, '96), the authoritative Encyclopedia Of Nature & Religion (Bron Taylor, 2005), and How Shall I Live my LIfe? (Derrick Jensen, PM Press 2008). Recent books by Hardin include both I'm A Medicine Woman Too! (www.medicinewomantoo.com) for budding child herbalists, and Old Guns & Whispering Ghosts for history buffs and outdoorsmen (www.OldGunsBook.com).
You can subscribe to his blog of latest writings "on every conceivable topic" for free (www.AnimaCenter.org/blog), and additional essays are available to be read at no cost on the Writings Page of the Anima School Website (www.animacenter.org/wolfwritings). Go to the website, also, to find out about his and Kiva Rose's life-awakening Home Study lifeways and herbal courses (www.animacenter.org/courses). Jesse is currently at work on a collection of writings delving into the very heart of healing, health and herbalism... and may release a second novel, The Kokopelli Seed if there prove to be increasing requests for more of his unique ecocentric fiction.

Both your sharing letters and quotes about The Medicine Bear are welcomed by the author:
JWH@TraditionsInWesternHerbalism.org

*Farewell, farewell...
never goodbye*

Made in the USA
San Bernardino, CA
28 November 2014